AF603793

RUINED

SONS OF SOLSTICE

ALYSON DAWN

Copyright © 2026 by Alyson Dawn

All rights reserved.

No part of this book may be reproduced, distributed, or transmitted in any form or by any means, including photocopying, recording, or other electronic or mechanical methods, without the prior written permission of the author, except in the case of brief quotations used in reviews and certain other noncommercial uses permitted by copyright law.

This is a work of fiction. Names, characters, businesses, places, events, and incidents are either the product of the author's imagination or used fictitiously. Any resemblance to actual persons, living or dead, or actual events is purely coincidental.

Cover design by Donnie Neuber
Editing by Jena Prall

Published by Chapters at Dawn

Trigger Warnings

Before you continue, please be aware that this is a dark romance containing themes and situations that may be upsetting or triggering for some readers. This story explores dark and difficult subjects and includes relationships that are not intended to reflect healthy real-life dynamics. Everyone's comfort level is different, and I encourage you to please read triggers with care. If any of the themes listed below may be harmful to your well-being, consider whether this book is the right fit for you at this time.

This book contains the following triggers:

Physical violence

Stalking

Kidnapping

Grooming

Dubious consent (dub-con)

Non-consensual sexual situations (non-con)

(On page) Sexual assault

Somnophilia.

Voyeurism

Explicit sexual content

BDSM and kink-related themes

Restraint and dominance/submission dynamics

Trauma and trauma responses

Anxiety, panic attacks, and mental health struggles

Self-destructive behavior

Death, grief, and loss

Murder and attempted murder

References to past abuse and childhood trauma

For all the girls who've been through
things they don't talk about.
For all the women drawn to the darkness.
For everyone who loves a masked man.

I

Silas

Bodies bent in devotion as mouths met through masks. Moans reverberated off the walls, colliding with the music as legs spread and eager Volunteers settled between them. The white masks of the Watchers glinted along the walls, each of them searching for what suited them.

From up here, they all looked the same.

Hungry.

It wasn't unusual for Ruined to be this full. Being the only club designed for anonymity, it was the one place that offered a choice in how to participate. The club created a unique type of darkness, a place where everyone could thrive. Most newcomers entered with the intention of just "trying it out" but left with an assigned mask and membership card. That was the whole reason this empire had been built—to offer you an experience that left you in ruins.

My favorite spot was *here*, above it all, where I was free to observe the chaos beneath me. Accessible by only one staircase, my office sat on a second story that jutted out over the main floor, engineered to appear as though it floated. Truthfully, the steel columns that held it up were more than capable of bearing

the weight.

Peering over the half wall that connected to the balcony, I wrapped my hand over the railing and looked down at the world beneath me. From this perspective, I had a clear view of everything I owned. The space was considerably large, every corner filled with pulsing music and smoke. LED lights traced the edges of the floor in deliberate paths, cutting through the darkness in bands of moving color. They shifted with the beat of the music, causing the entire club to feel alive as the light illuminated the haze. One minute, the room glowed soft and hypnotic; the next, it burned bright enough to highlight silhouettes. Here, each piece looked controlled, almost strategic—like the club itself was breathing.

The main floor underneath had many features, all anchored by the bar-top. A mix of low benches and polished tables curved around it, arranged as if drawn into its orbit. Smaller booths and couches lined the farther walls, offering pockets of privacy and a variety of toys, without ever fully separating anyone from the pull of the bar. A handful of dark barstools lined the counter, and black walls enclosed the rest of the open space. Vaulted ceilings stretched high above it all, feeding into an atmosphere that felt both expansive and deliberately contained. It was the kind of room designed to offer both solace within the shadows and security outside of them.

As I watched the people below me, my eyes caught a slight change in color and moved from my members to the slivers of light that filled the space between them. Just at that moment, the bass dropped and a silver beam shot up to the ceiling, exposing all the skin around me.

My world.

As the hue shifted again, the colors separated amongst the darkness, glinting off the mirrors and chains that were evenly spaced along the walls. I had always been intentional about each section, especially when it came to the layout. I wanted the experience here to offer different perspectives. No matter where you stood, the room revealed itself in fragments, through mirrors or openings into the spaces attached.

The song once again picked up speed as the beams of color around me dissipated. The few that were left over caught the metal-like ornaments in my cathedral of sin. Something inside me shifted at the sight, at how everything fit so perfectly here. A smile grew on my face as my eyes traced down the hallway, eventually finding the smaller play rooms—another exclusive form of privacy for my members.

I leaned into the hand braced against the rail and raised the glass in my other. The rim met my lips, and I took a slow sip. *Scotch. Neat.* The fact was that I had never been fond of drinking. Truthfully, I hated everything about the taste, but I always carried something to occupy my hands, especially when I patrolled over the fucked-up heaven I'd created.

With a sigh, I took another drink and lifted my line of sight toward the masks that adorned the upper wall near the entrance. *Masks were the absolute law here.* Not only did every member have to chose a mask, but they had to wear one while inside.

Depending on which one you chose, you were then labeled with certain characteristics and rules. At the start of every year, members voted on three new designs. As a result, the old ones were mounted above the door, creating a visual history of the club itself.

Voting had recently been finalized, and this was our first night with the new masks. Overall, I found myself quite pleased with the outcome

The first was a white porcelain mask—smooth and pristine, with wide mesh eyes and a smile carved into the mouth. These belonged to the Watchers, those who only wished to *observe.* People who chose this mask were usually new to the club or curious voyeurs who hadn't yet found the courage to step into their power. This mask was typically the stepping stone to the others.

The only thing I allowed on the wall beside me was a black mask I kept out on display. Kyrin bought it for me as a congratulatory gift for the club's opening. "*Cheers to being broken,*" he'd cackled, presenting it to me. I couldn't even stay mad about the comment because in a lot of ways, he was right, which made it perfect. The eyes and mouth were dark voids, a jagged purple crack split the surface over the right eye. The design was picked after our first round of originals, making it different from every other one worn by the members here. That uniqueness quickly became a problem when it became a blaring sign, I was the owner. I retired it to the wall as a trophy, dismissing the attention it brought.

Since then, I have permanently become a Watcher.

Watchers usually lingered along the walls and furniture. Some stayed fully clothed and simply observed their surroundings. Others touched themselves openly as they watched the main floor. Their rule was simple: if your mask was white, you could not be approached. Every Watcher was treated as if they were not there.

In a way, it was almost a luxury, and because of that, some members stayed Watchers forever.

Next were the Volunteers, people who wore the same color but in a red stitched design that fit close to the face. Where the Watchers design was simple, this mask was marked with an angular cut on the top and bottom, exposing both the hair and mouth for play. Volunteers were different because they existed to give themselves freely. Whether for pleasure or purpose, that mask meant the wearer was both willing and submissive. They moved through the space without hesitation, waiting for an offer from a Dom or performing for Watchers. Their silence wasn't mandatory, but it was often chosen.

The Volunteers one rule? *They had to obey.* Choosing that mask meant you volunteered yourself completely—no *exceptions.*

That left the Dominants. Characterized by darker leather and sharp lines, the design of this mask was made for control. A variety of buckles and buttons were sewn into the sides, allowing the mask to be removed in specific ways. There was something unspoken about the Doms, something that set them apart from the rest. They followed the same rules as everyone else yet somehow held more control. Their rule was a *safe word*—they had to have one, and if they heard it, everything stopped.

That was the foundation of Ruined. Everyone wore a mask, and everyone followed the system. There were no exceptions, not even for me.

Tonight, I wore my usual choice, *white*. I didn't want to be approached or bothered. My pleasure came from the energy here; I didn't find the need to be involved in anything else.

A quiet moan drifted up from below me, drawing my attention to a Volunteer kneeling at a Dominant's feet in offering. Even from here, I could see her tanned skin glistening beneath a light sheen of oil. Her mouth was slightly open, showcasing a smile full of wicked intent. A tattoo wrapped around her side and thigh, spiraling down to her ankle. She wore nothing else, a clear indication that she had no limits.

I watched as the Dominant's fingers brushed against her jaw in acceptance—a silent contract. She leaned into the touch, licking his fingers. Within a single movement, he pulled her off the ground and onto her feet, slipping into one of the rooms that lined the hallway.

I followed them with my eyes until they disappeared. Then I pushed off the railing and turned back toward my office. I'd only taken a few steps before the heavy steel door clicked shut behind me, the sound cutting through my thoughts and the music outside. The walls around me vibrated faintly, but most of the noise from the floor below was swallowed whole. I slid my mask off and moved toward my desk, inhaling slowly.

Instinctively, I ran my hands through my hair, the only thing I didn't demand control over.

I kept the sides shaved close in a clean, deliberate fade, while the top was left long and wild, thick enough for someone's hand to run through. I pushed it back out of habit, only for it to fall forward again, defiantly.

As I sat, I caught my reflection in the dark monitor of my computer. The stark contrast of my black hair against my light blue eyes echoed my bloodline, a family built on contradictions.

I shook my head at the image and focused back on the office around me. My desk was a matte black mahogany and sat dead center, flanked by two angular chairs that no one ever stays long enough to get comfortable in. A single lamp cast a low glow across the dark wood. The only other piece of furniture was a leather couch tucked into the corner. The walls were bare, covered in a deep charcoal gray. I didn't do photos or decoration, especially because I thought most were ugly. That meant that my space only had what it needed. A large filing cabinet sat behind my desk, and a simple rug tied together my monochrome palette. That was it.

My eyes grazed over the mask as I rolled my neck back and forth, popping several vertebrae. Raising the glass to my lips, I finished the last swallow of liquid just as the door creaked open. A low scoff of annoyance left me when the intruder pushed up his Volunteer mask, revealing a familiar pair of blue eyes.

Kyrin. Of course he hadn't knocked. *He never did.* Who needed common sense when you had brotherly privilege?

With a small *tsk*, my younger brother stepped inside and closed the door slowly behind him. With every step, a smirk curled the sharp angles of his face. "You need to learn to lock your door." He reached my desk and removed his mask, showcasing his dark hair that matched mine. Right now, it was messy in a way that made him look like he'd just come from a fight or a fuck. *Probably both.*

I raised an eyebrow at him as I set my glass down on an onyx coaster. "Like that would stop you?"

Looking at him felt like looking into a mirror sometimes, one that showed a two-years younger version of me with no sense of the word *control.* Many people assumed we were twins, but the truth was we couldn't be more different. Where my personality demanded quiet, Kyrin carried a presence that filled every space he entered. He'd always been so full of life, and when we were younger, it always drove me nuts. But still, I tried my best to foster it in him as we grew up.

A large smile crossed his face as he tossed something onto my desk, knocking one of my pens to the floor. "Probably not, especially when it's because of something like this."

I didn't even look down at what he'd thrown, just replaced the pen and moved my attention to my computer monitor. "And this couldn't have been a text?"

"Nope." Kyrin answered as he leaned forward to brace himself against the edge of my desk. Soon, his fingers began to drum on the wood, a clear indication he was excited over something. When I didn't play into it, he moved one hand away from the edge and placed it over my keyboard. My hand caught his wrist before he could press anything.

Same Kyrin, same games.

Another sly grin spread across his face as he pulled his arm back. "I'm so glad I have your full attention now, because"—he bent between his legs and pulled up a chair—"I know the votes were solidified, and I'm here to remind you that it's time for your annual masquerade."

The dude couldn't remember our monthly dinners, and yet he had this tradition circled on his calendar every year.

I pulled my eyes from him and finally glanced down at the paper on my desk, the one he had thrown. The square piece of paper was practically fluorescent and instantly irritated my eyes as I picked it up. Blinking at the glossy neon yellow, I realized it was a business card. *Who in the hell would voluntarily choose this to represent them?* The design was like something ripped straight out of a children's birthday catalog. Printed in a random blocky font, the name felt clumsy and completely lacked subtlety. There wasn't even a business logo, so I had no idea what this card was even for.

I looked up at him like he'd handed me a soiled napkin. "What is this?"

"My gift to you for the masquerade." Kyrin shrugged, leaning in slightly. "She's an up-and-coming photographer. Her work is raw and unfiltered."

I set the card back down carefully, as if it might infect the desk. "Pass."

"First off, I knew you would say that," Kyrin laughed, moving around the desk to grab my shoulder. "Which is why I already hired her."

Looking at his hand from the corner of my eye, I reminded myself that blood stains were hard to get out of this carpet. Inhaling, I pushed it off and brushed at the fabric where his hand had been. "I'm not interested."

"*Come on*, Silas. I can't have any fun like this at the bar. Besides, it's not about being interested," he said, leaning down and putting his arm around my shoulder. "It's about finding people who understand this place, people who can capture it in the way it deserves."

Kyrin wasn't the philosophical kind, more the type who went out of his way to find new ways to irritate people. There was always a selfish reason behind his choices, and I'd been unfortunate enough to learn that multiple times throughout the years. I could tell by just looking into his eyes. With the same blue as mine, he had a swirl of certain silver mischief that appeared whenever he was looking to cause trouble.

Whatever his play was, I didn't care. If he wanted to pay for absolute crap photography, he could be the one to pay again when it got redone.

I stood, pushing him off me. "Bullshit or not, I want to see proof she can handle the event, and tonight is as good as any other. Make sure she's here before the late rush, and we can do a test run. Matter of fact, you better be here too. I'm not dealing with"—I waved the card in the air before throwing it back on my desk—"Ms. Sunshine alone."

Kyrin watched the card slide across the wood. "She'll be here."

We both nodded in agreement as I turned to my cabinet and pulled a file out. A rough slap on my back made my blood pressure rise, and I looked toward the shit-eating grin that covered my brother's face. "I was planning on visiting some of your rooms anyway, I guess I'll just stick around until seven."

I exhaled, turning to face him. *Of course that was it, the little shit just wanted to let off some steam.* Regardless, no matter how I looked at the situation, there wasn't a downside. Best case, the pictures worked out. Worst case, I hired the most expensive photographer I knew. I nodded slowly. "Fine."

Kyrin grinned and pumped his fist into the air. "Fuck y—!"

"On one condition"—, My voice stopped him in the middle of his celebratory dance—"you actually come to dinner this week."

His jaw snapped shut, and I could have sworn I saw a slight eye roll at my stipulation. "We're not kids anymore. Do we really have to do the stupid dinners?"

"You're right. You're not a kid. That means you are more than capable of showing up on time and sitting still."

Kyrin swallowed whatever words were teetering on his tongue, and I took the silence as agreement. Dipping my chin at him in approval, I moved my attention back to my files.

"And throw that godforsaken card in the trash on your way out."

Chuckling, he snapped his Volunteer mask back on. "Sure thing. I'll be around if you need me."

2

Ember

The scent of espresso, cinnamon, and warm pastries filled the air around me. The aromas here were one of the things I enjoyed most at Clove. The coffee shop was rather new, and the only one built within walking distance from my house. Between the aesthetic and the short distance, it took me all but one visit to fall in love.

Because of the popularity, Clove was always slammed. I probably should've considered this before coming in today. Even the familiar smells did little to ease my anxiety as I tapped my foot against the tiled floor. My eyes flicked up toward the counter and around the crowd of people waiting for their orders. *Was I a patient woman? Yes. Was I about to be incredibly late to my job over a drink? Also, yes.*

Adjusting the intertwined straps that hung off my shoulder as I fidgeted with the keys to the bookstore. My brown hair, the barely tamed mess that it was, fell around my face in loose waves as I looked around at the horde of waiting people.

In hindsight, I'd accepted the photoshoot this morning knowing I would be pushing the limit with time already. When I got the text asking if I was available to take pictures at a dog's

birthday party, I assumed it would be quick. The owner ended up wanting their dog to change into *multiple* outfits, and I had, of course scheduled it right up against my evening shift.

Not only had I seen no rush in going straight there, but my fat ass also thought it was the perfect time to get a sweet treat. That was a sick joke because I didn't even register the amount of people until *after* I had ordered.

I crossed my arms and straightened as the black leather jacket I wore made a strange sound. I prayed it hadn't ripped. This day was already shaping up to be a rough one, and I didn't want to end it by being choked.

Well, not by *my roommate* anyway.

"Excuse me," I said, stepping closer to the counter where a barista stood. "Hi. Sorry to bug you, but do you happen to know how much longer the chai for Ember is going to be?"

He didn't even have the decency to look up from the cups he was marking as he responded. "It's in the queue."

I blinked. "Okay. Well," I gestured broadly to the crowd packed shoulder-to-shoulder behind me, "I'm just wondering if 'in the queue' means it's coming up next or if I should just take the loss."

That got his attention, because he looked up at me. Well, for a split-second anyway. "Can't you see how busy we are. You aren't special, lady. Go back in the line."

My eyebrows shot up in surprise.

Oh hell no.

I wouldn't have dealt with that on a *normal* day, and especially not on a day like this one.

I yanked my bag from my shoulder and threw it down on the counter in front of me. The items clattered loudly against the white granite, but I didn't care. The sudden movement claimed the attention of the patrons around me, so I exaggerated even more to make sure everyone noticed.

I pulled my purse to me and opened it to reach inside. The barista froze as he watched my hand search around, not exactly sure what to expect. After another moment, I raised my hand out and showed him exactly what I was looking for—my middle finger, which was now raised directly at him.

"Keep the chai and the money, asshole," I announced, grabbing my things and hoisting them over my shoulder.

Ignoring his widened eyes, I walked to the door and glanced down at my watch.

Shit! I was definitely going to be late now, and it was all for nothing.

I huffed and pushed into the blinding sunlight. As I lifted my hand to shield my eyes, my phone started buzzing in my pocket. Groaning, I used my chin to keep the straps in place, one hand still raised against the glare while the other fished around in my pocket. My keys threatened to slip through my fingers as I fumbled inside my pocket, finally pulling my phone from the depths. By the time I answered, my voice was tight with anxiety.

"Hello?" I said on a quick breath.

A male voice answered. "Hi, is this Ember Vale?"

"Yes?" I replied, exasperation creeping into my tone as I

hurried down the sidewalk, desperately trying not to drop anything.

"This is Kyrin Solstice. I got your name from a friend. They said you're good with photos and can handle *nontraditional* shoots."

His voice was deep, catching slightly on the second-to-last word. Curious, I stopped and resituated everything I was holding. I cradled the phone between my cheek and shoulder as I separated my bag, purse, and camera sling. "I mean"—my hip caught the corner of a brick wall, sending a sharp pain into my side. I sucked in a breath, my words coming out in a rushed jumble. "I do all kinds of shoots." I let out a small sigh as the pain subsided and refocused on the conversation. "This morning I was even able to capture a Great Dane in a bikini. What exactly are you looking for?"

He let out a short scoff, but whatever he said after was swallowed by the noise of the street around me.

"—looking for a photographer." His voice cut back in. "The club needs pictures for an upcoming event, a masquerade. Would you be interested?" A small pause followed, like he was considering his next words. "It's important that we find someone who can shoot atmospheric images of the models. Our whole goal is for the pictures to entice potential customers and create excitement among our members."

His request seemed common enough, and I could always use the extra money. "Sure. What day works best for you?"

"That's the thing. Your portfolio is rather impressive, but the owner wants you to come in for a trial run tonight to make sure you are comfortable with the environment."

Tonight!? I didn't respond immediately, quickly analyzing my schedule *and completely missing the part about the environment.*

"I will offer you a grand if you can be here at seven."

My thoughts slammed to a stop. "I'm sorry, did you just say a grand? Like *one* thousand dollars?" *That was enough to cover my portion of the bills for two months.*

Kyrin chuckled like that amount of money was an average transaction for him. "Yes. Normally, we wouldn't pay for a trial run, but I think you're going to love the vibes here, so I'll make an exception."

My stomach threatened to drop as I drew in a deep breath. "Yes. I'm available." I glanced at the time, panic rising again as I picked up my pace. "I get off at 6:30, and I'll head straight there. Just send me the location."

When he responded, his voice sounded almost triumphant. "Perfect, I'll text you the address and a contract link. Make sure to fill everything out beforehand, or you can't enter the building. The owner's kind of a dick about it."

What would a contract for photos have to do with entering the building?

My brisk walk had now moved into a jog as I answered between breaths. "Okay, got it."

Ending the call, I shoved the phone into the pocket of my dress as my mouth split into a grin. Bunching the fabric of the dress into my hand, I cradled my things and took off into a full sprint toward the bookstore.

When I finally made it there, the bell above the door didn't just jingle, it *clanged.* The noise was loud and accusing, like it had been personally offended by my entrance. I winced at the sound that echoed through the quiet space, ducking under the edge of the familiar doorframe—the same one I'd entered through for four years now.

Back then, I'd only come in for a few hours here and there. By the six-month mark, I was working every closing shift and loving it. I quickly learned that the morning shift brought the rush, and my only responsibility in the afternoon was to organize whatever mess was left behind. Most of the time, I could restock, clean, and have everything back to normal within an hour or two—which gave me the rest of my shift to do whatever I wanted. More often than not, I used this downtime to edit my photos.

Unless *Edna* came in, the owner's fifty-year-old assistant. Since day one of working with her, she'd made it her personal mission to make my life a living hell. Naturally, I tried to avoid her at all costs. The downside of that was the store was rather small, tucked between a yoga studio and a smoke shop.

From the outside, it seemed like any other small shop, but stepping inside was like entering another world. Books were everywhere, stacked on shelves that tilted at odd angles. Pictures of covers had been blown up and glued to the walls, sectioning each corner into a different genre. We were always playing some type of music, and not the boring elevator kind either.

As I reached the front desk, my eyes darted around for my arch-nemesis.

Empty.

Just as my body relaxed, I stepped forward to clock in when a familiar voice cut through the silence.

"You can breathe. I'm covering for her tonight."

I jumped, letting out a high-pitched squeal. Spinning my body around, I pushed into Atlas's chest. "You scared me!"

A grin spread across his face as his hazel eyes glimmered with excitement. Letting out a short laugh, he scoffed. "I *should* scare you. Maybe then, you'd actually get to work on time."

I rolled my eyes at the owner of the store as I set my things down in a lopsided pile. "It was less than ten minutes."

He didn't answer me as he walked by. Instead, he playfully raised an eyebrow before pulling a stick of gum from a small pocket in my bag. Shoving it into his mouth, he ruffled my hair and headed to a stack of books needing to be reshelved.

No one would ever guess that man was thirty-seven.

Closing the pocket he had stolen from, I feigned a dirty look and threw most of my things below the counter. After positioning my camera carefully in the drawer, I sat on the chair next to me and leaned in on my elbows as I watched Atlas. "If you could just shelve all of those for me and then the ones in the back, that would be great."

"Oh, sure," he scoffed, turning toward me. "Anything for you, boss."

I smiled at the sarcasm in his voice and silently thanked him for being the person he was. If he was *anyone* else, I probably would've been fired a long time ago. Through the years of being here, there had been a couple situations where I'd been called "hot-headed" by certain customers. At one point, I'd even found myself in a heated disagreement with security, but no matter the situation, Atlas always defended me—which was probably why Edna *loved* me so much.

A quick vibration from my phone reminded me of the conversation from earlier.

One thousand dollars.

The number settled in my mind like it held actual weight, and I wondered if it was too good to be true. Just as I started weighing the possibility of it being a scam, my phone lit up. Without even checking, I knew it had to be from Kyrin. To my surprise, he had sent two different texts. The first was a link to a secured drive, showing three different forms to sign. *He hadn't been kidding.* The second text gave a time and place.

Ruined. 7 p.m.

Well, an address would have been nice. Now, I had to figure out exactly *where* I was supposed to be at seven.

"Are you really not gonna help me?"

Uh-oh. My eyes shifted away from the screen and moved to Atlas. He was no longer being playful. Resting his elbow on the shelf, his fingers were hidden in his short brown hair, and it was clear he was actually agitated. I gave him a small smile and stood, shoving my phone into my jacket pocket. "Coming!"

Jogging to his side, I reached for the books he was holding. "Why don't I,"—I said, sliding the pile into my arms—"just take these."

Atlas gave a stern look as I quickly walked away from him to sort the books. For the next little while, we worked with only the sound of music surrounding us. As I went on to replacing the stock and organizing, Atlas mumbled something about having to set up his camera and headed to his office. The only time he went in there was when he was meeting with someone about the store, so I wished him luck as he walked away. Following him with my eyes, I let them flicker to the small clock mounted above the doorway.

2:27 p.m.

I couldn't help the spark of excitement that followed. In four hours, I'd have the chance to earn a shit ton of money by having fun and taking some cool pictures. With that reminder, I double-checked that Atlas was gone and pulled my phone back out. Opening maps, I typed in *Ruined.* It wasn't far—about a twenty-minute drive.

That was doable.

Snapping a screenshot of the directions, I tossed it back into my open bag and returned to my responsibilities.

3

Silas

My first mistake had been letting my brother stay.

My second had been entering a playroom I thought had been taped off to clean, only to walk in and find him sucking on someone's toes.

I wanted to burn my fucking retinas.

For a second, I tried to convince my brain it was someone else, *anyone* else. Lucky for me, my line of sight picked up on the stupid puzzle piece scarred into his chest—the jagged symbol that marked us as family. How ironic that ink that small was responsible for part of my sanity being destroyed.

For the next few hours, I threw myself into work, hoping I could forget the image, but nothing worked. Walking to my office, I shook my head and convinced myself he needed to find another place to experiment. Once inside, I went straight to my desk, taking a seat in front of the monitor. Pulling off my white mask, I placed my hand on the mouse and clicked twice to turn on the club's surveillance system. Small squares flickered across my screen in neat, obedient rows. As they focused, each square displayed a different room in the building. I hate security, but having a club like this meant I could never be too careful. Not

only did I need eyes roaming the main floor, I needed to be able to see all the rooms that were interconnected or within hidden spaces. To aid with this, security cameras had been installed in almost every corner.

Right now, I could see that room three was occupied by at least four people. Room seven was being used for an orgy, and room five was where I'd been absolutely blindsided by Kyrin. Moving my cursor over that square, I briefly disconnected it. *They would be fine for ten minutes... knowing him, it would probably be over in five.*

I watched over the other feeds for a few minutes longer than necessary. Seeing members in different positions finally allowed my brain to replace the mental image of my asshole brother. Some would probably call this an *abuse* of my power, but each member had granted me this freedom. By signing my contract, they agreed I could watch them as much as I wanted.

Did I ever actually *want* to? No.

The feeds from the rooms were never something I indulged in. I either did so out of habit or to keep my mind moving—like right now, when I needed to close my eyes and see something other than toes crammed into a mouth.

Once the image faded, I switched mental tabs and dove into the preparations for my masquerade. I had very few tasks left to complete before the event. I prided myself on not letting a single detail slip through the cracks. My mind didn't allow things like that to happen anyway, not when I was constantly analyzing everything. That's why the biggest decisions were always handled by me and my brothers.

Flipping through the stack, it seemed like those were the only types of things left to do. *Good, we could handle that easily.* Still, a familiar tension settled across my shoulders—the kind that never truly went away, no matter how prepared I felt. A ping from my desktop only tightened those muscles, and I looked over to see an email notification from Taya, my receptionist. I opened it, pushing the papers aside and clicked on the message. A file containing our finalized contract filled my screen.

I had requested she make some amendments to the original before the masquerade. After a few misunderstandings involving pompous dickheads, I needed a few things simplified. I'd only asked her to do this two days ago, so seeing it had been done already made me smile. This was now one thing I could push to the back of my mind—or try to at least, because *that* was a place that never seemed to rest.

Being idle was never my thing. I was always moving or thinking of the next thing to do. My brain was just that type, one that ran on stimulation and dopamine. If I didn't have something to take care of, I felt useless, and I hated that feeling. Taya understood that, which made things easier. She never questioned agendas I would send or how late I would stay. Running a business kept me in motion, and I liked it that way.

If I thought about it, that was the reason Ruined worked so well. I understood people, just like Taya understood me. There was never the need to explain things. Whether your mind was busy like mine or life had a way of suffocating you, my club gave everyone a chance to breathe, to feel.

A small smile formed at the corner of my mouth as I sifted through different sections of the forms she'd sent. On the side of the screen were her notes, outlining each change. The first piece that had been altered involved our actual application process for a membership. In order to gain entry, you would have to present your ID *and* have it verified through a new identification system. Due to this new protocol, we could easily check names against past convictions or any type of red flags that person might be associated with. If your name was put on the restricted list, you were denied entry.

It was that simple.

My phone made a quick buzz as I flipped to the next page. I didn't plan on bothering with it, but then it vibrated again, which meant I knew who it was. I could count on one hand the number of people who had my number, and only *two* of them would have the audacity to text me twice. *One of which was somewhere in this very club, with god knows what in his mouth.*

With a half-irritated sigh, I opened the text.

Kyrin: *Count me in for dinner this week. I'll bring the appetizer.*

I snorted under my breath knowing he was *here*, yet texting in our family group chat.

Greyson: *If the appetizer is that blonde you brought last time, count me in. But I swear to god, if you bring that nasty* *asparagus shit again, I will light you on fire.*

It was mere seconds before three dots appeared and another response chimed.

Kyrin: *Well, the appetizer was going to be vodka. Also, don't threaten me, you're making my dick hard.*

"Idiots," I muttered, though there was no heat behind it. *There never was with them.* My brothers were the only ones allowed to be a constant, unavoidable, and annoying headache. I switched my phone to silent and set it face down on the desk. *They could sort out whatever details they needed to without me babysitting.* As I pulled my hand away from the phone, my eyes landed on a half-hidden business card in the trash. My body once again tensed in reaction to the color.

What an ugly thing. Gaudy. Like it had been designed specifically to test me. I could practically feel it staring at me, right there from the trash. I could swear whoever created it did so just to taunt me.

I exhaled sharply and looked away, forcing myself to focus on the contract edits. Skimming the pages until I found the other altered sections, I read them aloud.

"After being granted entry, one must select an assigned mask and obey its role according to the rules." *Yes. Very black and white, very simple.* "Masks cannot be switched during visits and are not allowed to be removed." Another easy one, *you would think.* "Upon leaving the membership area, one consents to being filmed while in the building."

I nodded as I glanced through the remaining pages, the ones

that hadn't been revised. They outlined basic things like the members' information and a waiver, releasing us of any liability. As my eyes reached the last portion, the music in the club intensified, and the muffled pulse of it bled through the reinforced walls around me. Glancing at the clock, I noticed the time.

Shit.

I grabbed my white mask, stood, and locked my computer before heading toward the door. Whoever Kyrin hired would be here in the next few minutes, and I wanted to make sure I was present for every opportunity to rub that choice in his face. Taking the stairs down two at a time, I thought about the mere satisfaction I'd get from watching her failure.

In the short time I'd been gone, the club had filled. Every inch of the floor was now covered in sweat and skin. Not entirely a bad thing for *me*, but I hoped it would be for whatever walking highlighter was coming soon.

I cut across the main floor and opened the large door to our member entrance. This small waiting area was where we decided if you were worthy of being ruined. From the street, the space gave *no* insight to what waited behind the next door. In fact, the walls were a bright white, almost *glowing* against the few black geometric patterns that hung sparingly. There were no chairs anywhere, just the desk where my receptionist sat. It was similar to mine, with dark wood, clean lines, and a low light which filled the room.

Taya noticed me right away and stood, her green eyes giving away the smile underneath her mask. The black fabric stayed tight to her mouth as she dipped her head in recognition. To anyone else who came in, the mask she wore seemed almost normal. It mimicked the medical ones that were used to ward off sickness, but we both knew it was an inconspicuous way for her to follow the rules.

"How can I help you, Mr. Solstice?"

"The contracts look nice," I acknowledged, watching the clock hit seven. "I like your revisions. I'll need digital copies archived by morning and our physical copies replaced."

She nodded and bowed slightly, as if I was graced to be in her presence.

I couldn't help but shake my head at her behavior, a trait that often reminded me of Kyrin. For some stupid reason, I had hired her fully knowing I would have to deal with that everyday.

"Oh, and there will be a guest here tonight," I added, as she looked up at me. "I'm granting her a one-time entry without membership, but make sure her paperwork is completed and her name is pushed through our system. She's a potential photographer for the masquerade."

Her head tilted just a fraction, and I caught the desire that flooded her eyes. "Is that the one Kyrin mentioned earlier?"

Bringing my fingers up to my face, I rubbed the bridge of my nose and slowly exhaled, remembering that her being a raging lesbian was also one of the reasons we got along so well. "I am this close to enforcing restrictions on both of you. Just try to keep it in your damn pants."

She laughed through her mask. "Don't compare me to that child. Besides,"—she moved her hand, gesturing between her legs—"I can't help the fact that she's a hunter, okay?"

Mental note: find a new receptionist.

Dismissing her with one look, I glanced toward the entrance leading back to the street. Then, turning away from her completely, I let my feet guide me back inside the club. I adjusted my cuffs as I walked, grounding myself in preparation for tonight.

Whatever trouble Kyrin thought he'd found wasn't strong enough for what was coming her way.

4

Ember

After his meeting, Atlas came back with a lot of information for us to cover. We discussed new inventory coming, the seasonal hours, and the possibility of hosting up-and-coming authors. Even though it always involved work, our conversations amused me. He was the type of person that started with one topic and ended on a totally different one. As the hours passed, the discussion fell away and he became more of a body double, sinking into his chair as I shuffled around helping customers.

After waiting for me to finish ringing up one of our regulars, he called to me from across the room. “Want me to grab some dinner, and I’ll close with you tonight? That one Chinese place you like has a deal if I order in the next thirty minutes.”

Normally, I would absolutely take that offer—especially since he always splurged on a dessert for us. Unfortunately, this was the one night I had somewhere to be.

“I can’t,” I replied, crouching down to the cabinet beneath the register to refill our bags, “I have plans. Rain check?”

“What?!” Atlas clutched his chest as if my words had wounded him. “But who will I share my Mooncakes with?”

Rolling my eyes, I separated the bags and placed them on the

counter. "I'm sure you'll manage just fine."

"*Manage* is different than enjoy." Dramatizing his long face, he pushed himself up from the chair and walked toward the door. "But I guess I'll just go by myself." Pausing with his hand on the doorframe, he looked back at me. "I wonder if your boss knows just how mean you are."

I fought the urge to laugh at his childish behavior. *Thirty-seven years old, I swear.* Turning my head away, I shrugged. "Good question. If you see him, you should ask."

Flashing a quick smile, he chuckled softly before opening the door and walking out. Shaking my head at the man who signed my paychecks, I hurried through the last few closing tasks.

Not long after that, I pulled the shop door closed, locking the building up for the night. As the key turned, I tapped my home screen to check on the taxi. The address I'd bookmarked earlier was in the next town over—definitely *not* within my normal walking distance.

Most of my adult responsibilities fell within the same ten-block radius, which meant I'd never really found the need to have a car. In the rare case things were farther, like tonight, I normally just used my roommates.

Unfortunately, I wasn't in the mood to explain where I was going tonight—mostly because I wasn't even sure of that myself. Plus, I would be subjecting myself to five different lectures from the boys and whatever questions Kinsley would have. *No thanks,* I preferred the driver.

As I stepped toward the curb, the universe decided to test

that theory when a strong wind swept in. Instinctively, I pulled my camera tight to my chest and cinched my jacket closed. I squeezed my eyes shut just as my hair whipped around my face. Thankfully, the wind settled as the taxi pulled up.

Reaching for the handle, my reflection in the window caught my attention—or rather, the wild lioness mane spilling around my head. I sighed at the image, smoothing my hair as best as I could before ducking into the car door.

The driver's eyes met mine in the rearview mirror, and just as his eyebrows started to lift in question at my appearance, I held my hand up, stopping him from saying anything. The look I gave him must've been a clear indication of just how much I didn't care for what he had to say because he quickly cleared his throat, looking straight ahead again.

Settling into my seat, I pulled up the information I'd found and read the address aloud. As the car pulled away from the curb, I realized I'd never looked at the attachments from the text, meaning I still hadn't filled out the paperwork he had mentioned. *Shit.*

Blowing out a quick breath, I scrolled to the files he'd sent. If Kyrin hadn't specifically mentioned the owner being "kind of a dick," I probably would've brushed it off. People forgot things all the time, and that was an easy excuse, but for a thousand dollars, I could take a few minutes to get it done.

Opening the forms, I was met with one word in bold, italic letters. ***Contract.*** At this point in my life, I wasn't afraid to admit that I'd signed my life away on countless dotted lines.

Between numerous side jobs and the bigger photography gigs, signing things like this had become a regular thing for me. Contracts were as common in business as handshakes—the whole purpose was to manage risks and ensure legal compliance. For a club, though, I wondered why this would even be necessary.

Glancing over the first few sentences, I found my answer. The contract began by promising a safe, respectful space for *play*—highlighting the property as an environment designed to test boundaries with anonymity. *Interesting.* In order to gain access to this property, one had to sign the contract and apply for a membership. If accepted in, access to the space came with conditions.

From the first portion alone, I had so many questions about how this place worked. *I mean, who would pay for a membership like that?* However, the second section was where those questions faded as my eyes halted on the word **masks**.

What the..

I let my eyes skim through, quickly understanding this part of the document outlined the mandatory rules for membership. The very first stipulation highlighted three different masks that had to be worn at all times.

What the fuck had I gotten myself into.

Blinking a few times to gather my thoughts, I lowered my phone and looked around the car I was in. I had no idea that places like this even existed. Regardless, I was capable of taking pictures anywhere, so I mindlessly scrolled to the end of the document and typed my signature. I didn't need to know every little detail because I wasn't signing up to be a member. I didn't need to know any specifics because frankly, I didn't care. My name on this was for a paycheck. I'd only be there long enough to earn a grand.

Just so I wasn't completely shooting myself in the foot, I pulled up my messages and sent a quick text to my roommate. **Heading to a photo shoot. If I go missing, look up Kyrin Solstice.** I knew she probably wouldn't see it right away, but it was the evidence needed if I ended up in a ditch somewhere.

Letting my mind wander, I swiped to my search engine. My fingers hovered for a second before I typed Kyrin's name, then the club. Scrolling through, I realized there was barely anything on either. I had to go through multiple pages to even find the name Solstice, and when I did come across it, there was only one article. It turned out, Kyrin was one of three brothers who each owned a business under the family name.

That one page led me to Silas, Kyrin's older brother. He was the owner of the club I was headed to, but I only knew that because his name was connected to the address. The weird thing was the club's address wasn't labeled as anything specific. There were no photos either—of the club *or* Silas. It was like there was *no* record of any place called Ruined.

Just then, Kinsley's name flashed on my screen with a thumbs up emoji, and I felt the tiniest bit of reassurance. I turned to the window beside me, watching the blurred colors of the outside world rush by. The closer I got to the address, the more intrigued I became with this whole situation.

When the car finally came to a stop, I handed the driver some cash and opened the door. To my disbelief, the club's exterior was disappointingly bland. So much so, that I second-guessed the address altogether and sat there for a moment to retype it. When my phone showed the exact same destination, I stepped out and slung my camera over one shoulder. *Was this a joke?*

Matte black brick covered the tall building, rising close to two stories high. A few dark windows were scattered across the wall, but none granted any hints to what was inside. Besides those, there were no other signs of anything remotely inviting. The only indication that something was actually inside, was a single, thick metal door framed by two narrow sconces with flickering light.

"This is it?" I muttered to myself as I stepped toward the building. "Who in the hell would pay for something like *this*?"

A wall of muscle in a black shirt stepped out from around the corner, "Can I help you with something?"

"Yeah, actually. I'm looking for—" my eyes dropped to his nametag. **DUSK**. "Is that really your name?"

The corner of his mouth lifted in amusement, "Yup. My mom loved sunsets. What is it that you're looking for exactly?"

I wasn't sure what I felt more, empathy for the man in front of me, *or pity*. I answered without taking my eyes off his nametag, "A club. I'm here to take some photos."

Dusk seemed to have no idea what I was talking about as he looked around at the buildings surrounding us. "I'm sorry. There's no—"

"She's with us," a smooth voice announced as someone else stepped around him.

I immediately recognized the tone, knowing it was the man from the phone call I'd taken earlier. Turning toward the sound, I found a tall, bronzed figure standing there in a black tank top and ripped jeans. *Kyrin.* My eyes scanned over his body, locking in on the tattooed sleeve that covered his right arm. Moving my gaze to his face, I found it completely covered by a white mask.

He stepped toward me and held out his hand. "You must be Ember."

I blinked once, my attention still glued on the mask. "Yeah," I answered, drawing the word out. "That's me."

"Nice to meet you, *sunshine*," he replied, spinning me and making my dress fan out before handing me a mask of my own. "I presume you read over things and understand this is required." I frowned, shifting my camera as he turned and gestured for me to follow. "I'd put it on now, *before* we walk in. It will ensure that no one will approach you."

"Is this really necessary?" I asked, slipping the mask on.

Kyrin laughed, deep and warm. "Yes."

I didn't respond as I followed him around the corner and past a wall that looked exactly like the others. The only difference was *this* side had a door that was bigger and a metal sign next to it with a large silver S, almost like a monogram.

Pulling open the dark door, we entered a small lobby—an area that definitely did *not* match the aesthetic outside. The walls were actually cute, fitting the generic cookie cutter mold of an office. Kyrin approached the desk I quickly realized was for registration. A woman in a strapless dress sat behind it, her black hair hanging far below the medical mask she wore. A light tapping sound came from her fingers as she moved them across her keyboard. The sound stopped as soon as we entered, and her attention settled on me. "You must be the photographer."

When I nodded, she asked for my ID before motioning to the keypad on the edge of her desk. "Please put in your birthdate and zip code."

Punching in the numbers, I glanced over at Kyrin. "I draw the line at my social security number."

Kyrin opened his mouth to respond, but it was the receptionist that spoke. "Cute *and* funny, I see why you hired her."

Shaking his head at her comment, he tapped the pad. "Sounds like you're already looking for a membership card." When I held his stare through my mask, he shrugged with one shoulder. "It's just how we do things here. There's no walk-ins and no exceptions to the rules, even for temps."

Holding my tongue at that term, I looked back at the woman behind the desk. After a few seconds, she handed my ID back, and the door beside us buzzed. With a wink, she motioned toward the door. "Have fun, beautiful."

As soon as it opened, the music from inside swallowed us. I couldn't see right away, but as my eyes adjusted to the darkness, it felt like my senses were hit all at once. This wasn't like *Clove*, where the subtle warm scents wrapped around me. My *entire* body reacted the moment he opened that door, even my feet began to vibrate with the pulse in the floor, alive with the music. My eyes moved quickly, making out different people who weaved within the shadows. The door didn't just open into another room—it opened into chaos.

Beautiful chaos cloaked in different forms of stimulation. At first, it was the music that caught my attention—a seductive metal track layered with violin. Next, the neon lights traced the floor, piercing through the low-hanging fog. No matter where I looked, something else demanded my attention, pulling my gaze deeper into the club.

Everyone inside wore a mask, but for some, that was *all* they wore. Most were *completely naked.* Not only naked, but in the middle of various sexual acts.

Looking at everyone around me, I realized two things. One, I now understood why everything here revolved around privacy, including the masks. Two, I also knew why there had been no pictures in my research.

This was a sex club.

I had been hired to take pictures in a *sex club.*

I swallowed sharply as my gaze snagged on someone across the room, someone who had clearly been watching us. Being one of the few people that was fully clothed, he wore a white mask like ours. Leaning against a metal column next to a flight of stairs, his attention stayed set on us. If not for the mask, I might not have noticed him at all. Dressed in a black long sleeve with his arms folded across his chest, he nearly blended into the surroundings. The more I focused, the more I made out his dark jeans and army boots. My mind recalled the internet article I'd found, and somehow, with one-hundred percent certainty, I knew this had to be *Silas.*

His head dipped in acknowledgment before he turned toward the stairs and motioned for us to follow. Kyrin moved before I did, obviously seeing the same instruction. Grabbing my hand, he led us through the large crowd of people that filled the space. Looking around us, I became hyper-aware of just how bright my outfit was to those around me. Not only did I seem completely *overdressed* compared to the other guests, but my yellow dress stuck out like a sore thumb. I suddenly felt like a streetlamp in a graveyard.

Was that why he had called me sunshine? Because of my dress?

I squeezed his hand to get his attention. "You could have told me there was a dress code," I yelled over the music.

"I guess I didn't want to scare you by saying clothes were optional here," Kyrin replied, turning toward me and squeezing my hand back. "Besides, *I'm* not the one you should be saying that to. I like yellow."

Even though his mask covered it, I knew he was smiling. It was that moment that I decided to stop caring about how I looked, since it was obvious that no one else here did.

The top of the stairs opened into an office resembling a penthouse. Everything inside was immaculate, no stains, no impressions on the seats, *nothing.* Every item had its place, as if nothing within the four walls had ever been moved. I was immediately uncomfortable, especially with how sterile it felt. There was no color—no life. The room reminded me of a hospital, *or a prison.*

A voice deeper than Kyrin's pulled my attention toward the desk, where the man who had been watching us now stood. "I want to make my expectations very clear. You were invited here tonight because we're testing you on your skill. We want the atmosphere captured. If you can do that, we'll talk about the next steps." Pausing for only a slight second, he continued, "We're looking for headshots and members in motion. We want the masks—and what we *offer* here—to be the primary focus. Do you think you can handle that?"

I cocked my head to the side, stuck on the fact he hadn't even introduced himself. Holding out my hand, I stepped toward him. "I'm willing to bet you're Silas."

He made no attempt to move. "And I'm willing to bet you don't survive tonight." Instead of shaking my hand, his head moved up and down slightly, like he was sizing me up. "The darkness here tends to destroy anything that it deems too bright."

So, he was the one who had a problem with yellow. I pulled my hand back and straightened, making it clear he didn't intimidate me. "Is that what this club offers—what I'm supposed to capture? *Darkness*?"

Silas's answer was immediate, his voice seeming to fill the space around us. "What we offer here goes deeper than that.

Our darkness is one that invades without you knowing, a slow kind of ruin. A type that eats at you until you're ready to admit exactly who you are. You don't strike me as someone who would understand that."

My eyes locked onto his mask as his words echoed inside my head. Each time I heard them, my anger rose. *Who did this man think he was*? "And *you* don't strike me as a people person. Tell me—did you go with the masks because you're ashamed of your dick size? Is that what your whole attitude is about?"

When he answered, his response was to Kyrin. "Huh. Color blind and childish, nice choice." The words were dismissive, his tone bordering between disinterest and disgust. With his head inclined toward me, he continued. "Are you sure you want to be responsible for her? There are a million other photographers we could use."

The anger in me magnified, and I didn't know whether I wanted to swing at him or just leave his presence altogether. Steadying myself and the growing irritation, I responded with a clipped voice. "*No one* is responsible for me." Then, I softened my tone as I turned toward Kyrin. "Let's just get started, yeah?"

Silas watched the interaction and scoffed as Kyrin let out a loud laugh. "Yeah, sunshine, let's go."

The repeated nickname was enough to push me over the edge, and I pointed my finger at him as he crossed the space in front of me. "*Don't* call me that."

Silas stepped around us, ignoring the interaction, and led us back to the main floor. Exiting the stairs, I noticed a group of naked models lined along one of the walls. I immediately knew they were waiting there for me. I studied each of their bodies before turning to Silas, who seemed to already be watching me.

He was expecting me to fail.

A large smile formed beneath my mask as I faced the models. Looking around, I scoped out the areas around us and scanned for the best backgrounds.

Fuck him and his stupid darkness.

One by one, I took the model's hands and repositioned them, gauging the light. Within seconds, my instincts kicked in and several visions formed in my mind. I began directing the women with silent gestures as the bass of the music picked up and thundered around us. They followed my cues easily as I aimed the camera toward each of them and started shooting. After checking quality with a few test shots, I angled myself to catch the fog and the gleam of leather props hanging behind them. After a few simple poses, I encouraged them to move with each other instead. Eventually, I pulled away from staging them and just observed from the side with my camera. I'd just captured a few amazing close-ups when I heard an eruption of throaty moans nearby.

Looking to my left, I followed the sounds until I reached a room filled entirely with green light. The hue cast a haze over everything, including the people inside. Everyone was fully immersed in play with someone and unbothered by the fact that I had entered. I couldn't stop watching them, completely lost in the moment. It was captivating, even to me. *Maybe the darkness he was talking about was this. A feeling that left you intoxicated and full of adrenaline.*

It took me half a second to decide that *this* was what I needed to capture next. Lifting my camera toward the group in the middle, I dismissed all the models around me besides two. My eyes widened beneath my mask as I moved closer to document their passion. Every movement was real and raw, filled with a feral need.

That exact feeling was what I needed to produce for these pictures to turn out—the feeling that stripped away all simplicity and turned up the intensity.

Steadying my camera, I stepped further in and directed the models to join them. The people in front of us gladly welcomed the company, grabbing at them with low groans and lapping tongues. Immediately, one Volunteer dropped to her knees as a Dom pushed inside her mouth.

I watched until I found an opening, slightly adjusting the models themselves to caress the back of heads or squeeze thighs. Seizing every opportunity, I went to work capturing the feeling within the room. I didn't hesitate as I moved around, letting Silas's doubt guide me on what to do next. Soon, my simple suggestions turned into instructions on how to please one another, and I captured that as well—all while keeping my camera angled so the masks were fully visible.

I used the room too, moving around to catch their reflections in the mirrors surrounding us. Kneeling, turning, and stretching, I focused on anything that would help catch the unique energy here. I was completely in my element, and I knew the pictures would prove that, but I also planned on succeeding just to slap the shit out of Silas with my worth. *Other photographers? He could suck my metaphorical dick.*

For all I cared, they could leave the room, *the whole building,* and I'd be just fine. As for now though, they were probably still watching me intently. Honestly, at this point, I was barely paying attention to their existence anymore. Especially because the more I watched the people in front of me, the more everything else seemed to fade into nothing.

As they groped each other, I bent them into position, guiding hands, and opening mouths. With each choice I made, the pictures came out better than I initially imagined. Each shot caught a different form of euphoria, at one point I was even able to capture one of the women as she hit climax, her head thrown back in ecstasy.

When I finished the last round of shots, I stepped back until I made contact with one of the walls. The rigid surface grabbed my attention, and for a moment, I lowered my camera and allowed myself the opportunity to step out of my job and be a *Watcher* for a moment.

I could immediately tell why this mask existed. The air in the room was pure electricity, crackling with every movement and I was able to witness it all. From my corner, I watched the people in front of me unfold into a blur of skin and tongues.

The more I watched, the more I understood this place, how it could be a craving to some and a need for others—*myself included.* The realization made me angry, because there was no way in hell I was admitting that to the devil who owned it. Silas Solstice was already a big bag of smug.

I crossed the room and headed back toward the two men who followed me in. Sliding the camera strap over my head and settling it securely against my chest, I stopped directly in front of them. A sudden rush of confidence, along with my growing irritation, fed into my petty side as I locked in on Silas. Slowly using my hand to move my hair to one side of my neck, I paused at my chin and slipped the Watchers mask free from my face.

Silas's reacted almost instantly, his entire body going rigid before shooting off the wall. Trying to hide what happened, he forced his muscles to relax again and I internally celebrated. *Ha. Ha. Mother fucker.*

I met his gaze and held it through the mesh fabric between our eyes. "Do me a favor," I said loudly, "and tell the darkness it can choke."

I didn't wait to see how that landed. Instead, I turned to Kyrin, handing him the mask I'd worn. "You'll have the proofs in a few days but just know I have some requests for when you ask me to finish this job. First off, it will be a hard pass if you plan on calling me *'sunshine'* again and that's only if I don't immediately decline based on the fact I'll have to work with *him* again." I turned to Silas specifically. "And if you're the one who reaches out, make sure to look up the word *decency.*"

Taking my phone out of my pocket, I requested a ride home. As my finger tapped the button, I felt Silas's eyes burning through me, but he said nothing. Turning my body away, I refused to look back at either one of them as I left the club, and the asshole who owned it.

5

Silas

I sat alone, twirling a pen between my fingers at my desk.

For three days, I'd waited for this exact moment to come. I'd spent most of that time envisioning this very package being delivered, but more often than not, I found myself thinking about the woman who sent it. At this point, it felt like my thoughts were beginning to consume me—each one consisted of her.

Now that her photos were in front of me, I almost didn't want to open them. Instead, I watched the light from the setting sun move across my desk, cutting long slats across the manila envelope.

Proofs.

Ember Vale.

Resting one elbow on my desk, I ran my thumb along my jaw before leaning forward and pulling the envelope closer. As curious as I was to see the pictures inside, seeing her name angered me. I'd convinced myself she would crumble inside my walls. Instead, she *thrived*—taking control of the whole goddamn room we had been in. It hadn't been enough for her just to piss me off by proving me wrong, she had then

chosen to openly defy me in my own club. On top of all of that, this delivery meant that she had downloaded, edited and printed this portfolio within *three* days. That was the fastest turnaround time I had ever experienced from a photographer, which was even more infuriating.

Pulling the tape off the envelope, I slowly slid the glossy 8x10s free. A fresh wave of irritation rose when I quickly realized Kyrin had been right about her. Through the camera lens, she found a way to capture the beautiful, feral mess here. Somehow, she'd taken hidden faces and transformed them into intimate moments that felt raw and haunting.

One photo screamed lust, showcasing the veins running up a man's arms as he gripped the open thighs in front of him. The bottom half of his Volunteer mask showed his tongue hanging out, ready to please. Another highlighted a man who was being ridden, the woman on top staring down with such intensity I could see it through her mask. The third showed a Volunteer licking the curve of a spine as each bead of sweat reflected the colors around them.

Each pose position only highlighted the mask being worn. They were all remarkable in their own way, and I had zero notes on her technique. In fact, I took my time, enjoying and analyzing each picture. Soon, I realized they only grew in potency, and a strange feeling settled over me. Each time I came across a new photo, I knew it wasn't the artistry that made my grip tighten—it was the person *behind* the camera.

I kept finding her at the edges of the frames and in reflections of mirrors. Without even realizing it, I was searching for her in each one. My mind moved on its own, looking for the blurred silhouette of a woman with wild brown hair, just out of focus. She was everywhere without ever being the intended subject.

I set the photos down on my desk and felt my hands curl instinctively into fists. This brewing feeling was not one of irritation or anger. What was building inside of me now was stronger. Each second that passed, I only felt it grow as it ignited inside my veins. I needed to do something, and *fast.* This feeling was overwhelming, and I needed to channel it somewhere. Naturally, my mind chose anger.

Not only had she treated my rules as if they were *suggestions*, but it was as if nothing could touch her—like her entire presence was a fire that refused to go out. The fact that she walked around that loud, that bright—maybe it would be best if I was the one to show her exactly how the world would eventually treat her.

Flipping through the photos in my hand, it now seemed like every image she'd sent was a deliberate challenge, a quiet smirk aimed straight at me. She hadn't just disobeyed me. She'd disrespected my club, my space, the order I'd built and protected.

No one did that. *Ever.* My jaw tightened as my mind replayed the last interaction I had with her. She hadn't just taken her mask off but *casually* exposed herself to everyone in an act of defiance toward me.

I felt the back of my teeth grind together as I thought about it, all because I couldn't get that damn moment out of my head.

At first, I didn't understand why, but now, seeing these photos, I knew—it was her *and all her chaos.* She was uncontained, like fire in its purest form, and as much as I tried to fight it, I was drawn to her unpredictable heat.

Rolling my shoulders, I tried to release the tension building in my body, but the more I thought about her, the more my blood boiled. She hadn't even bothered to make herself presentable before coming here. Her hair had been unbrushed, and she'd worn that damn yellow dress and leather jacket. Just like her annoying business card, her fashion sense also got under my skin.

A low growl escaped me as I brought my fist down on the desk, the sound cracking through the room. It wasn't just about my rules anymore—it was about *her.* A fire like that was dangerous and needed to be controlled. Closing my eyes, I pictured her as a raging inferno that burned everything I stood for. She was too much, too intentional to be anything but a provocation. I drew a slow breath in through my nose, allowing my thoughts to settle.

It all made sense—why her wild hair, her unmasked face, and the defiant look in her eyes refused to leave my thoughts. She thought this was all a game, but she hadn't been face-to-face with actual darkness before, not like *mine.* All I needed to do was smother her with it. No oxygen meant no flame, and no flame meant that she would know what it was like to be ruined, to be torn down to her very core. If I could get her there, I could rebuild her with my own hands, piece by piece.

I'd barely spoken to her the night of the shoot, leaving Kyrin to handle everything after. I convinced myself she wasn't worth anything, but now, watching her flame die out meant everything to me.

I sat up, a new determination settling deep in my chest. She would learn what it felt like to be stripped of confidence, to be left bare and vulnerable. Like a sign from whatever demon possessed me, her business card once again caught my attention from the trash can beside my desk. I picked it up, turning it between my fingers as a slow grin spread across my face. The color didn't even bother me anymore because I planned to bleed it dry.

EMBER VALE

877-555-4890

Pushing the photos aside, I logged in to the club's database and pulled up the record from her ID.

Ember Vale.

Female.

25.

Employed- multiple
No criminal record.

This was going to be *too* easy.

A small part of me hoped there was more I couldn't see. Either way, I needed the full picture before I put any type of plan into place.

I picked up my phone, tapping a contact I used quite frequently, my cousin Knox. He was my go-to for this kind of work, including things like finalizing my staff roster. All club members ran through a general database for their background checks, but for my employees, I recruited someone who could find every secret. Having an extensive background as a P.I., Knox had initially been hired specifically for *staffing,* but now, I used him to find any type of information I needed. The dude could hack any electronic, find any face, and uncover anything that was hidden. He lived for it and looked forward to most of the tasks I gave him.

The line rang once, then again before it clicked softly. Knox's voice was low as he answered. "Lay it on me."

"I have a name. I'm looking for a full workup."

The steady click of a keyboard filled the background. "What do I have to work with?"

I glanced at the card again, slowly dragging my thumb over her first name. "Ember V-A-L-E."

More light tapping followed, then a small click of his tongue. "What are we looking for?"

"I want everything. History. Records. Real name, if that isn't it. Bank accounts. Web presence. Social. Family. Anything you can find."

He hummed in approval. "I'll need a few days. I'll send it in a file like usual."

"The faster, the better." With that, I pulled my phone away from my ear as the line went dead. Because of him, I'd be able to get everything I needed. As soon as I had that file, I'd know exactly what method to use on her. The more I let my thoughts stray to possible scenarios, the more excited I became for her downfall. Pulling up my email, I secured the next step in my plan by typing up a quick message—or more so, an *invitation.*

The email was quick, methodically typed to elicit the reaction I knew she'd inevitably give. Only after confirming the delivery did I gather my things, my mind shifting back to what was in front of me, specifically the dinner I was expected at soon.

After checking in with the bartender and going over the next shift with Taya, I stepped into the night. Cold air scraped against my skin, my body erupting in goosebumps. I smiled as I watched them spread, knowing I would soon be able to claim the same reaction from *her.*

My body quickly adjusted to the temperature change as I walked to the garage around the corner where I'd parked my Lexus. The car itself wasn't anything special, but the details I'd installed on it were. Wrapped in a special vinyl, the color came off darker than most blacks and the windows were all tinted to prevent anyone from seeing inside. Aesthetically, each decision I'd made about the appearance was solely based on my personality, but the fact that it fit so perfectly for my current situation, wasn't lost on me. Turning the engine on, I settled in and tried to think of anything but her.

The drive *should've* helped, but it didn't. In fact, it only made things worse. My head felt full of static—clearing only to show glimpses of her face as I hit the freeway. Those damn brown eyes, so full of life. *I wanted to carve them out with my fingers.* No matter what I tried, she stayed at the forefront of my thoughts, like she had every right to be there.

In response, I turned up the music until it was louder than necessary. I didn't stop turning the dial until it reached a volume that rattled the mirrors and drowned out all thoughts. I focused on the road, and the red lights blurring together. When that didn't help, I tightened my grip on the wheel and forced my mind elsewhere. *The club's inventory. The dinner I was approaching. Security rotations.* Anything that didn't feel like heat behind my ribs.

By the time I pulled onto my street, my jaw ached from being clenched for too long. As my house came into view, my body relaxed slightly. This was the residence where I'd grown up, my home away from the club. Being here always gave me a weird sense of comfort. Maybe it was because it was the only part of me left that was sentimental, or maybe it was because this house was the only thing I had inherited from my mother...*other than my brothers.*

Pulling into my spot in the driveway, I recognized the two cars parked out front. Each vehicle resembled its owner in different ways, Kyrin's truck was bold, just like him—the burnt orange color reflecting a warm type of strength. Greyson's Jeep was red and open on all sides, a running joke of how empty he was inside.

Pulling my keys out, I prepared myself for whatever was waiting for me inside. Each time we had dinner, I ended up walking into some kind of shitstorm.

It wasn't until the last ten feet of the driveway that Ember's face finally started to fade from my mind. Lucky for me, all thoughts of her vanished completely as I pushed my front door open. The air inside hit me, thick with a mix of paint and something chemical, close to bleach. The scent was followed by quiet laughter coming down the main hallway from my living room. Kicking off my shoes, I set them by the door and closed it behind me. Walking toward the familiar voices, I guessed at what my brothers could be doing.

In no world, was I expecting that to be *Twister.* Yes, the children's game, except in my brother's ridiculous minds they decided to up the ante with *paint.* The furniture in my living room had been moved, and in the middle was a gigantic tarp where each dot on the mat was smeared with a different combination of colors. Fingerprints streaked my table and unmistakable handprints stamped the floor.

I didn't have to think too hard to guess Kyrin was the leader of this, but then again, Greyson was never *always* the innocent one. Coming in at 6'2", that barbarian was a whirlwind of scarred skin and blond hair that didn't say no to anything. Even now, he stood barefoot with streaks of red across his cheeks like war paint. Kyrin was there too, right next to him, bent at the waist, while a girl I vaguely recognized stretched over his back as she tried not to topple over. I watched them laugh for a moment before my gaze dropped to the floor beneath them. The white tile surrounding their game was stained with a series of mixed blotches. I glared at the multiple spots where paint had very clearly spilled and then attempted to be cleaned.

I walked to the hall closet and pulled the wooden door open, reaching inside. Sorting through the supplies, I grabbed my mop and some rags. Returning to the *children* in the living room, I cleared my throat and shook my head in their direction, *as if they actually had the ability to process disappointment.* Then, in one smooth motion, I threw the supplies at their feet and walked straight past them to the backyard. I wasn't their father, nor was I in the mood to deal with whatever excuse they were about to give.

The deck I'd built out back overlooked nothing special, but it was still nice to stare out at the trees beyond. The sounds around me blended into something calm, and right now, I much preferred them to the ones inside.

After what felt like only a few minutes, the sliding glass door behind me opened, and Kyrin stepped up beside me with a plate of food. "I wasn't sure if you were still pissy or not, but I made you a plate."

The sarcasm in his tone reminded me of Ember, and her eyes instantly filled my mind. "I'm pissy because you guys seem to forget the fact that you're both grown men."

He raised his hands in submission, already retreating back toward the door like he had no way to defend that comment.

I called out to him right before he pulled it open. "Where exactly did you find Ember?"

Kyrin stopped immediately and looked over his shoulder at me. "*Ember*? Could she be the reason you're so uptight tonight?"

As usual, I didn't feel like playing his mind games. "Just answer the question."

His smile loosened as he rejoined my side. "I found her card on a table in a coffee shop I visited. When I was looking at it, the waiter swore she was the best thing around and bragged about how she always brought things to life. Then she mumbled something about that only being true if you could *handle* her. I had a good feeling about her and thought she might be good for you. So, I decided to take the chance." He shrugged before a sly, stupid smile covered his face. "Plus, I knew she would end up bothering you, and I kind of live for things like that."

Huh.

Well, at least now I had someone else to blame for her demise. Realistically, what was coming for her was his fault. The fact of the matter was, he decided her outcome by playing this dumb game of his. "So, you knew how she would act, then?"

My question made him pause for a moment, like he was replaying that night. "It's because she took off the mask, huh?"

When I didn't respond, he nodded like everything made sense. "I had nothing to do with that, man, so don't put me on whatever shit list you've created in your head. I told her it was mandatory."

His reaction confirmed my original thought about her. *She had willingly chosen to act like that.* Regardless, none of that mattered now. I'd made up my mind about her and exactly what was going to happen.

Physically, I was here on the porch with him. Mentally, I was already devising every way I could tear her apart.

6

Ember

Almost four days since I had experienced *Ruined*—an experience that had settled deep into my bones.

I knew coming home that night I had ventured into dangerous territory, but as I walked through my front door, I found myself trying to fight the pull to go back.

The second I was inside, Kinsley and Kolby were there waiting for me. Neither of them were thrilled with my decisions, and walking in felt a whole hell of a lot like coming home to your parents after missing curfew, but in this case, it was my roommates. I answered all of Kinsley's questions and avoided Kolby's glare before popping in some headphones and deciding to use my boost of energy wisely. I rode through my adrenaline high that night by cleaning every surface in the house.

The whole time, I just replayed the night in my head. I was so proud of the pictures I'd taken, and I *knew* they were going to be amazing. Ruined had so many unique elements, but my favorite moment of the night had nothing to do with the club. Seeing the flicker of irritation within Silas? *God, it had been beautiful*—the absolute highlight of my week.

About an hour later, Kolby had found me with a controller

in his hand. Pretending to take a piece of paper out of his back pocket, he unfolded the air and cleared his throat. "You have been challenged to a duel involving kart racing and trash talking. Please proceed to the couch where you will be thoroughly destroyed."

I couldn't help but snicker at his choice of presentation. Setting the rag down, I crumpled the imaginary paper and threw it into the trash. "You're going down."

My answer must have surprised him, because his face lit up as he took off toward the living room where we eventually settled into our competition. Inevitably, one match turned into hours. Every time one of us won, it became a "best two out of three" situation, then best five, then best seven. At some point, snacks even appeared between us.

By the time I blinked up at the clock, it was 3:57 a.m., and my extra energy was fading fast. I set the controller down to signal I was done and fought off Kolby's repeated attempts to get me to go to his room. By the time I closed my eyes, I was still buzzing with adrenaline.

Fast forward to now, where I sat at my vanity, still somehow feeling the aftereffects. I never reached back out to Silas or Kyrin, but my proofs were scheduled to be delivered today, and in some weird way, I almost wished I could be there to see their reaction.

Twisting a brown curl around the metal rod of my iron, I frowned at the reflection staring back at me. The morning sunlight streaming in was bright and a little too honest. The pale light highlighted every single part of my exhausted face. Every freckle and every ghost of a blemish screamed for attention within its rays.

I set down the iron to section off another piece of hair when my phone buzzed, alerting me to a new email. I held my breath as the name flashed across the screen.

Silas Solstice

Masquerade Details

I couldn't help the smug smile that spread over my face as I read the name of the sender again. However, that smile faded as my eyes moved to the actual message. The email was precise and polished but also *arrogant*—much like the person who'd sent it.

Ms. Vale,

It seems that I have misjudged your talent. Therefore, your presence is requested for the masquerade at my club. I hope you understand we have certain expectations involving a strict time schedule and dress policy. The event will take place in three days with your scheduled arrival at 6 p.m. Payment for your services will be sent via invoice.

Decency; a behavior that conforms to expected standards of morality.

Example- I hope you have the decency to keep your mask on the entire time.

Not asked. Not invited. Requested—as if I had no choice. Clearly, he was used to people simply following his demands, no questions asked.

Fuck that guy and his god complex.

I set my phone back down and stretched my legs out from underneath me. Placing my feet on the cold floor, I pushed down into my heels and raised my arms, stretching out the stiffness in my back. The hard wood beneath me was stable and real—unlike whatever fantasy world he seemed to live in.

I was ashamed to admit that for the briefest moment, I was actually excited to see the email come through. That initial reaction suddenly felt like a traitorous emotion, and I scolded that part of myself as I weighed the options of accepting his offer. The whole event intrigued me for multiple reasons. Not only was it an exclusive event, but I liked the environment, and I knew it would be a good payoff for me in the end.

I reached for my mascara as I felt my jaw clench. Regardless of my interest, the email hadn't asked if I was available, it hadn't even asked if I *wanted* to participate. I curled my lashes and blinked a few times in the mirror before moving the small brush to my left eye.

I hated that man, and I knew for a fact that in his twisted mind, he saw no reason I wouldn't be there. The most annoying part was that he wasn't wrong, which made me hate him even more.

Straightening in the mirror, I ran my fingers through the curls I'd just put in my hair. I then stood and crossed the room to my closet to find my outfit for the day. Hangers scraped against the wooden rod as I searched for something that fit my mood for my shift. I pulled out a black top and paused with it in my hand. *Black*. The color of his club walls, which meant that would probably be one of the colors of his masquerade.

Ugh.

Lowering the shirt, I sighed. If I was being honest, it would be stupid to not take the job, especially for *that* kind of money. If I could focus on something other than my growing hatred for the owner, I could probably let myself get excited. Maybe I wouldn't have to deal with *him* to get the job done, or at all, for that matter. I clung to that thought as I dressed quickly, pulling the shirt over my head and tugging my jeans up with sharp movements.

"You look like death."

I jumped from Kinsley's voice, the one that came from my doorway, where she stood staring at me with her arms crossed. Her blonde hair was twisted into a lazy topknot that somehow still looked runway-ready. Silk pajamas clung to her body, and two green gel pads sat perfectly under her eyes.

"Any word from the demon boys?"

A small sound escaped my throat, something between a laugh and a scoff. "They want me to come back."

Raising one eyebrow at me, she pulled herself off the doorframe and stepped into my room toward my bed. "Just wait until Kolby finds out. You know he thinks you belong to him." With a dramatic sigh, she flopped onto the edge of my purple comforter. "The electricity bill is due today, and it's your turn to pay. You still good with that?"

"Yeah. With the money from the club, I'll be good for two

months."

At the mention of the club, she shot upright like she'd been electrocuted. "Oh no, absolutely not. I can just use my trust fund. There is no way you are paying with cash from the demons and their—what did you call it? The den of sex and assholes?"

I snorted as I packed up my make-up, realizing she actually *had* been listening to me that night. "Yup, pretty much."

Her questions about the club had been pretty direct, and I answered most of them, but we really hadn't talked since.

"I just don't understand why that place would even exist, Ember."

That made sense. Kinsley wasn't exactly *that* type of person—more so the hopeless romantic, with the meet-cute in a coffee shop. "You don't have to understand it."

She wrinkled her nose like the mere thought of the club offended her whole existence. "I don't like it."

I turned slightly and gave her a small smile. "You don't have to *like* it either."

"No, I don't accept that. I'm taking care of the bill." She leaned forward, resting her hand on my shoulder. "You know it won't even make a dent in the account. That way, you don't have to go back—"

Before she could continue, another presence appeared in my doorway.

"*Ugh.* What do you want?" Kinsley deadpanned, staring at her brother, who now stood in the same spot she had moments before.

Kolby didn't acknowledge her. Instead, he nodded in my direction as he strolled in with his usual grin and tousled blond hair. As he reached the bed, he pushed her legs over to create space for himself. "Not *you.*"

I rolled my eyes at him before clearing the rest of my vanity.

Giving me a lopsided smirk, he threw himself onto my bed beside Kinsley, shoving the pillows on the floor like he owned the place. "She probably wouldn't have bothered you if I had been in your bed this morning."

"*Kolby—*" I scoffed, making eye-contact with him through the mirror.

"That's seriously never going to happen." Kinsley half-yelled as she kicked him off the bed.

His body hit the floor with a hard thud, followed by a dry laugh where he'd landed.

As Kinsley turned back to me and opened her mouth to continue our conversation, Kolby's hand shot up over the bed. My eyes immediately moved to what he was holding. Wrapped in his fingers was a pair of my silk underwear, probably taken from somewhere under the bed. "Can I pretend this was a souvenir from last night?"

"You. Are. Such. A. Freak." Kinsley shrieked before rolling over the bed and throwing punches that hit him repeatedly. He blocked her, but she yanked the underwear from his grasp and tossed them back to me. Kolby grunted in pain as she smiled at me.

In the next moment, he ripped a pillow off the bed in retaliation, smashing her in the face with it.

A flustered scream escaped her before she erupted into a whirlwind of smacks and squeals. "*Out.* Get out, you big fat *idiot*!"

Kolby just laughed in response, as if her temper tantrum meant nothing. Dodging her attempted attacks, he stood and winked at me before making his way toward the door. I just sat and watched everything unfold like I normally did with them. Arguments like these weren't uncommon, especially with them being only six minutes apart. With twins as roommates, I'd already learned their life was either a constant competition or an impromptu wrestling match.

Just as his foot crossed the threshold into the hallway, Kinsley ran to the door and closed it by throwing her body weight into it. "If mom wasn't visiting in a few weeks, I might actually murder him. Too bad I have to keep him around for brownie points. He may be *my* twin brother, but he's still *her* baby boy."

I laughed, enjoying the sarcasm in her tone. "He's not that bad."

Raising her eyebrows, she folded her arms. "He just had your underwear. Your *underwear*, Em." Pulling away from the door, she swung it open and peered down the hallway to check that it was empty. From there, she turned her head slightly, looking at me from the corner of her eye. "And we'll be finishing this conversation later."

I responded with a nod of confirmation.

I was thankful for our friendship, even though sometimes it felt strained. Kinsley came from money; her whole family did. A few years ago, they put out an ad for a roommate which I'd found in between places. Upon meeting, I realized they needed to prove to their family they could live on their own, and at that time, I knew I just simply *couldn't.* It was a situation that worked for both of us, and living with the twins had worked out. Our house was a constant carousel of people, but I didn't mind it one bit. I could probably afford to live on my own now, but I liked it here with them—they kept things interesting.

Bending down to grab my shoes, I glanced back at my vanity. A large photo was shoved into the frame around the mirror—me, Kinsley, Kolby, and the rest of the football team after they'd won the state championship. To celebrate, Kinsley and I had been hoisted onto their shoulders, our hands raised in victory for them, smiling like nothing in the world could touch us.

I kept my eyes on the picture as I pulled my shoes on. The Ember in that photo was the same woman I was now, someone who was built to withstand anything. Taking out my phone, I shot a quick reply to Silas's email before grabbing my bag and leaving the room, closing my door behind me.

7

SILAS

Almost a week had passed since meeting Ember, and I was starting to get antsy about how long Knox was taking. Luckily, the masquerade was tonight and preparations for it had kept me busy. Even now, my brothers and I were finalizing the last details of the floor plan.

All three of us moved around the silent space as we worked, securing lights and different fixtures. The stillness clung to me, only adding to the restlessness within my body. I knew this time, it was necessary to make sure everything ran smoothly, but I still missed the vitality from a full crowd.

Having the company of my brothers helped as we worked to secure the steel frames for the dancers. The large metal cages had just been hung, and we were in the middle of making sure the attachments to the reinforced beams were secure. Kyrin tested their chains twice but was still perched next to one on a ladder, tightening one of the bolts.

"You know," he said, glancing down at me. "You could probably put a camera in this thing and livestream it."

"The club is interesting enough without that," I replied, kicking the bottom rung of the ladder.

Kyrin grinned down at me and steadied himself on the steel door of the cage. "Nothing can ever be *too* interesting."

"The members have enough to watch here." Shaking my head, I caught the wrench he tossed down to me and glanced over at Greyson, who was clearly done contributing. He leaned against the bar with one boot hooked on the foot rail, pouring tequila into his mouth from the spout of a random bottle.

Making a mental note to switch that one out before the event started, I turned back to Kyrin as he climbed down the ladder. Now that the cages hung straight, the tables were all that was left.

"We just need to line the walls now."

Kyrin nodded in understanding and looked up toward the middle of the ceiling. "Is that where the silk will be?"

"Yeah, so we need to measure the space on both sides and make sure she has enough room."

Greyson snorted behind us as he switched to another bottle. "For what? All the debauchery below her?"

I ignored him as the tables scraped softly against the floor. A couple more small adjustments later, and the entire space around us was done, our final task complete.

Kyrin looked around, wiping his hands on his pants. "We good?"

My phone vibrated in my back pocket as I replied. Pulling it out, I saw Knox's name flash across the screen.

All information on Vale has been sent.

Perfect.

I looked up at them and quickly nodded before I headed for the door. "I'll have the staff handle everything else. Just make sure to be back around five."

Kyrin threw me a half-assed salute while Greyson grabbed the bottle he was drinking and wedged it under his arm. I was so anxious to open the file, I didn't even care that it was one from the top shelf. *I just wanted them out.* As the door closed behind them, I grabbed a nearby chair and sank into it, opening the message. I let the silence fall around me, finding solace in the quiet this time. For once, I was thankful there were no members here, or anyone else in general. Like this, I had no distractions, and that was exactly what I wanted. I watched my finger hover over the attachment.

Ember Vale.

There were four pages, each one outlining a different part of her life. The first included documents her name was legally attached to—a lease agreement, a petty theft when she was sixteen, and several online resumes. There was no title listed anywhere, so it was clear she wasn't married and had no corporate designation. Everything I read fit her personality completely, exactly what I'd assumed would be in here. I could tell by just reading over the first few things that Ember was someone who existed on her own, without anything else or any type of context. I laughed under my breath when I realized her name wasn't even connected to a vehicle registration. I blinked, like it had to be a joke, then laughed again when I realized it wasn't.

True to Knox's personality, he'd included a note next to this section. *"Who doesn't own a car... or a bike for that matter?"*

In terms of her family, things were pretty blank. Neither parent was listed anywhere, but a grandparent showed as a previous address.

Interesting.

Moving to the next page, I came across her occupations. Most evenings, she worked at a local bookstore but was also under contract with a freelance photography company. The shifts there were sporadic, making me think she was able to make her own schedule. Digging a little further, it seemed that even with both jobs combined, her paycheck stubs proved to be *just enough* to pay her bills. What money she did have left was usually spent on books, chai's, and a few pharmaceuticals that were delivered monthly—anxiety medicine and birth control.

I read the second prescription again and felt all the amusement drain from my face. As proud as I was of her for being prepared, that also meant that someone out there might already believe they had some sort of claim on her. The realization settled wrong in my mind, awakening something territorial. If someone out there actually thought she was *theirs* to take, *theirs* to touch—that would be an easy problem to eradicate. Whatever hands had reached for her before had been operating under a time limit, one that had recently expired.

Finding no mention of a boyfriend anywhere in the file or in Knox's notes, I decided to sort those details out later. Pushing those thoughts aside, I moved on to the rest of the information. The property she lived at was tied to Kinsley Monstat, but they seemed to have no familial relation. Interestingly, Kinsley's last name had been flagged as part of a well-known family and was attached to a string of multi-million-dollar companies. In other words, Ember's roommate had money, *a lot of it.*

So why was it that Ember didn't even have a savings account?

On paper, it seemed like her personality bled into her everyday decisions. There was no retirement or savings. No insurance. She lived off impulse and blind optimism. Even her bank statement was proof of this, the last few months full of small purchases that weren't needed. Ember's a perfect example of someone who lived in the moment and left her future up to chance. The money in her account was usually gone before her next payday, and to make matters worse, there was no one listed as her emergency contact. That alone told me everything I needed to know.

I closed the file and exhaled slowly through my nose. Everything about this girl was chaotic, even the reply I'd received from the email I had sent.

If I can make it work, I'll be there. If not, I'll send another photographer in my place.

In her place? As if she wasn't the whole entire goal.

I stood, smoothing my jacket and moving toward my office. If it wasn't Ember Vale who walked through those doors tonight—if she thought just anyone could stand where she belonged... there would be hell to pay, and I would enjoy every second of it.

8

Ember

My life had turned into a game of keeping myself busy so that I wouldn't think about Silas Solstice. Anytime I took my camera out, anytime I checked my email—his stupid mask would pop into my mind.

Any sane person would have replied to his ridiculous email and moved on, but I didn't. Over time, I realized it was the opposite for me. The irritability I felt at the thought of him was like poison, seeping into every part of me. I racked my brain to understand why I couldn't shake him, but I eventually gave up—only after ordering the dress I'd wear *if* I ended up going to the masquerade tonight.

That was a lie, and I knew it.

There was no "ended up".

I would be going.

As I rounded the corner toward my house, a voice pulled me from my head. "Hey, doll."

I froze for a moment, before letting my entire face split into a grin. "Bodhi?!"

I took another step toward him as he pushed away from the wall, and I could immediately tell most of his practices had been

outside. Every inch of him had darkened in just the short time he'd been gone, including his usual backwards cap and faded jersey. The circle of teammates around him opened as he moved toward me.

"Bodhi!" I squealed louder. Before my brain caught up, I bolted down the remainder of the sidewalk and launched myself at him.

He laughed, catching me and lifting me clean off the ground into a tight hug. "I wanted to surprise you and Kins," he said into my shoulder. "We're off for the summer. I thought I'd come spend that time with my girls."

I leaned back, my hands still hooked behind his neck. "She's going to lose her mind! Having you on the weekends is never enough for her."

"I know, now she'll have to deal with me for two months," he retorted, smirking.

I squeezed him once more before stepping back and looking at the grass stains covering him. "Dude, come on. Isn't there a team rule for showering?"

Without warning, Bodhi pulled me into his armpit and wrapped his arm around me. I half-laughed, half-screamed as I pushed him away and gagged.

"Save it for your girlfriend."

Grabbing for the door handle, he bumped me with his hip, and a small cough from behind us reminded me of his company.

"Oh, these are some of the guys from my team. I offered Kolby's bedroom to them."

I waved to each of them. "Oh goodie, he'll *love* that." Reaching for the door, I looked back at them. "Cover your ears," I instructed, as we all stepped into the hallway.

From the kitchen, Kinsley called out to me, "Em, did you get—" She turned the corner and screamed. "BODHI?!"

Dropping the empty bowl in her hands, she sprinted across the room, throwing herself at him. He barely had time to brace before she wrapped herself around him, legs and arms locking in place.

"Oh my god, what are you doing here?!" she yelled.

"I missed you," he laughed. "Surprise, baby."

"I thought you had training until Tuesday!"

"They let us off early."

Excitement lit up her face as she kissed him everywhere.

"Okay, okay," he muttered between each kiss, "at least let me shower first."

She laughed back in response, pulling him down the hallway toward the bathroom.

When they disappeared around the corner, I turned to the men and pointed to the living room. "I call dibs on the remote."

The next couple of hours unfolded easily. Instead of resting like I'd planned, I ended up on the couch, squished between random men that were now friends and pizza boxes that covered our living room. Kolby showed up halfway through and threw a whole ass fit when he learned he'd been kicked out of his room.

Checking the time between bites, I debated *staying* home. Bohdi being back had turned the house into something full of laughter and comfort, while being around Silas would probably evoke the opposite. I finally gave in to the nagging in my head and stood, knowing it was well past the time I should've have left by. *Maybe showing up late would be a good thing. Maybe it would do him some good to have to wait on someone else, for once.* "Sorry guys, I have to get ready for work."

Kinsley looked over at me from Bodhi's lap. "What?! You're ditching us?"

Picking up my trash, I nodded. "It's another photo gig."

A look of confusion and then recognition washed over her face. "Oh, no!" she yelled, hopping off his lap to follow me into my bedroom. "Absolutely not. You're going *there* again!?"

By the time I came out of my closet, I was met by a small crowd. Kinsley stood directly in front of me with her arms crossed. Bodhi was close behind her, sitting on the edge of my bed. Even Kolby had come to see what was going on, leaning into the doorway.

"Ember, come on. Do you really think this is a good idea?" Kinsley's tone was short, a rare occurrence, but nothing that made me second-guess my plan.

"It's just work," I said, before moving into the bathroom and stepping into my dress. From the mirror, I could already tell the yellow color I'd ordered was perfect, mimicking the same one I wore last time. This dress, however, had an added layer of glitter, which made it even more elevated.

Kolby's hand dropped from the doorframe he was leaning

against as I entered the bedroom again. His eyes scanned over me, landing on the slit in my dress exposing my thigh. "You're wearing *that* to a work thing?"

Bodhi stood, stepping toward me. "Wait, am I missing something? Did you get a new job?"

"No,"—I said, reaching for the brush on my dresser, "and I'm not sure if you guys are aware of this but I'm actually a big girl and can handle myself." I brushed through my hair a few times, deciding to leave it down. "If it helps, don't feel like you need to wait for me this time. The gig is slotted for the whole party. I'll be fine, even if I'm late." None of them replied, but they remained rigid. I could tell they each had something to say, a different reason for me to stay home. I honestly understood, but this wasn't their choice, *it was mine.*

After another minute of silence, Kolby walked across the room and caught my attention in the reflection. With zero regret, I watched him through the mirror as I applied my lipstick. He sighed in response, he tone a weird form of defeat. "Who are you wearing that for, Em?"

I smiled up at him before standing and turning toward him. "Myself."

Stepping around him, I grabbed my camera and purse before nodding at Kinsley and leaving them all in my room behind me.

9

SILAS

The club had never looked more alive.

Gold foliage swallowed the dark walls, layered with textures that caught the lights. Taya had done well choosing the silver accents that bled through what darkness was left. The color had been meticulously placed, swirling in strategic strokes and lining the mirror fragments embedded into the centerpieces. The prominent shades were picked to match the chandeliers now hanging between the suspended cages—a fixture that dripped with thick black crystals.

A dancer now occupied each of the custom-forged shapes that hung overhead. Outside, the metal was decorated with curling filigree, making the whole thing look like an art piece. Both swayed with the beat, giving glimpses of the painted bodies moving inside them.

The silk performer was stationed at the central beam of the room, already at the beginning of her performance. Each time the spotlight hit, and those silks unraveled from the rafters, the entire floor tilted up to watch, regardless of what they were in the middle of.

The final touches had elevated the club into something wor-

thy of damnation. It wasn't just the rooms or the experience, we decided to upgrade the masks as well—a privilege that was only for tonight's celebration. The edges of each one were elongated into elegant points, their surfaces lacquered in midnight finishes or dusted with metallic sheen. Some bore delicate etchings that only revealed themselves when the light struck just right.

Then there were specific accents chosen for each one. Dark chains draped from the corners of the Dominants, swaying softly as their wearers moved. Diamonds glittered along the stitching of the Volunteers. Fishnet veils covered the foreheads of the Watchers, accompanied with silver swirls on their cheekbones. Even the one I wore, the one that marked me as the owner, had been lined with purple light. Each one caught my attention as they passed, but my focus kept drifting to the one specific person who still hadn't arrived.

My gaze cut through the crowd from my balcony, where I'd moved for a better view. I kept scanning the floor, unable to stop. The music throbbed, but it did nothing to settle the restless edge creeping under my skin. The masquerade had started an hour ago, and my photographer had yet to show up.

Even without seeing her face, I'd know the moment she arrived. As annoying as it was, I had memorized the energy she gave off, I could feel it a mile away. Like the air adjusted when she walked through it.

I checked my watch for the twentieth time and let out a frustrated growl, debating on just calling her. My fingers flexed at my side as irritation sharpened into something more dangerous.

Reaching for my phone, I formed her name in my mind. Just then, a bright shade of *yellow* stole my attention.

The flash of color hit my peripheral vision like a strike of lightning. Instantly, I turned my head to the east corner of the room and saw her standing with a group of people. I wasn't sure what irritated me more—the fact that she hadn't been hiding from me or the fact she wasn't looking for me.

The dress she wore fit like it had been made exactly for her. The color, a multi-layered yellow that mimicked the one she'd worn when I first met her. I knew she had chosen that outfit on purpose, just to rile me. I didn't dwell on that for long. My attention instead shifted to something else she was wearing—a *Volunteer mask.*

I hadn't noticed it at first. While taking pictures, her camera and arms hid most of the design, but now she was standing still, and I could see her face. Now, *everyone* could see the blaring message that apparently, *she was available to play with.* A slow, possessive heat settled low in my chest as I watched her direct members of my club with a confidence that made me bite my tongue.

It was as if she belonged in this chaos far more than she should have.

I bit down harder as the first man approached her. The metallic taste of blood spread across my tongue as my eyes locked on their exchange. He leaned in too close, saying something I couldn't hear over the music. She gave a small, professional laugh and lifted her camera again.

The second man came only minutes later, followed by a third.

Each time, my grip tightened on the railing as something feral clawed its way out of me. By the time the fifth man appeared at her side, I moved to the stairs, barely able to control myself. Walking toward her, the number had already moved to eight. *Eight* men in total, drawn by curiosity and the way she existed so fully in her element. It was a miracle none of them had touched her yet. According to my rules, she would have to obey, to *listen*—which meant these men had approached, but none had propositioned her. *Yet.*

Mine.

I reached her just as the ninth man did, my eyes snapped to his hand, where a tattoo marked his skin. I recognized it immediately. This was one of our usuals, one that came here often with a preference for obedience so deep, it bordered on obsession.

My body moved before my thoughts could finish forming, and I closed the space between us. Just as I reached her, his fingers intimately brushed her shoulder.

I turned to her, making my voice deliberately louder than it needed to be. "Your membership here has been revoked," I said, my voice cutting sharp through the music. "You need to leave."

She turned toward me waving her camera. "I don't have a membership. I'm here to work, remember?"

The man I'd been watching just moments ago, leaned in and grabbed her elbow. "I'd like to enter a contract before you leave."

Ember looked at him, tilting her head as if she didn't understand.

Of course she didn't.

I stepped fully between them and yanked his arm away from her. "She is no longer a member," I said coldly. "Which means she cannot accept."

The bass pulsed around us as my adrenaline rose, the moment between us stretching thin.

I calculated how quickly I could end this, taking notice of everyone surrounding us. My muscles coiled at the ready, but to my surprise, he looked at me at once before turning away. I watched him until he disappeared back into the crowd, just to make sure his decision was genuine. I turned back to face Ember feeling a sharp impact against my shoulder.

"What the hell was that?!" she snapped.

I looked down at her slowly, letting my pent-up fury meet hers. Closing the gap between us, I held her gaze. "What the hell is that *mask*, Ember?" My voice dropped to a dangerous level. "Do you even know what you're doing—what you're *saying* to everyone here?!"

She recoiled, letting out a sharp, disgusted sound directed straight at me. Hearing that come out of her mouth lit up every nerve in my body, and red bled into my vision. *It's time for her first lesson.* The thought disappeared as my body moved on auto pilot. I bent down and hoisted her over my shoulder in one swift motion. She screamed out at the touch, clutching her camera and securing it against her chest before it could fall.

"Hey! Put me down, asshole!"

I locked my arms around her, ignoring her kicks and twists. Maneuvering her legs, I pinned them so she couldn't hurt anyone as I carried her through the crowd and up the stairs. Masks turned, and whispers followed us, but no one said anything, and I realized why—it was my mask. *That's* why no one tried to stop me. *That* was why the man from earlier left without a fight. They knew I was the owner.

Halfway up the stairs, I caught Kyrin's gaze through the crowd. He'd witnessed everything and moved quickly to follow us as I jerked my chin up toward my office.

Once inside, she only fought harder. Adjusting my grip, I heard the door click shut behind me. Kyrin entered just as I set her down. She spun immediately, her fist aimed toward my face. I caught her wrist, spinning and pressing her chest against the wall. I stepped in close until I was pushing into her back. I wanted her to be scared of what could happen. I *needed* her to understand, to feel my presence caging her in.

I lowered my mouth to her ear, deliberately clipping my voice. "You are not allowed to wear any mask besides that of a Watcher." I pressed into her harder, pulling a small grunt from her as I flattened her against the wall. "Better yet—you are not allowed to return here *at all.*"

She scoffed beneath her mask, the sound sharp and fearless. Somehow, it only fed my need to tame her. Gripping her arms, I swung her around and placed her back against the wall. Taking both her wrists, I pinned them above her head and watched her pulse start to escalate in her throat.

I swallowed down the exhilaration she was giving me and forced myself to stay calm. Breaking her would take time, and multiple efforts, but that process would be starting right now. She was no longer allowed to do whatever the fuck she wanted, and I would make sure of it.

Lowering my forehead to hers, our masks met with a soft clink. "Do you really want to experience being a Volunteer?" I asked quietly. "Or did you show up in that mask just to piss me off?" My voice was a hardened replica of my normal one, but even this low, it came out absolute.

I tightened my grip for a moment, deciding to release her and take a step back. In the foot of space now between us, I presented her with just enough room to think she could run. If I were smart, I would use this space as an opportunity to retrain certain parts of her, but right now, that was not what I wanted—*not yet, anyway.* Tonight, I wanted to test her fire.

"Take your dress off."

Every muscle in her body tensed at my request, sending a jolt of excitement through me, one I didn't expect. For a second, I watched as she remained absolutely still. Even without speaking, I guessed at exactly what was happening behind her mask. Her anger started to fizzle out, and the heat she felt toward me was now transforming into something else entirely. Confirming my thoughts, her chest began to rise and fall in a steady rhythm. Adrenaline flooded her system so strongly I could practically taste it. Still, she stared at me through her mask, defiant and uncertain all at once.

I tilted my head and lifted my hand to her bare shoulder. Carefully, I traced a finger along the skin above her left collarbone before pausing and moving to the other side. "I know you chose that mask on purpose, Ember," I said, letting my fingers lazily drift over the fabric on her chest. "So don't make me ask again."

Within seconds, her breathing slowed, and I could tell she was ready to ignite. Lifting her hands, she began to peel the dress from her shoulders. I carefully watched every inch of skin she exposed, the energy between us catching sparks with every movement. The more fabric she pulled away, the harder it was to stop myself from touching her. When she stopped at her chest, she paused to look between me and Kyrin.

Time to light the match.

"Keep going, baby."

As soon as the words left my mouth, her gaze locked on to mine, and I knew I had her. I'd chosen that specific term of endearment, not because I wanted to encourage, but because I wanted to enrage. Right away, I could tell that one simple word had done its job. The unwelcome nickname helped push her past whatever had stalled her, and now she was back to herself. There was no hesitation now as the yellow fabric slid down, revealing her chest to me. I kept my attention on her mask, imagining her eyes and how right now, they were probably glowing with no remorse. I wanted to witness it, and even more so, I wanted to make them roll back for me. I fought the thought and the need to remove her mask. At this point, the need to ruin her had begun to shift into something else, and that was problematic.

I needed to stay focused.

I zeroed in on her movements, my eyes locking onto her perfect body that was now completely free from her gown. This was the first step in making her vulnerable. In the first few moments, I thought I had succeeded. She seemed uncomfortable, maybe even afraid, but then things changed. Slowly, she dragged a finger along the dark lace that clung to her skin—the lingerie she'd chosen to wear underneath. The way her finger moved made me feel like she knew she'd be showing them off tonight, and I hated how that made my mouth water. As the fabric caught the low light, she pulled them down slightly and my heart rate spiked even further.

What the fuck was happening.

Before, I'd only witnessed one side of her—the side that caught my attention without my consent, due to her infuriating ability to be so damn loud and obnoxious. The woman standing in front of me *now* was the same person, but in a different way. This part of her still claimed attention, but it was like she was pulling it from the shadows around her. In the darkness surrounding us, *my* darkness, she remained absolutely radiant. The more I looked at her, the more something dark and possessive twisted in my chest.

Fuck. I needed to feel her skin.

I crossed the space again, but this time, I didn't trap her

against me. Angling my body, I positioned her in the corner, turning her just enough—so that from Kyrin's position in the room, all he could see was my back. The movement looked casual, almost accidental, but it wasn't. Initially, I'd allowed Kyrin to be here as part of the lesson, but now I needed him here to keep me from completely devouring her.

The voices in my head began to scream for her, and I no longer had the control to fight them. *What I needed was to see her explode.* Lifting my hand to her throat, I gripped the skin and turned her head to the side whispering into her ear. "You don't look away when you fall apart for me, do you understand? Welcome to your ruin." In the next second, my fingers moved on their own as they slipped beneath her mask and pulled it up over her head. I immediately locked in on those brown eyes that had haunted me. There was no sign of fear, just pure anticipation for what was coming next. My pulse thrummed in my ears even louder as I realized the emotion within them, *excitement.*

I looked down at her through my mask, trying to contain myself in every way possible. The inferno within her was intoxicating, and if I wasn't careful, I would be burning tonight. I slowly dragged my fingers over the skin of her thighs before letting them rest for a moment. Next, I pressed my palm against the inside of her legs, clearly signaling to her exactly what I wanted. She took a moment to debate, as if granting me access was a choice. I smiled at that, knowing her reasoning was now futile. She didn't have a choice in what happened. If anything,

I would make sure she felt exactly what she was doing to me. When I had my way, she would be burning right alongside me.

I leaned into the curve of her neck. "Do as you're told, Ember."

Her eyes dilated at her name as a shudder ran through her body, goosebumps scattering across her skin. Under my mask, my smile grew as she finally opened her legs for me. I moved slow at first, taking in the fact her breathing had turned shallow. When my hand finally rested between them, she held her breath as I traced the thin fabric covering the space there. Small, light moans soon filled my ears. Those sounds encouraged my fingers to explore, circling the area. Each time I swirled them, the lace under my fingers became slightly more wet.

I continued my slow, tortuous movements until a slight whimper escaped her. Looking up I saw a slight twitch in her eyebrows, making me guess the sound she'd made was involuntary. I let out a dark chuckle, moving the lace aside. The skin beneath was smooth, another sign she had expected this in some form. My dick swelled as my fingers explored further, the pain a direct result of playing with her.

With each stroke of my finger, I thought about how I'd been so sure that I had her figured out. Now, I knew better. No matter what form she took—she was invigorating, a goddamn fixation.

Tracing every curve of her, I paused just long enough for her breathing to become rushed and erratic. I liked the sound, and apparently, she liked the way I played because her arms reached up to grip the back of my biceps. Her fingers dug into me, trying to ground herself in any way she could. Each time her nails clawed into me, I teased her opening. After three rounds of this, her body started to shake.

Tilting her head up toward me, her eyes locked on mine, flaring with need. I gave another soft chuckle as I pushed one finger inside but stopped just short of my second knuckle.

Time to burn.

Her body instantly convulsed, like she was craving more just as much as I was.

After a stuttered breath, she spoke through clenched teeth. "I hate you."

Her tone was sharp, but her body betrayed her as she tried to move against my hand. The contradiction instantly made me want to fuck her.

"I really fucking hate you, Silas."

This time when she spoke, it was as if she was trying to convince *herself*, not me. Either way, I wasn't letting her deny whatever this was. Plus, she needed to know that I did not tolerate lying.

Without warning, I pushed two fingers inside of her, and a scream ripped from her throat. "Then why are you so goddamn wet for me, *Ember*."

A soft moan escaped her as I started to pump my hand. Just as another one threatened to come out, I grabbed her jaw, pulling her eyes to mine.

"You don't get to pretend that I don't have an effect on you, not when I plan on breaking you." Directing her chin over my shoulder toward Kyrin who was still watching from the corner. "You're going to come until I say stop. Do not break eye contact with him."

The words landed heavy in the room, ripping through multiple boundaries. Kyrin stilled as he registered them. His Volunteer mask did well at hiding his expression, but I knew he would still listen.

Ember's breath hitched as I leaned into her ear, keeping my voice low enough that only she could hear me. "Right now, you're my Volunteer, and he's going to be the Watcher. Do you understand?" I pulled my finger out and aggressively pushed it back in again before finding her clit with my thumb. "I know you do because you came here wanting this to happen, didn't you?"

Her body was the first to submit, as her hands tightened around me for support. She said nothing though, as her eyes moved to my brother—who was now taking off his pants.

Pausing my hand, I asked her again. "*Didn't. You*?"

Ember released another whimper she tried to disguise as an exhale. Then, a low "yes" filled my ear.

The answer wasn't enough for me, not when she was still actively trying to fight us, to deny me the right of tearing her down. I needed the truth, and I needed to hear it from her lips. "Is it me that you want inside of you? Or just anyone?"

I could practically hear her thoughts as she fought for an answer, but I remained silent, ready to reward her if she chose the truth this time. To encourage her, I pumped into her again with one hand as I gripped her waist with the other.

The sudden movement overwhelmed her, throwing her head back in pleasure. "You!" she screamed.

The confirmation was enough to send me over the edge, and a tingle started to spread through my limbs. It was as if her fire had erupted within my own body. "Good," I cooed, "then answer one question for me. Why did I watch nine other men approach you tonight?"

Ember replied with a groan, like she was losing the ability to think.

Accepting the sound as an answer, I finished my thought. "You will learn that none of them get to touch you anymore. *None.* Of. Them."

A mixture of garbled sounds flood the room as my fingers moved faster. I was half surprised to know she had listened to my demand, keeping her eyes on Kyrin only until she felt herself build. Once she hit a certain point, she grabbed my chin, bringing her forehead to mine as she came on my fingers. I was at number seven when her legs finally gave out, but that didn't mean anything to me. "Two more, Ember. That would make nine, and then we're even, baby."

"I'm *not* your baby," she argued, as she threw her head back.

"You are going to be whatever the fuck I say you are, sunshine." Unbuckling my pants, I picked her up at the waist and wrapped her legs around me. She tried to hit me, but I grabbed her wrist and slammed it against the wall as I held her up.

Repositioning us so her body was still hidden from my brother, I pushed her into the corner where the two walls of my office met and watched as she struggled to open her eyes. "When we first met, you told me I wore this mask to make up for my dick size. Why don't we test that theory out, huh?" Impulsively, I decided to lean into the firestorm she created within me, I turned toward my brother. "I want you done by the time she screams."

Ember's eyes opened fully at that statement, her mouth dropping open in disbelief. She was about to protest when I drove myself inside of her. Covering her mouth with one hand, I muffled the scream that tore from her.

She fit me like a fucking glove.

"Shhh, baby, didn't you hear me? You can't do that just yet. You have to stay quiet until you hit nine, and then you can be done." Her response was a needy moan that filled the room around us. " Ember. I need you to listen and understand. No other man will be allowed to experience this again. No one besides me."

I began moving, and with each thrust, I could feel my entire reality burning. The plans I had for her, the assumptions of who she was—all of it charred, along with my will to suffocate whatever magic she possessed. Instead, a smoke-filled euphoria filled my mind like nothing else I'd ever experienced. Before I knew it, I was doing everything I could to not completely lose myself in her.

At one point, she tried to push me away and signal that she

couldn't take anymore. I simply readjusted, taking more of her weight. Catching her eyes, I watched as the flames built one last time. I could feel a change then, the exact moment she fully submitted to me. In doing so, she hit her biggest orgasm yet and screamed out my name as her body thrashed.

10

Ember

No words described how I felt the next morning.

Not only had my body refused to wake up from whatever coma Silas put me in, but my mind kept trying to convince us that we should be mad about it.

Were we?

No.

Especially not when all my focus was needed just to move. Every muscle of my body seemed unconcerned with the fact I needed to be able to function today. Last night had been anything *but* average, and my body was still reeling from the experience. I had walked into the club with the intent to cause some issues, but never in a million years did I expect *that.*

Now I found myself stuck between a wall of self-loathing and leftover ecstasy. Accepting Silas's demands had been a special kind of stupid in the first place, something I *probably* should have fought back harder against. I knew that now, considering I could still feel him in all the spots he had touched, like my skin was still burning from his grip. I couldn't compare that experience with him to anything else.

The way he made me feel—I had never had that reaction

before, *ever*, to anyone. I had given him the control he so desperately sought, and I reaped many benefits because of it—*nine*, to be exact.

A wave of heat flooded my cheeks and suddenly, I felt stupid. Wrapping the comforter tighter around me, I buried my face into the pillow underneath me. That one word bounced around in my head. *Stupid.* Could I just use that as an excuse? Chalk last night up to ovulation and stupidity? No.

Before I entered the club last night, I had made decisions I knew would push every one of his buttons. Every choice was intentional, and it all started the moment I asked the receptionist for a different mask. So I couldn't blame this on stupidity. I knew what I was getting myself into.

Thinking about it now, I probably could've handled things differently. I *could have* went in with the full intention of just doing my job. However, that's not what I'd wanted. I wanted to do my job and see him suffer, to beg. Two steps into the club last night, and I was a goner. My camera was instantly out, and I was capturing shots I *never* thought possible. I'd instantly been transported to heaven, operating on pure adrenaline by the time Silas showed up. I squeezed the blanket around my head as I felt a pulse between my legs at the mention of his name.

What he had done—What had happened in that room—

Everything I hated about him had been the very things I let unravel me. The control he needed, the arrogance he always wore—every sharp edge of him repulsed me, and yet somehow, I had practically begged for them to carve into me.

I closed my eyes and tried to swallow whatever emotions were trying to form. I had no idea what he looked like, and even more so, I'd left that room in a state of pure delusion. He had fucked me stupid, and all I could picture now was the mask over his face. *That* image, and the feelings he evoked in me while wearing it, seared into my mind. Everything else about the night had turned hazy.

I knew Silas drove me home. I remembered him helping me into the car when my body started to feel heavy. The drive had been quiet, until he said my name once, low and certain. I also vaguely remembered a warm hand on my thigh at one point, but that could have been my imagination.

After leaving his car, the blurred fragments dissolved into nothing. I had no idea I'd even changed my clothes. And yet, when I shifted to look down, I was wearing my pajamas. My eyes scanned over the tiny, frosted donuts scattered across the fabric on my body. The irony wasn't lost on me, in fact, it hit more like a cruel joke.

Last night, Silas uncovered a side of me that *I* didn't even know existed. I'd offered myself to a man I barely knew and thought I hated, with his brother watching us from only a few feet away. Now here I sat, the very same girl, wrapped in cloth confections and absolutely no regret.

Taking a deep breath, I let myself stretch out under the thick blanket and opened my eyes to the almond-colored ceiling. Almond, a color very different from dark grey. The smoky grey that had been behind Kyrin, the color that surrounded us as we—

I pulled the blanket off me and pushed myself upright.

No. He did not get to just snap his fingers—or in this case*, use* them, and think he could have me. The whole reason I was in that room to begin with was because I was proving that I was the one in control. He had thrown me over his goddamn shoulder like a bag of trash. He probably thought he could do that to just about anyone, and they would melt. A familiar irritation rematerialized for him and replaced everything else that had begun to manifest. I was *not* that type of woman, one that he thought he could manipulate. I was not just a toy to play with. *Despite the fact that he could play really well.*

Silas Solstice was the farthest thing from special, and someone needed to prove that to him. Persuading myself to never partake in anything with him again, I shifted off the bed. As I moved the blanket and turned my body, I immediately noticed something strange.

Facing my window, I noticed it was open. Not completely, but wide enough to let the air in from outside. The curtain swayed gently with the light morning breeze, as if mocking me. I straightened my spine as I watched it move again.

Ever since a rogue bird had flown into my room, I never opened that window. Not at night, not *ever.* In my mind, it had been glued shut.

A chill crawled up my spine as I continued to stare at it, my mind scrambling for excuses. Maybe I had simply forgotten. Maybe Kinsley had been in here while I slept. Maybe I'd been too out of it last night and opened it, just needing some air. All I knew was that it couldn't have been Silas. *There was no way.* Dismissing me from his car, he had watched me just long enough to see me unlock the door. Once I closed it, he drove off.

I knew that for sure, *right*?

Rubbing my temples, I let myself settle on one of the explanations and forced myself to stand. My bare feet made no sound as I crossed the room to my window and grasped the bottom of the pane. Pulling it down, I locked it, letting my fingers pause on the latch. After looking over it for a few more seconds, I let go and moved the few feet to my closet. Convincing myself to forget about the window, I decided to focus on the day ahead of me and grabbed some jeans with a light blue shirt.

I had just pulled the fabric over my head when I caught a swirl of color in the corner of my eye. Turning toward the vanity, my eyes landed on a pile of flowers that had been haphazardly laid across the top. No vase and no wrapping, just a variety of petals and stems stacked on top of each other. My eyes moved back toward the window as I pulled my jeans up over my hips.

Instinct kicked in, and I readied myself to yell at Kolby, the only one dumb enough to do something like this. Opening my bedroom door, I was hit by the sweet smell of blueberry pancakes and was instantly less irritated. Inhaling deeply, I stepped back inside my room and walked toward the vanity. Grabbing the flowers, I simply tossed them into the trash bin before grabbing my things and leaving the room.

The sound of warm laughter echoed as I entered our kitchen to see everyone awake and already eating breakfast around the table. Kinsley, Kolby, Bodhi, and the random members of the team all crowded together around the large wooden oval. I watched for a moment as syrup bottles were thrown back and forth and plates were stacked high with pancakes.

"Turns out I survived last night," I announced, setting my things on the counter and sitting down next to Kinsley. A chorus of greetings answered back as Kinsley waved her fork at me like she didn't want to hear anything about it. I wanted to say more, but a blueberry hit my face, courtesy of Kolby. When I looked up, it was clear that he was trying to grab my attention with a mouth full of food.

"He's *lucky.* I would have scoured the world to find you."

Bodhi handed me a plate, looking over at Kolby, "Dude, you can't even find your keys half the time."

I smiled at their banter as I accepted the plate in front of me. Setting it down, I immediately stabbed the pancake and let my eyes drift across the table. They're met with ones of honey brown, a color belonging to one of Bodhi's friends.

"I saw the dress you left in last night. You looked really good."

I didn't even get the chance to respond before Bodhi smacked him in the back of the head. "Behave."

"Yeah?" I said, keeping my tone casual even though I was already over his whole personality.

"Yeah. Good enough that I should have given you flowers the moment I saw you," he responded.

The wording seemed off, like he might have been the one in my room, and suddenly, I wasn't so sure it was Kolby. "Well do me a favor and just *don't* next time, okay?"

"How else is a dude supposed to try?" he asked between bites.

I didn't respond as I let the discussion fade back into whatever they had been talking about before I'd entered. Taking another few bites, I sat and watched the conversation around me. I was in the middle of enjoying the exchange when I realized the honey brown eyes had yet to leave me. Snapping my head up, I met his stare. "Can I help you with something?"

Bodhi choked on a laugh as he looked between me and his teammate. Lifting his cup, he bowed his head in introduction. "Uh. Em, this is Archer. Archer, Ember." Taking a drink, he swallowed before adding, "Be careful, she tends to bite."

Archer's reply was clipped, almost void of emotion. "And what if I like to bite back?"

Two things pissed me off about that answer. First, his arrogance was undeniable—much like Silas's. Second, I was surrounded by men who were full of themselves, and I was *over* it.

I stood abruptly, done with the whole conversation. Brushing crumbs from my pants, I rolled my eyes at the man across from me. "Yeah, I'm gonna pass on that." Taking my plate to the sink, I nodded in Kolby's direction. "Feel free to bite *him.* I'm willing to bet he's into that."

Kinsley giggled and raised her hand to offer me a high-five as I passed her. The sound of our hands colliding brought a smile to my face, which only grew wider as Kolby stuck his tongue out. A small chuckle escaped as I grabbed my items and left the room to head to the front door.

I stepped out onto our patio when I felt my foot crunch against something plastic. Looking down, I froze before pulling my leg back slowly.

More flowers.

The ones in my bedroom had been simple, almost like they'd been pulled from the ground, but *these* were on a completely different level. Each bundle featured a different flower, all neatly tied together with various ribbons. My eyes roamed over the floor, catching everything from sunflowers that were speckled with bright colors to roses that had been dusted with glitter. Together, they covered the entire space in front of our door—hundreds of flowers, just lying there.

Scanning each one, I noticed a folded note stuck inside one of the bouquets. Taking a quick breath, I moved my camera to my back and crouched to read over my name that was typed onto the front. I hovered there for a few seconds, my mind drifting to Silas and the off chance he had done this. He absolutely did not seem like that type, but then again, I didn't even know the man's eye color.

Opening the small piece of paper, my eyes immediately moved to the seven words on the back. They were hand-written in black ink:

I will <u>ruin</u> you for anyone else.

Heat filled my face as I stared down at the one underlined word. To me, that was enough proof to tell me exactly who had done this. Could that mean the window might have been him too? I never outright asked Archer if he was the one who'd left the flowers in the first place.

Crumbling the paper in my hand, my mind drifted back to Silas and the fact I had already promised myself that I'd stay away from him. My body fought back at the reminder, recalling images and feelings from last night. Suddenly, my mind filled with his voice, and I remembered how he had been very clear that no other man would be allowed to have me. There was no way he had been serious, right?

Standing up, I brought my foot down on the flowers, smiling when another satisfying crunch filled my ears. I didn't belong to *anyone,* and despite the fact he had quite literally *destroyed* me last night, that included him. Moving out of instinct, I grabbed as many flowers as I could and walked them over to the large trash at the side of our yard. Hurling them inside one by one, I didn't stop until every last bouquet was gone from our porch. Then, I straightened my bags and started toward my shoot.

Nice try, motherfucker.

II

Silas

My mornings usually consisted of a smooth, defined ritual, but all normalcy burned away last night when I experienced Ember Vale.

I hadn't slept because of it, still trying to heal from my own personal form of cauterization.

After taking Ember home, I drove around, trying to clear my mind. When that didn't work, I laid down for more than an hour trying to release myself from whatever hold she had put on me. Each time I closed my eyes, I pictured the way hers had rolled back for me. I fought the pull and the visions for as long as I could before my body started to protest. Then, it was as if she was wrapped around me again. It took one second of trying to adjust my dick before my hand wrapped around it, and I closed my eyes to the thought of her riding it. The flames I hated, the ones I had vowed to suffocate, ended up welding us together.

That possibility, that outcome—had never been my intention. In fact, I'd started last night with a completely different plan, one I'd placed my confidence in. Unfortunately, within thirty minutes, *that* plan had somehow been completely derailed. To be honest, I was still a little dazed from the whiplash

of my own thought process. One minute, I was in complete control, and the next, I wasn't.

One thing was for sure, last night had changed everything for me.

The spark inside of her that I thought needed to be extinguished? I had caught a glimpse of it, and now I needed more. Her soul. Her anger. Everything about her made me feel alive in a way I couldn't explain, and I already wanted to watch her flare again. *No, it was more than that.* I wanted to nurture the flame until it consumed every piece of me.

I had been misguided in assuming that I'd be the one to ruin her. It was clear to me now that even then, my obsession had been solidified. An obsession that had originally been born out of anger but now, fueled by something else.

I had lived my life in darkness. A vast, hollow wasteland where I continuously searched for anything that would make me feel. Yet, in one night, I had experienced it all. By awakening my anger, Ember had involuntarily caused me to thrive. I wanted to feel more. I wanted to experience everything she could offer. Most importantly, I wanted her.

In fact, I *needed* her.

A flash of her skin from my memory caused my blood to smolder. Last night she looked at me like I was the gasoline she needed to light herself on fire, and yet I was the one who had willingly been burned alive. My skin itched just thinking about it, and a small groan escaped me as I realized just how fucked I was.

Rolling off my couch, I reached for my phone and sent a silent prayer to whatever deity was listening that I'd at least been able to bridge the connection that was formed. Scrolling to the app on my screen, I clicked on the icon I was looking for and immediately found her marker. A slow grin spread across my face as I looked down at the blinking dot. No matter where she went now, I would have her location, and that settled something in me.

The emitter was specially designed, smaller than a grain of rice and extremely hard to notice. Knox and I had come up with various plans on how to plant it but lucky for me, I had completely worn her out. That made things pretty easy for me on the drive home when I installed it under her phone case.

Clicking on her picture, she was at the same address I'd left her at last night. Rolling my head around in a small circle, I locked my screen and moved to my desk for the small bottle of pain relievers in my bottom drawer. *The lack of sleep was starting to affect my mind, along with my muscles.* Chasing the pills down with the only water I had, I found some extra clothes I had stored near my new favorite corner—the same one I'd held her up against.

Then I checked my phone and the multiple texts I'd sent Knox throughout the night. The first one wasn't that bad, but as the hours passed, so did my desperation. It was clear to anyone who could read that I was obsessed, and I was positive that he would have something to say about that, especially with what I was asking. I sent one more text asking him to call me, before I dressed quickly and headed downstairs to assess the aftermath of the masquerade.

Taking the stairs, I could immediately tell that most of the mess had already been cleaned by my crew. While *I* had spent the early morning hours spiraling in my office, *they* had started disassembling. Mostly everything had been taken down or removed. The only things left were some decorations and scattered glasses strewn across tables. Grabbing as many as I could carry, I moved them to the sink at the bar and filled it with water. A soft snoring grabbed my attention from somewhere under a table. I followed the noise and soon found myself standing over my brother.

Kyrin was fast asleep, sprawled out like he had fallen at one point and just stayed there. It was no surprise he had slept through the cleaning, he had always been like that.

I sat down on a chair across from him and nudged his shoulder with my foot. "Get up."

He groaned, then cracked one eye open to glare at me. "What day is it?" he muttered to himself as he pushed himself off the floor.

I leaned back into the chair and watched him, letting out a quiet sigh. A small part of me envied him for whatever amount of time he'd been able to sleep.

Rubbing his eyes and blinking rapidly, he looked over at me speaking through a yawn. "I'm glad Ember showed up. I thought you were gonna go on a killing spree."

Her name coming from his mouth triggered a whole-body

reaction from me I didn't see coming. The feeling was instant and almost violent. *That's not good.* "Yeah," I said slowly, forcing myself to breathe through it.

Kyrin's head tilted slightly, as if my short answer amused him. "Nothing else to say about that? Nothing *at all*?" He stretched his arms out in front of him before moving them in small circles. "Okay, so we're just gonna pretend that *nothing* happened?"

I looked at him for a few seconds, debating on which way I wanted to go with this conversation. Knowing she would eventually be a part of his life too, I chose the truth—just like she had last night. "Ember happened. She showed up in that mask, and I couldn't just let it go... I can't seem to let *her* go."

He nodded, as if my short explanation was enough to make him understand everything. "I get it. It's always the ones that drive us a little crazy, huh?" Shrugging his shoulders, he pulled his eyes away from me and stood. "You don't have to explain anything else to me, including the fact that last night has been permanently erased from my memory. The number nine? It means nothing to me now."

I couldn't help but laugh. Throwing a punch into his shoulder as he passed me to collect his things, I mumbled a quick "thank you."

A ping from my pocket alerted me that Ember had left her house. Without any direction to do so, my hand moved on its own. Soon, I was looking down and following her dot as it moved.

Glancing back up at Kyrin, he was just standing there, smiling at me. *Asshole.* I ignored him and the smirk that formed in the corner of his mouth as I grabbed my keys off the counter. Closing my hand around them, I swore I heard him laugh. His amused voice hit me just before the door shut. "Just keep doing the finger thing, she seems to like that."

I didn't know whether to be thankful for who he was or beat the shit out of him for not knowing boundaries. Just as I was debating the answer, Knox called me.

I answered, putting him on speakerphone while I shot a text to my lead manager, explaining that I had some business to attend to and outlined instructions for the rest of the clean-up.

"Hey," I said, typing the last of the message out.

"Oh, hey there. I'm looking for Silas Solstice? I think his phone might have been stolen or maybe he acquired a certain head injury that left him unstable."

And here we go.

"Can you just let me know if it's doable?" I locked the door to the club and started walking to my car, pulling up the map that showed Ember's location.

"D*oable*? Yes. But do you really want me to 'hack anything needed' so you have a full-time feed to her? That's a bit much, don't you think?"

He's not wrong, but I needed to be able to see her. "Is it a yes or a no, Knox?"

The line went silent for a few seconds. "Are you on drugs?"

I was already irritated from this conversation, but if anyone could help me, it was him. "Knox."

"Do you plan on killing her?"

"KNOX!"

"Okay! Okay. I was just making sure! This will be a little bit tougher than your last request, so I might need an extra day. Do me a favor and don't go too crazy, okay?"

I was twenty-two minutes away from her location, but I could probably make it in eighteen. "Yeah, got it," I answered, as my foot pushed harder against the gas pedal.

He hung up once I agreed, leaving me with the silent map on my screen. Within seventeen minutes, I found myself parked in a small lot listening to the engine tick as it cooled. Flexing my fingers over the wheel, I pushed the button to uncover my sunroof and surveyed the area around me. Everything here seemed common, including the high school that Ember was inside of. Considering the time of year and her photography contract, I put together that this was something to do with graduation.

In an effort to relax, I looked up to the open sky. Watching the clouds hover, I laughed once, sharp and humorless. *I* was supposed to be the storm, the one who controlled things— and yet here I was, a shadow circling its fire.

A slight movement in the corner of my eye grabbed my attention, turning just as a group of people in robes walked out from behind the building. They stood there for a few moments until a woman stepped out from around them. Moving quickly, she positioned them one by one, just like she had with the members from my club.

“Okay, on three!” she shouted, voice bright. “One, two, THREE!”

The line of graduates threw their caps into the air as tassels flickered in the sunlight.

Click-click-click.

Moving around, she captured them from different angles all while pushing her wild hair from her face. Grabbing another lens from the pack on her back, her fingers moved automatically as she changed settings and shifted between different rays of light. Just as she finished and capped the lens, a man walked up behind her.

I was getting real sick of seeing that happen.

He moved close, greeting her with a wide smile. The motion was smooth, like they had an established connection. My body stiffened at the contact. *How dare he touch her skin.* I felt my hand tighten on the steering wheel as the leather creaked, and I imagined snapping his fingers off one by one.

I guess we're starting another count, Ember. Apparently the first nine weren't enough for you.

The thought of making her repent was enough to calm me as I watched them. I knew that while he was talking to her, she was thinking about me and what I did to her last night. With each passing second, he became more animated with her. Ember's reaction stayed the same though, only nodding her head in response to what he’d said. Her body was stiff, and it was clear she was just trying to be polite. There was distance in her eyes, and her body closed off as she angled herself away from him, searching for a way to end the conversation.

My fingers twitched in response, knowing that was the opposite of how she was for me.

That's my girl.

Watching her, I realized how much her energy could expand. She had the ability to easily influence those around her, to feed into their emotions. Earlier, she helped the students be comfortable and encouraged them to relax. They fed off that positivity and listened. Even now, I knew this guy could feel it, the way she had shut down.

My eyes narrowed as she laughed once out of courtesy, hugging him again before excusing herself to head across the street. He watched her the whole way, just until she entered a coffee shop. Then he ushered the students back to where they'd come from.

I didn't like the feeling of not seeing Ember, and as the moments passed, I told myself to stay put. I knew I needed to stay in the car. *I knew that.* So, I made sure to apologize to myself as I opened the car door and walked into the street. As I crossed over the sidewalk, I realized it didn't matter anyway because she *didn't know my face.*

Within a few seconds, I'm filed in line a couple people behind her. I quickly realized that I was not only close enough to see she was on the phone but also lucky enough to hear the conversation.

"No," she said firmly. "I don't want to go out, regardless of what type of bar it is." There was a slight pause, before her voice turned brighter, teasing. “Because I’m tired, okay? And I can take care of those things *myself.*”

I almost smiled at the conversation. With that tone, I could only imagine what “things” she was talking about, probably the very things I took care of for her last night.

She shifted, stepping back to take out money. As she moves again, she bumps into the man in front of her.

“Oh! I’m so sorry!” she said quickly, her apology genuine.

The man in front of her turned, and I could tell he was instantly interested in what he saw. I watched it happen in real time—the way he looked her up and down before deciding to make a move. He smiled, saying something I couldn’t hear, gesturing to the menu.

Ember glanced up at the board pulling the phone from her ear. “The chai,” she said, like it was no big secret. “And the croissants. They’re stupid good.” She gave him a simple nod and turned back to her phone, completely unaware of his interest.

He watched her for another second before smiling, then turned back around. When it was his turn, he did exactly what I expected, ordering his drink, along with her chai and croissant.

It took everything in me to not intervene. The lack of sleep was feeding the voices in my head, making them harder to ignore. Half of me wanted to remove her from the situation like I had last night. It would be easy to throw her over my shoulder and make her leave with me.

When Ember finally registered what he’d done, she protested of course, but it lacked her normal ferocity. If it had been me, she would have simply walked away or *hit me,* but for some reason, he was able to wave her off. I continued watching until Ember caved, but that wasn't all because then she actually *smiled* at him before ending her phone call. They talked until their drinks were ready, handing hers over like it was some type of offering. When she went to leave, he had the balls to ask for her number. For half a second, I stifled a laugh, but it faded quickly when she took out her phone.

She couldn't be serious.

I forced myself to turn away before I did something irreversible. I left the shop without looking back, mostly because I didn't want to see what happened next. No matter what the reasoning was, she had made the wrong choice, one that I would apparently need to watch for. The faster Knox was at his job, the better it would be for her overall. She would soon learn that I was all she needed.

From the sidewalk, I glanced back at her once through the glass. She looked content, sipping her drink as she took a bite from her croissant.

I had no control over myself, and I knew it was because of her. Taking out my phone, I sent her a text.

One word. All caps.

TWO.

12

EMBER

Sitting at the little round table, it wasn't long before I popped my shoes off and pulled my legs up to sit cross-legged. My chai was almost gone, and I was already wishing I'd taken smaller sips. The drink itself had been delicious, but this one tasted especially sweet.

At first, I was going to deny the drink and the man who'd bought it for me, but then I realized how perfect an opportunity it was to think about someone other than Silas. In some twisted way, I was aware that accepting the offer and giving out my information would upset him—that was the whole reason I'd gone through with it. Plus, he had manners, striking up a conversation before hitting on me. *That* was how women should be courted, not by being trapped in a corner, naked where others watched. Silas could probably take some notes from him.

But then again, maybe I didn't want him too.

I picked up my phone to block the thought. I wasn't doing this to myself again. I refused to think about *that* or the man responsible for the ache within me, especially after what he pulled with the flowers. I wasn't *his*, and he needed to learn some boundaries.

Apparently, that was a common theme tonight, seeing how I also had to rein Kinsley in from going full party mode. The guys were out at some practice thing, and she had scored tickets to some new bar that was close. Fortunately, I had zero interest in going and had convinced her to make drinks at home with me.

My phone buzzed in my hand, and I looked down at the text notification. Whoever that guy was worked fast, considering he walked out the door about ten minutes ago.

I raised my eyebrows at the message that had just been delivered from an unknown number. As I stared down at it, I somehow knew it wasn't from the guy in the coffee shop.

TWO.

What?

Taking the last bite of the croissant, I looked around, like the person texting me was somewhere in the room with me. Letting my fingers glide over the screen, I settled on the most generic response I could think of and hoped that my gut was lying to me.

Wrong number.

Hitting send, I looked up from my phone to watch the people on the sidewalk pass the window. A few children skipped by that were clearly related and in the middle of some sort of tag game. A few seconds later, a teenage couple who seemed to be in the early stages of dating came into view. I watched as she made a move to hold his hand and a light shade of pink blossomed across his cheeks. I smiled at that, at the innocence of what love could be.

Pulling my headphones out of my bag, I pushed them into my ears and turned on my music. By the time I hit the sidewalk, I was humming along with Chokehold by Sleep Token. Each step seemed to loosen my shoulders, and soon, I was feeling pretty good. I timed my movements to fall in line with each beat, turning the walk home into a game. By the time I reached my house, I had just finished the last song on my playlist. *Perfect timing.* Clicking the side button, I waited for the screen to turn on so I could shut off the music.

Three messages came through during my walk, the music somehow masking the notification sounds.

I don't have the wrong number, but I had the wrong idea. Nine wasn't enough for you to learn. Because apparently you still feel the need to give out your number.

I scanned over each message, the oxygen in my lungs disappearing. I tried to function, to breathe, but my brain refused to process what I was reading.

It was Silas *again.*

But this time, he had been *watching* me. He knew what happened, what I had done at the coffee shop.

Throwing open my front door, I beelined straight toward my room. I wasn't going to reply. I wasn't going to let him know he had succeeded in making me flustered. In fact, he'd done nothing besides solidify how I felt about him. Stomping across the floor, I flung my closet door open and yanked out the shortest skirt I owned. I wasn't the one who needed to *learn.* He did.

The skirt I grabbed was gifted to me last year, jet black leather with a zipper crotch. I'd worn it once to a bachelorette party, then stored it, knowing it barely surpassed my moral dress code. *Tonight, he had ripped that inhibition in half.* Stripping out of my pants, I shoved the skirt up my hips with violent purpose and reached for the matching top. The corset-like front was perfect, a message that I knew he would receive loud and clear. *Fuck you, Silas.*

I worked a closing shift tomorrow which meant I had plenty of time for what I was about to do. This wasn't just about the text he'd sent. This was about proving he was not the boss of me. If he wanted to watch me, I might as well do something interesting.

I sat down at my vanity and brushed out my hair, maximizing every inch of volume. Stretching over to grab my make-up bag, I chose a crimson lip stain, like the color of blood. Taking the cap off, I traced over my top lip and then popped my mouth a few times before smiling into the mirror.

This was going to be fun.

When I finished getting ready, I headed to the kitchen where Kinsley was dancing with a half-cut lime in one hand and a salt shaker in the other. Stepping up next to her, I snatched the tequila bottle off the counter. "Still want to go out?"

Kinsley sighed in disappointment, turning toward me, "What—" Her eyes moved across my body, bulging as they hit different parts of my outfit. After a few seconds of pure glitching, she reset and looked me up and down. Taking my hand, she spun me and whistled. "Who are you, and what have you done with Ember?"

A grin slid over my face. "*I'm* the girl taking you out to the bar tonight."

Her response was a high-pitched squeal that bounced off the kitchen walls. Covering my ears, I motioned toward her bedroom.

"I'm leaving soon, with or *without* you." Then for added drama, I took a long swig straight from the neck of the bottle. She gawked at me before jumping up and down. Then, she opened the cabinet and pulled out two small glasses. I took them from her without hesitation, pouring each of us a shot.

Kinsley's eyes widened with happiness as we clinked our cups together. Knocking hers back, she set the empty glass down on the counter before bolting to her room. "You better not change your mind! Give me twenty minutes!"

Pouring myself another shot, I watched her close the door. There was *no way* I was changing my mind. I planned on making whatever choices I wanted tonight, and he could sit there and watch every single one.

With that thought, I replied to him.

I guess that means you didn't do it for me, huh? Maybe the next guy can.

Taking another swig, I felt the warmth from the alcohol as it settled into my chest.

13

Silas

The drive back to the club became an internal war between staying awake and not turning the car around to go back to Ember. All the windows were down, and the radio was on full blast—anything to keep me awake and stop me from sending more text messages to the woman I was close to strangling. The anger was back, but for a different reason. Something in me warned that I would always be mad at her for something.

I could just envision it. Every time she misbehaved, I'd pin her up against the wall with my hand around her throat. The way she'd look up at me, the absolute rage it would put her in. *That thought alone sent a tingle through me.*

By the time I reached the garage, my eyes were heavier than I wanted to admit. I fought against them as I parked the car and entered the club. My staff was so focused on the tasks I'd left for them that no one noticed my maskless face as I snuck back into my office.

My body hit the couch as my phone fell to the floor, and I was fully asleep within thirty seconds. I was okay giving myself just a little time to recharge here, because then I could be at full capacity to get back at Ember. I would need to be at full strength

for that, because I knew she'd put up a fight with whatever I chose to do.

One second I was picturing her face, and the next I was somewhere else entirely—some half-formed dream where nothing made sense but everything felt real. There were voices, I think. *My brothers maybe?* I was only there for a matter of minutes, or at least that's what I felt like before something started ringing.

At first, it blended in entirely, just another sound stitched into the dream. My brain twisted it into a phone call at one of our family dinners, but the sound didn't stop, even after Greyson walked away to take the call. It kept cutting through, louder each time, like it was trying to claw its way out of whatever fog my mind was buried in.

Soon, the sound was coming from my phone at home, and I was standing there above it, lifting the receiver to talk to the police about my mother.

The next time I heard it, it was the principal calling about how Greyson was fighting at school again and how he was seriously close to being suspended...*again.*

Ringing.

Ringing.

Ringing.

I was finally able to break through the cycle, consciously realizing the ringing was coming from my own cell phone somewhere around me. "Alright, I get it." My voice cracked out as I peeled my eyes open.

In no way was I ready to wake up, but my arm obeyed, sliding out from under me to pat the floor blindly. I struggled for a few seconds before my fingers finally brushed up against my phone. It was vibrating hard against the wood floor, the generic ringtone magnified from the confined space underneath the couch.

I grabbed it, nearly dropping it in the process. Squinting against the glare of the screen, my eyes watered, and I had to turn my head away to blink rapidly. I fumbled to swipe the answer button but missed. Swearing under my breath, I opened my eyes fully and tried again.

There was a silent pause that quickly ended, and about half a second later, it started again.

"Jesus." I dragged a hand down my face, trying to wake up enough to function. I hit accept this time, barely managing to get the phone to my ear before my grip started to loosen again. "Hello?"

There was a pause, then loud music filled my ear. "Silas!"

Kyrin.

I answered him as I closed my eyes again. "What do you want?"

"We have a problem," he said, loud enough that I had to pull the phone away from my ear, "and you need to come solve it. *Now.*"

Keeping it at a distance, I used my other hand to rub my eyes. "What happened?"

His response was a click, and then my screen filled with a live feed from his bar. Trying to adjust my eyes as fast as I could, a light moved across the screen as the picture settled on a booth. A familiar shade of brown hair moved across my vision, and my eyes narrowed on the face it belonged to—a face that had no reason to be there. Kyrin's voice carried through the speaker, even though I couldn't see him. "*Ember* happened."

I was instantly pissed when I saw my girl wedged between two men, laughing loudly with her head tipped back. What really did me in though, was the leather zip-up skirt that hugged every inch of her like it was spray-painted on. Her top, made of the same material, clung just as tightly and left *nothing* to the imagination.

"Kyrin," I said flatly, suddenly very awake. "What the fuck am I looking at."

"She's drunk," he said quickly. "Like *drunk*, drunk, Si."

One of the men next to her leaned in, his mouth brushing the skin on her neck. Her reaction was inviting, but too sluggish. It was clear to anyone with eyes that she was *way* past her limit.

My anger had become palpable as it pulsed under my skin. "Get her out of there. N*ow.*" I growled.

"I tried that already," he replied, his tone suddenly short. "She can barely stand. and it doesn't help that she has no idea who I am. She thinks I'm just some dude trying to steal her fun."

I watched as the man on her right slid his hand to her waist. I don't remember starting to yell, but my throat suddenly burned, and Kyrin was shouting my name through the phone as I grabbed my mask off the wall and headed downstairs. Throwing the keys at the bartender, I called out to him. "You run everything until I'm back," I barked, already moving out the door.

Bringing my eyes back down to my brother, my voice dropped low. "Do *whatever* you have to do to get her out of that situation. If you allow any of them to touch her more than they already have, I will kill them in front of everyone." With that, I shoved my phone into my pocket.

The evening air hit me like a slap as I tore across the lot. One second, I heard my tires burning, and then everything blurred. When I finally slammed to a stop, Kyrin was already outside waiting for me. I closed my car door and listened as he began explaining everything. Turns out Ember had shown up already close to drunk and her mind set on making trouble. She had given quite a hassle to the bartender and most men that approached her.

I heard her before I could see her—the sound, a feral scream, followed by banging. Approaching the door it was coming from, I looked over at my brother. "You locked her in a *supply closet*?"

"Look," he explained, his hands raised in the air. "I was able to convince her friend that she left with some guy. She was fine with it, but then a couple of men showed up and started asking questions. Apparently, they were her roommates. It was the only way to keep her contained until you got here."

His words replayed in my mind as I stared at the wooden door. *She lived with other men?* Knox failed to mention that.

The door handle jiggled before a barrage of bangs followed.

Kyrin listened for a moment and then continued, "I'll handle them and give you time to get her home."

Pulling my mask from my back pocket, I put it on as the familiar weight settled over my face. When I opened the door, she must've recognized me because she began to fight harder. In those first few moments, it took everything I had to hold her without hurting her. After a few minutes of her constant struggle, it was clear I'd have to restrain her to get her into the car. Just as I started to think about the best way to move her, Kyrin reappeared at my side. We both just stood there, watching her flail around like a wounded animal.

I moved my eyes to him and immediately knew he had followed my thought process. Blowing out a small breath, he nodded. "I guess I'll go get the side exit ready."

While he was gone, I managed to stifle her movements with one arm before shimmying out of my jacket. Deciding to throw her over my shoulder for the second time, I used the jacket as a wrap to cover her bottom half. "Knock it off Ember, or someone is going to see up your skirt."

"So what if they d-do?" she hiccupped, her words slow and slurred. "As long as it's not you, you big stupid i-idiot."

"Yeah, *I'm* the idiot." I replied, adjusting her weight on my shoulder.

"You a-are the idioch," she yelled, hitting my back as she tried to repeat the last word a few times. Ultimately, she was unable to do so, which made her burst out laughing. "You think you can just stay in my head, but you're not that cool. Cool guys aren't mean like you."

As If I had been mean to her at all.

I reached up, slapping her ass. "All I'm hearing is that I'm in your head."

"Hey, don't t-touch—", her body stilled as she pushed her hands into my back. "I think I'm gonna be sick."

Oh, great.

I tensed, expecting vomit to hit my back. To my pleasant surprise, it never came. Instead, Ember's body tensed and then went completely slack in my arms. I realized she had passed out the moment Kyrin returned.

"Fuck man, did you kill her?"

Why does everyone keep thinking that?!

"No! Just help me get her in the damn car."

With one nod, he trailed me as I took the side door out of his bar and headed toward my car. Once I reached the Lexus, he pulled open the passenger door, and I eased her into the seat. Adjusting the belt across her chest, I pulled away as my eyes locked onto a rectangle clasp attached to her necklace. Without needing to look at it for too much longer, I knew exactly what it was. I snapped the chain off between my hands and popped open the piece of metal, watching as a small microchip fell into my palm.

Another tracking device, *one that didn't belong to me.*

Kyrin peered over my shoulder as his voice went quiet. "Please tell me that's one of yours."

I straightened slowly but didn't answer his question. "I need a camera I can place that has live access. Give me whatever you have that will work."

Understanding flashed across his face as he pulled a small device free from the inside seam of his jacket. "This links to the security team for the bar, but I'll disconnect it from them."

I nodded briefly as I pocketed the microchip and the wired camera before closing the car door. "Thanks. I need an hour."

He said nothing but backed up, pulling a small radio from his pocket.

Ember stayed asleep for the drive, which gave me some time to sort through my thoughts. My hand moved to her chest every few miles, checking for any type of change in her breathing. I wouldn't be surprised if she ended up having alcohol poisoning.

That's how out of it she was.

I sighed into the space between us, because it was *this* exact thing I found myself drawn to. There was no warning label with her, just that damn fire that burned without apology. I was still so eager to watch it, to press my hands into the heat and see who screamed first, her or me.

Looking over at her now, I could see it. Through her matted hair and faded make-up, she was still that same burning chaos but in a different shape. Tonight, she had been too reckless. I thought the fire within her had burned me on purpose, but the truth seemed to be that she had no idea how to control it. Her flame didn't just destroy what it touched, it was the kind that consumed itself if left unchecked. Seeing her on that video, it was clear how close she was to turning herself into ash.

Her fire was something sacred to me now, but the truth was she was damaging herself too. With that realization, something in me shifted. My need for her didn't soften but redirected into something new. The urge to destroy her curled in on itself, reshaping into something heavier. This new feeling was possessive in a way that sank deeper than desire. She wasn't just mine. She was mine to tame. If her fire was going to rage, it would do so within the boundaries *I set.* I would be the restraint she wasn't giving herself. Settling into my new purpose, I drove the rest of the way with a calm mind.

Night had fallen by the time we arrived. From the outside, the house seemed completely empty which meant Kyrin had kept his word. It seemed that everyone from her house was still at the bar. Once I was parked a little ways down the street, I stepped out and walked to her side. Opening the door, I gathered her into my arms and carried her the few yards to her house. As I tugged at her doorknob, it clicked, and I immediately knew she had left the house unlocked. *Yet another thing I'd have to fix—her common sense.*

Moving inside, I guessed at which room was hers. The first one had bubblegum pink walls and a bedazzled comforter. *Nope.*

Moving into the second one, I turned on the light. This one fit her personality more, with simple designs and a purple comforter. Walking straight to the bed, I laid her down and covered her with the blanket. Looking down at her for a moment, I decided to let my impulses win, *yet again*. Shifting her to her back, I carefully pulled off the outfit I'd planned on burning later. Once it was all off, I turned toward the closet to find her something else to wear. After sifting through a few things, I finally settled on a large shirt.

Once she was dressed, I tucked her back into bed and took out the camera that Kyrin had given me. It was small and attached to a wire, similar to the ones that my bodyguards wore at the club. Looking around the room, I tried to find possible locations to place it. I already knew this would just be temporary—a placeholder until Knox had this all figured out.

I eventually found patterned molding on the farthest wall that would hide the wire well. Angling it straight toward her bed, I positioned it to catch most of her room. This model wasn't great for long-range vision, but it would do.

The bed dipped as I sat next to her, watching her sleep for a few minutes. Every now, and then her eyebrows furrowed, as if a headache was already forming. Part of me wanted to go search for pain relievers, but ultimately, I denied myself. She deserved whatever repercussions her body had in store for her—much like the ones she would be receiving from me.

I eventually stood and pulled my eyes away from her, determined to use my remaining time here wisely. Taking a lap around her room, I let my hands skim over her piles of clothes and scattered books—things that made sense now that I understood her. In some places around the room, there were pictures of her and other people, which I admit I didn't *hate*.

A loud vibration pulled my attention to her phone—which to no surprise, was *also* unlocked.

Add that to the list.

A text from Kinsley, wishing her *the best kind of orgasms* and notifying her that they were headed home. *Fuck.* Scanning through her inbox, I found that most of her texts were from her boss at the bookstore and random clients about edits. I read through each one, deciphering the other male roommates my brother had mentioned from different threads of conversations. It was clear she didn't *love* to be on her phone, at least not to communicate with others. Annoyingly, it was also clear that one of the men she lived with was into her.

That list of names was too long at this point.

Her web history was where I looked next and where she spent most of her time. The pages were full of activity, showing a wide variety of searches—from lenses to chocolate to...*me.* An instant smile spread across my face, especially because despite her best efforts, she had found nothing more than a few articles where the name of the club was mentioned.

Once I was done there, I moved to her pictures. Her gallery full of random things that showcased her passion for photography. Different things like trees, clouds, and flowers made up many albums. There were some selfies scattered in too, but those seemed to be quite rare.

A random thought crossed my mind then, and it provided too much dopamine to dismiss. Smiling, I walked over to her dresser and found a permanent marker amongst her things.

Taking a seat next to her in bed, I pulled her thigh over my lap and popped off the cap to the marker. Moving in slow, repeated patterns, I began to write my name in large block letters across her skin. Once I was done, I pulled up her camera and bent to take a selfie with my signature. The last thing I did, just because I felt like it, was assign the photo as her new wallpaper. I only wished I could be with her when she saw it. Lucky for me, I now had a front row view to her room.

The sound of tires outside ruined my excitement. Moving gravel meant I'd have to leave. Thankful I'd made the decision to park farther away, I closed her phone and tucked it inside her bag. I then moved to the window, watching as her roommates arrived. As each person stumbled out of the car, I readied myself to exit through the window as soon as they entered. Once the front door closed, I moved fast, crawling over the small ledge and lowering myself into the dark.

14

Ember

I woke up to a headache that felt like a personal attack. My heartbeat thundered in my ears, each tick of my pulse like a bass drum pounding against my skull. Stronger than anything else was the instant regret that hit me. I groaned in response, rolling to my side, only to gag at my own breath. The sudden wave of nausea forced me upright.

"Fuck," I muttered, forcing my stomach to calm down. Opening my eyes fully, I prayed I'd made it home to my own bed. A sigh of relief left me as I registered the world around me. I was surrounded by *my* blankets, a confirmation that I hadn't gone home with a random stranger. Not that that had been the plan, but the night had started with a simple promise to myself—to do exactly what I wanted.

I must have succeeded in some form, because I could barely remember leaving the house. By that point, we were already a few shots deep. If I thought about it too hard, I could probably admit that I was lucky to be *here* and not in a freezer somewhere.

I pulled the blanket up around me and watched as something fell off the bed. Right away I could tell it was a different fabric than my comforter. Looking down, I realized that it was a black jacket. Holding it up in the morning light, the tag read "men's" and I knew that it didn't belong to me. *Oh god, had I invited someone back here?!* There was a faint scent of cologne that lingered to the piece of clothing, one that was oddly familiar to me. Balling it up, I tossed it into the corner of my room and told myself that I would deal with it later.

Moving slowly, I shuffled off my bed and headed toward my bathroom. Every step felt like a personal challenge, as if my body was fighting me tooth and nail. When I flicked on the light, the mirror hit me like an additional slap of hell.

My makeup had melted into something straight out of a horror movie. Mascara streaked down my cheeks in thick black lines, and bronzer smeared along my jaw like I'd been laying in dirt. My lipstick, what little was left, dragged across my cheekbone like I'd lost a fight with my own face. I took one last look before splashing some cold water on my face and peeling off my shirt. *My shirt.* My arms were still in the middle of the air as a brief memory flashed in my mind of the leather I had worn. *Where had my clothes gone?* Trying to find an answer to that question, I pulled my shirt the rest of the way off and leaned over the counter, bringing my hands up to my face. Slowly exhaling through my fingers, I convinced myself that a shower would help.

Turning on the water, I stood there watching the steam collect. After it was hot enough, I stepped inside, letting water beat down on me. Washing my body, I breathed through waves of nausea. The warmth had just started to feel nice against my skin when my stomach flipped and the walls around me started to shift. Placing my hands against them in defense, I looked down as my eyes caught something on my leg. They narrowed even further as I registered the five letters that were written there.

A name.

Using my hand to wipe away the residual soap that fell from my hair, I stared down at the word that now branded me.

Silas.

Red infiltrated my vision, and I yelled out every single cuss word I could think of. The headrush brought even more nausea, and I had to hold myself up for a second to think clearly. I could either make myself puke in preparation for fighting him, or I could brave breakfast and figure out what the hell happened last night.

Pressing my forehead against the tile, it took me all of five seconds to decide against the forced tequila exorcism. The best answer was breakfast or at least some answers. Wrapped in a towel and still dripping, I reemerged into my bedroom and sat on the bed. Rubbing my temples in slow circles, I fished my phone out of my bag and turned it on.

I watched as the start-up screen faded and then did everything I could to stop myself from screaming. There, as my wallpaper, was a picture of a masked Silas with my fucking leg—a leg that he'd *apparently autographed.* The picture faded as notifications came flooding in.

Twelve missed calls.

Three voicemails.

Nineteen messages.

I dismissed a few, only to have more pour in.

Kolby: *WHERE ARE YOU?*

Bodhi: *You left with a random guy? Kolby is freaking out. Just let us know you're safe.*

Kolby: *It looks like you did come home. Thanks for letting us know.*

Kinsley: *I'm dead. I've died.*

Kinsley: *Seriously, plan my funeral.*

Kinsley: *Promise me that you'll make sure I never drink again.*

Kolby: *You alive?*

Bodhi: *We have food for you whenever you're ready.*

Unknown: *Last night was a bad decision but at least I got something out of it. Can you send me that picture when you get a chance?*

My thumb stopped over the last message.

I'm going to kill him.

I furiously typed out a message, just to delete it and then retype it again. Nothing I wrote encapsulated my fury quite like the feelings that were storming through my mind. After a few more minutes I finally settled on one and hit send.

Touch me again and I'm calling the police.

15

SILAS

The police?

I laughed at her text as I took a bite of my sandwich, watching the feed from the camera that was now in her room. The picture sucked, and there was no audio, but it was something. I almost choked when I watched her pick up my jacket. Realizing I left it in her room had been quite the surprise. My priority last night had been taking those god-awful clothes off her and getting rid of them. I turned to where they were now, looking at the remnants of them in my trash can. Annoyingly, the leather turned out to be real and not easy to ignite.

The fact I had left my jacket in the first place showed how much she affected me. *Was her chaotic behavior starting to rub off on me?*

The answer was clear as I let my eyes scan over the name that now adorned her thigh—my name, the one that should be tattooed there.

My phone vibrated against the desk, cutting through my thoughts as Ember began to get dressed. Not taking my eyes off the screen, I answered. "Yeah."

"You're welcome," Knox immediately replied.

I leaned forward a fraction, resting my jaw in my hand. "For what?"

"Getting you full visuals," he replied. "Within a day."

On the monitor, Ember was now walking through her room, brushing her hair. As she threw her hair up in a ponytail, she hit the corner of her dresser and winced.

"On Ember?" I asked.

"Yup. You now have access to everything."

My fingers tapped my cheekbone as I continued to listen to him and watch her. I couldn't decide if I was entertained or mildly concerned for her coordination, because she ended up hitting the same corner three more times. Either way, I kept watching and counting the hits in my head like some personal scoreboard.

"Security cameras for her house were the obvious starting point, but I went further and hacked into the smart appliances inside too. Fridge, thermostat, anything that's connected. And the bookstore? Every camera feed there now also belongs to you."

Ember pulled on her shoes, disappearing out of frame. "How do I get to it?"

"Same app as the tracker that's on her phone."

I pulled the phone away from my face and switched through the many different feeds I could now access. They were all labeled with different areas and items. Clicking on 'kitchen' I caught her again like I'd never lost her.

"Oh, and last night?" Knox added. "Handled."

"And what exactly did you handle?"

"I wiped you. Every camera you passed—gone."

Fuck. Something else I hadn't thought about. She was actively destroying every thought process I had. "Huh. Has anyone ever told you that you're pretty good at this stuff?" That thought reminded me of the next thing I needed him to work on. "Speaking of," I said, picking up the chain that I had piled on my desk. The delicate metal was cool against my fingers as I palmed it to snap a picture. Then I took another picture of the tracker that was hidden inside.

There was a pause on the line, then Knox's voice was back. "Where did you find that?"

"It was in her necklace," I said. "Very similar to the ones we looked at before, right?"

Another pause, shorter this time. "...yeah," Knox muttered. "That's a standard one used for general tracking."

Glancing back up at the monitor. Ember disappeared down the hallway toward her bedroom.

I switched feeds and followed her.

"Could it be that she uses that as a safety precaution? That's a thing, right?" I asked.

"Not with that one," Knox said slowly. "There are other cheaper types for that. The way that one was hidden makes me feel like someone didn't want it found."

My grip tightened around the chain.

"I can trace it," he continued. "Figure out who bought it, maybe where it was activated. I can use the number from the picture you sent me. Although, if you don't plan on returning it, I would smash it."

I rolled the small piece between my fingers, feeling the weight of it. "Why?"

"Because if it's active, it's talking," Knox snapped. "And if it's talking, someone might already know where to find it."

I glanced down at it again, then back up at her. On the screen, I was now watching from her TV.

"Where are you right now?" Knox asked suddenly.

I intentionally didn't answer him, knowing exactly why he asked.

"...Silas."

"At the club," I said on an exhale.

A sharp groan sounded on the other end. "You brought it to the club?! You don't move unknown trackers into populated places. If that thing pings—"

Then they will come to me, and it will make things so much easier.

"At least I didn't take it to my house."

Knox went silent for a moment, probably assessing how far to actually take this conversation. "Yeah. That would've been worse."

I leaned back in my chair again. "Thanks for getting me access to her. Let me know when anything comes back from the tracker."

Knox's response was him cutting the line, but it didn't bother me. Taking the microchip between my fingers, I wondered who could be following her. In the end, it didn't really matter. She belonged to me now, and anyone who had a problem with that would be taken care of.

Standing, I moved to the balcony outside my office and dropped the chip on the steel floor. Placing my foot above it, I ground my heel into the small square over and over again. I didn't stop until it cracked beneath me. When I picked up my shoe, the tracker laid there broken, shattered into several pieces.

With that taken care of, I could move on with the rest of my plan. Step one, Ember. Step two, making sure whoever planted this, stayed far away from her.

Resting my forearms against the cold metal railing of the balcony, I looked down over the floor. The main room was packed once again, alive with bodies—exactly how it was supposed to be. My gaze drifted through the people, and somehow, I knew that all I was searching for was that wild brown hair and exuberant energy.

The bass crawled up through the floor and burrowed into my chest. That feeling used to be my favorite, but now it didn't compare to what Ember triggered in me. Realistically, I knew I couldn't be in three places at once, so I'd to have to figure out a way to temporarily make this work. Taking a minute to watch the havoc unfold below me, I should've felt satisfied, but I didn't. The club almost felt like noise—it was *her* that I needed right now.

More importantly, I needed a few days to get things settled. Then, I could just bring her back here.

The idea settled in my head like it had been waiting there all night.

If I could manage to create enough time to step away and clean up whatever mess this was, I could make this work. I knew the club would be just fine without me. Still...walking away, even for a couple days, felt wrong. This was my home, but now, I belonged here *with her.* I exhaled slowly and pushed off the railing.

The best option was to give myself time and use it wisely.

I crossed through my office before switching out my mask for the Watcher. By the time I went down the stairs, I'd already figured out the perfect way to say hello to Ember tonight. The main floor surrounded me as people brushed past without a second glance, exactly as intended. I moved through them like part of the background, heading straight for Taya.

The music dulled the second I pushed into the small room. A few more steps, and I was directly beside her desk. She'd been in the middle of flirting with a new member—a girl who looked like she didn't know whether to be impressed or nervous.

I stepped closer, stopping their conversation. "Taya."

She turned her head slightly, eyes landing on my mask.

"Boss," she said, smooth as ever. The girl glanced between us, clearly trying to figure out where she stood now.

"I'll be in and out for a little bit," I told her, offering nothing more besides that information.

Her expression barely shifted, but I still caught it—the understanding. She straightened just a fraction and gave me a small nod.

"I'll call if anything happens."

"Good."

I held her gaze for a second longer, making sure she was confident in me leaving. Then I turned and headed straight for the door. The outside air hit different, cutting through everything I'd just walked out of. Even the music faded into a distant pulse behind me.

I walked to my car, my mind quieter than it should've been. My hand rested on the door for a moment before I got in and started the engine.

Just a few days, that's it.

It felt necessary.

It *was* necessary, especially if it meant I came back with her.

16

Ember

Pushing up off the wall, I convinced myself I needed to get ready for work. To my surprise, my body actually listened. Sorting through my clothes, I tried to find something that covered the permanent marker that refused to come off.

The next time I saw him, I was going to junk punch him.

Besides pants, the only option I had was a dress that barely covered his stupid handwriting. Opting to be cooler in this weather, I chose to deal with the length and hoped I didn't expose it. After applying some foundation and throwing my hair up, I made my way into the kitchen to grab something to eat.

Kinsley was the first one to see me, standing in front of the stove and dancing around like she was 100% sober. *How she was capable of that? I had no idea.* Bodhi stood next to her, holding out a spatula for her like a microphone.

Kolby sat at the table with Bodhi's teammates and was the first to see me come in the room.

"Hey," he said sharply, his tone laced with anger as he stood and moved toward me. "You can't just leave Kinsley for some random dude, Em. We had no idea where you were."

I nodded, wishing he'd turn down his volume. With my head pounding, I squinted toward him. "I didn't leave with anyone. I came home."

Kolby seemed to relax slightly. "You were here the whole time?"

I nodded again, bringing my finger up to my mouth to quiet him as I sat at the table. I had just grabbed a cup and poured some orange juice when Kinsley let out one of her signature squeals, and my headache instantly worsened. Looking over at her, I realized she'd taken the spatula from Bodhi and was now pointing it toward my leg.

"You dirty, filthy liar!" She ran across the kitchen to me and started shaking my shoulders, making my head want to physically explode. "*Silas*?! Is that who you were with last night?"

Oh, shit.

Pulling the fabric over my leg to conceal his name, I ignored Kinsley as she danced around me. That was easy to ignore. What was harder to dismiss were the looks I received from the boys. Kolby's face twisted into one of contempt, which mirrored the same one as Bodhi's. *They must think I lied to them.*

I couldn't do anything about the situation, or their feelings, so I decided to leave for work early. Standing, I moved straight toward the door and away from this conversation. Bodhi tried to stop me, but I just didn't have the energy to explain anything to them. Making sure not to look back, I waved goodbye and slipped out the front door.

The walk to the bookstore was quiet for once as I tried to

process through my own thoughts. In one area of my life, I was hiding things that I just couldn't explain to my roommates. In another, I was not only provoking a stalker but plotting his murder. As much as I liked having my plate full, I was now teetering on dropping the whole thing and creating a big mess.

Letting my mind wander, I followed the familiar route. A safe and predictable part of my day, *the opposite of what I'd recently encountered.* Left at the cracked sidewalk and then straight past the café until I saw the bookstore. My hand lifted to my necklace without thinking and stopped when I felt bare skin. My fingers curled slightly before I forced my hand back down, but I kept walking like nothing happened.

Except something definitely did.

Silas.

I wouldn't be surprised if he was the one responsible for it missing, the asshole who'd claimed me with permanent black marker. The necklace had been a gift from Kolby, but he probably knew that already, which was why it was gone. My jaw tightened as I turned the corner, the bookstore coming into view at the end of the block. Usually that was enough to settle the unease in me, but that was exactly what scared me—it was like I couldn't settle now that I'd experienced him.

I slowed as I approached the bookstore and stepped inside to start my shift. Placing my bag down, Edna's voice found me from behind the counter. "There you are, I thought you were probably going to be late with how *reliable* you tend to be."

I looked over at her but didn't force a smile. "Morning,

Edna."

She didn't respond, just peered at me over her half-moon glasses before turning away with a frown. I watched her as the contents of my stomach threatened to come up. For a split second, I debated letting everything come out in her direction.

I managed to suppress the nausea long enough for her to walk out, the bell over the door signaling my freedom from her. Folding my arms, I bent and rested my forehead on the wood grain counter for just a second. My body taking that moment to inform me exactly how mad it was that we hadn't grabbed something to eat. A loud cry came from my stomach.

"Well that sounds painful."

Atlas's voice made me jump, which forced my stomach to do another somersault. I groaned slightly as I brought one hand to my belly and the other up to wave him away. Naturally, he didn't listen. Instead, I felt hm at my side as he rubbed my back.

"You okay?"

"Yeah, I'm good. Just not feeling great today."

"You look green." Guiding me toward the chair behind the desk, he made me sit. "Do me a favor and do not throw up. I don't do well with bodily fluids."

Normally, I would've rolled my eyes at him, but my head was pounding too hard to care. I sank onto the chair with a groan, leaning forward with my elbows on my knees.

Atlas disappeared for a minute before returning with water. "You eat today?"

I shook my head, ready to apologize for being hungover.

"Ember, we've talked about this. You can't just survive off caffeine and spite."

I huffed a small laugh as he crouched down next to me, and cocked his head to see my hidden face. "Atlas, I—"

"Hey, it's okay, Let me take care of you for once."

I barely reacted at first, but then he moved his body between my legs and sat on his knees, rubbing the outside of my thighs.

Atlas was touchy sometimes, it was just the kind of person he was. There were side hugs every time I would come into work or brief moments of him walking by where he would make physical contact. Looking back, it was always casual things that never seemed weird before. *Not like this.*

So when his hands moved to the inside of my legs and he started massaging them, I tried to fight the red flags that formed in my mind. "I'm okay, really. I just—"

"You're really tense," he said quietly as his hand moved in slow circles, "I hate seeing you like this."

I swallowed hard as I battled another turn of my stomach. I needed to get out of this situation and then find something to eat. "I'll survive."

"I know." His fingers moved to my calves, and he looked up at me. "Doesn't mean I like it."

Something in his tone confirmed the next wave of red flags that flooded my mind. He was looking at me and not as a friend or boss.

I shifted uncomfortably and pulled my legs away from him as I sat up straighter. The movement caused the fabric of my dress to fall off my leg, where Silas's name was now exposed.

A look of disappointment filled his features before he sighed and looked up at me. "Have you just pretended not to notice? Or did you really have no idea?"

I stared at him blankly for a second because surely I'd misunderstood him. When he reworded his question again, my nostrils flared. *Fuck.* Realization crashed into me all at once. The dinners, the banter, the way he always found reasons to hang out with me until closing—I pulled back from him instinctively.

"The truth is that I've been trying to get your attention for a long time now. I thought you would catch on the more we played." He let out a short laugh and ran a hand through his hair. "I mean, even Edna knows. The desserts, the time together, the *flowers.*"

Double fuck.

"Atlas, I love working here and I love our friendship..."

"I love it too," he leaned closer, resting his forearms on my knees as he gestured down to the dark marks on my skin, "but the question is, do you love it more than others?"

The way he said it made my skin crawl, like friendship had simply been a bridge for this. I wondered how long he had waited for this opportunity. Looking down at my leg, I envisioned a masked Silas, and for some reason, the mental presence made me feel comforted.

Another somersault came from my stomach, and this one brought the threat of dry heaving along with a fire in my chest. I stood, shaking my head as I walked around him. "I love you—just not, *like that* and if that's going to be a problem, I need to know now because I'll find a different job."

I watched as his lips shifted into a sad smile and then tightened into a thin line as he stood. "I'm sorry for my behavior, and I understand if I'm the one who caused a problem. I hope you'll stay here with us."

I said nothing as I watched him leave. For a while, I just stared at the door, trying to figure out how I had missed all those signs. For the next few moments, I just stood and contemplated how I would find another job like this one. As all my thoughts swirled together, the bell chimed again, and I expected a customer.

"Delivery for Ember?" a voice called out.

My eyes landed on a delivery driver from Clove. "That's me."

Nodding, he stepped up to the counter in front of me, holding out a small paper bag with a cardboard drink tray. The smell enveloped me like a familiar blanket, and I immediately knew what the drink was, a spiced chai.

I eyed the items in his hand as I tried to stop the drool forming in my mouth. "But I didn't order anything."

The short man shrugged, "Please just take it, it's already paid for." Raising his phone, he confirmed the order before handing me a paper. "Chai latte and croissant. Here's the note."

I put my hands up in another refusal, but he just set everything down in front of me before turning away. "I don't—"

"Have a good day!" he yelled back, already halfway out the door.

I sighed loudly and looked down at what had been delivered.

My head throbbed harder now, picking up speed as I ripped away the paper that was stapled to the bag.

You didn't eat.

Take care of yourself or I will.

My hand crumpled the paper, not out of shock, but out of irritation. *What the fuck was my life?!*

I was so tired of this, of everything, especially *him*. This might be how he functioned, how he lived, but it wasn't how I did, and I was sick of it.

I pushed both items to the side, where they now sat between the register and the new display of bookmarks. I *had* to accept the delivery, but I didn't have to *eat* them. As if in response to my refusal, steam started to curl out of the chai in soft spirals. I growled at the cup imagining that it was Silas. Boundaries existed for a reason, but clearly, no one in my life knew that. My fingers dug into my palms as I clenched my fists.

I imagined how I could take it all back into my own hands. The first part was easy, I would walk away from Atlas, but Silas was different. The thought of beating him at his own game sent a dark thrill through my chest, a feeling I couldn't quite place. The moment of victory was ruined when my stomach lurched hard enough that I dry heaved again.

"Fine," I hissed, yanking the croissant from the bag and tearing into it, not even trying to be graceful. Flakes scattered across the counter as butter coated my fingers. My stomach immediately thanked me by calming down, and that made me so ridiculously angry that I chewed louder. *This wasn't surrender,*

I said to myself as I swallowed some of the chai, welcoming the burn as it slid down my throat.

With every bite, I contemplated the different things I could do to him, ways to make him feel like this. The thoughts lingered as the treats disappeared, and I helped customers as they arrived. The next couple of hours went by fast, and in the small moments of stillness, I planned all the things I would need to do. By the end of my shift, I felt better about everything and was ready to go home to put my plan into action. When I glanced up and noticed I only had ten minutes left, I started packing my things. As I grabbed my keys to lock up, the dumb bell chimed again.

I glanced toward the front as I set my things back down. "We're actually closing—" My words faded when I realized the area was completely empty. Unease crept in, and I could feel the hairs on the back of my neck start to rise. Stepping away from the counter, I walked to the floor and looked around slowly. My eyes scanned down every aisle, my ears strained for the faintest sound, but there was nothing. I stopped when I got to the front counter again. A slight movement to my left made me turn, and that's when I saw him.

A masked Silas leaned into a stack of books that were tucked in the corner.

My whole body lit up, and my breath stalled as he tilted his head slightly in my direction. Even through the Watchers mask, I could see it—his damn demeanor. I reached for my bag to grab my phone, but he clicked his tongue and held something up in his hand, my wallpaper back to the picture of us.

"In the past twenty-four hours," he said, his voice dangerously calm, "I have learned a lot of things." He moved to the door and slid the lock into place. "One, I'm very much in your head." With that, he turned and walked toward me, brushing his fingers against the books he passed. "Two, I now have full access to you which means I can watch you anytime I want, *even here.*" A small nod to the cameras in the corner confirmed my suspicion about him. "Three, it seems you need another lesson in who is allowed to touch you." He paused for a brief second before crossing his arms over his chest. "I thought you learned before with the men from the club, but tonight it was your *boss.*"

My eyes narrowed in fury. "Tonight was *none* of your business."

After another moment, he resituated and pushed each of his sleeves up, exposing tattoos I didn't know were there. "There's also the little problem," he whispered, ignoring me as he closed the space between us, "of you having no idea what the word *mean* is. Isn't that right, baby?"

Every word landed like a bomb, and my mouth curled up into a snarl. I pressed my back against the counter, eyes darting around for an escape, but every aisle felt like a trap, and I already knew he was probably waiting for me to run. He must've known what I was thinking, because he made a warning sound that promised consequences for whatever decision I made. Quickly weighing the ideas from before, I eventually landed on one.

I scoffed, trying to keep the fear from my voice. "Cute speech, wanna add that to my leg too?"

He didn't flinch at the mention of where his name was on my body, but there was a slight shift in him, a tension I could feel. I took a slow, measured step to the side but not too far. I didn't want to give him the thrill of me panicking. "You think this scares me? That you do?" I challenged. "Try harder."

He advanced one step, and I threw my hands up, ready to push or throw something but he just laughed at me. The sound was low and sharp, like he was enjoying this far more than necessary.

"I've missed you," he murmured as he circled me, stalking me like I was prey he couldn't decide how to kill.

I refused to watch him, so I just looked straight forward. "Should I be expecting this kind of irritation every night then?" Planting my feet, I gripped the edge of the counter, refusing to give him whatever satisfaction he was getting out of this. "Because truthfully, I'm kind of over it." Maybe it was stupid, but the thrill of the anger, *of my defiance*, steadied me. The more I stood up to him, the more *I was winning.*

I continued to stand there as I refused to budge. Even though a part of me started to feel like I should. Every sharp instinct I had fully awakened, telling me to put space between us, but I didn't.

"You don't scare me." My statement came out strong, better than I'd expected.

His head tilted again, like I'd just said something mildly interesting. "I don't want you scared, baby." There was something in his voice now, an emphasis on the way he said certain things. "I want you vicious."

Lifting my chin just a little, I realized any choice that involved defiance only interested him more.

"Tell me something, Ember," he said quietly. "Do you always fight this hard for control, or just when you know you're about to lose it?"

My lips curved, but I forced the reaction away. "I don't fight for control," I said, meeting his gaze without hesitation. "I have it."

Tilting my head slightly, I mimicked his previous movement, just enough to make it deliberate.

"Maybe with your boss, or your roommates, but not with me. Let me prove to you just how wrong you are." He moved closer, fully aware that he had my attention. My heart kicked a little harder with each step he took, but I ignored it. "Better yet, let me show you what it's like to give up that control. I'll even let you choose how you say sorry."

A scoff left my mouth before I could stop it as my face morphed into one of pure confusion. "*Sorry*?!"

The first word of his answer was a hum, one that vibrated through his body. "Yes, for letting someone else touch what belongs to me."

My tongue glued itself to the roof of my mouth as I clenched my teeth together.

"I'll even let you choose this time," he whispered at me as his fingers traced my hip. "Which do you prefer," he said, "laid out on the counter for me to eat or up against the books for me to feel?"

A slow heat formed in my lower body, the same deep need I had experienced at the club with him. I hated myself for it, and I fought against the feeling but soon, I couldn't even do that. When I spoke, my voice was quieter this time—not weaker, just aware and cautious. "Neither."

He pulled my body tight to his, and for some reason, I didn't hit him. I physically couldn't, not when everything inside me was screaming for him. I tilted my head up to keep eye contact with him. I refused to look away because if I did, I *lost.* I didn't even know what that meant exactly, but I knew I couldn't let that happen.

"I like you vicious because it makes me feel alive, Ember," he said slowly. "Y*ou* make me feel alive."

"Stop," I muttered, but my breath didn't cooperate. It caught, just a little, like my body overlooked the whole fact we hated him.

The silence between us stretched for a moment, and I knew he was doing it deliberately. He didn't even try to touch me because he didn't have to. *That was the fucking problem.* The closer he was, the more I felt everything—my pulse climbed, heat crept into my face, even my fingers wanted to curl just to give the tension somewhere to go.

"Make me," he replied softly, "and pick one." He leaned in,

just enough for me to feel the shift of his chest, the contact that almost happened.

"You aren't—" I started, but the words fell apart halfway through. I didn't even know what I was trying to claim.

His hand lifted, and every part of me noticed. I didn't flinch away like I hoped I would, and I knew it was because my body craved him. When his fingers brushed my arm lightly, it was like a spark ran straight through me. *Damn it.* His hand lingered before intentionally running up along my arm like he knew exactly what he was doing to me.

By the time his fingers reached my neck, my pulse raced. As his hand wrapped around my throat, the feeling within me amplified—immediate and undeniable. I could feel the proof underneath his fingertips, my heart, completely betraying me. Although on the outside there were no signs, just my eyes locked on his mask.

"Still not scared?" he murmured.

I shook my head because I didn't trust my voice anymore.

His thumb shifted slightly against my neck, and goosebumps broke out across my skin.

"You're right," he said quietly, as his other fingers moved between my legs, "that's not fear."

I refused to reply, to make any type of sound that would answer his question. In response, he turned me around and pushed me up against the wall like he did in his office. With one hand around my throat and the other between my thighs, his voice rose, "Tell me how I'm going to take you or *I will choose*

Ember."

Before I could stop it, a small moan escaped me. The sound immediately made him growl.

Wrapping his palm in my hair, he backed me up to the counter, lifting me on top of it and spreading my legs. Looking down between them, his voice came out clipped. "Then I'll take you both ways and let your boss fucking watch."

This time, I replied with a sarcastic scoff. "I thought no one else was allowed to see."

I knew I had angered him because he ripped the underwear off my body in one clean movement. "Shut up and close your eyes."

I laughed but I listened. Just like in the club, I'm reminded that following his direction felt an awful lot like accepting his darkness. As that thought faded away, I felt him secure his mask to my face. "This is the last chance I'm giving you. I told you before, you belong to me."

My mouth started to form a nasty insult, but that's when I felt his hot breath between my legs. Before I could even brace for what was coming, he pushed two fingers inside of me and swiped his tongue. The pressure was instant and aggressive, like he'd been waiting for this. The touch was far from gentle, but it was everything that made Silas who he was—everything that I thought I was starting to need.

I couldn't help but buck as I pushed myself into his face. He accepted the movement and groaned louder into my center. His other hand slid up over my belly and held me still as his tongue moved faster. I had no time to debate whether or not this was the wrong choice. Before I knew it, the pressure started to build and my muscles clenched. Just as the tension threatened to snap, he pulled his mouth away, and I slammed the back of my head down on the desk in defeat. Another low chuckle from him made me want to open my eyes, but I knew if I did that, this would stop.

I inhaled through my nose as his fingers traced my opening. He wanted something, and I knew I'd have to deal with this torture until he got it.

17

Silas

I wasn't one to lose focus. If anything, I hyper-fixated on things in my life.

I'd always been told it was a toxic trait, one that would eventually get me in trouble.

That was one of the first things I learned about myself as a child. In the beginning, it was over small things, items that held my attention long enough to grant me a temporary dose of happiness. As an adult, I struggled to find something outside of Ruined that gave me that same rush... but now I knew, it was all because I was waiting for her.

She was it, the one thing I never saw coming. Ember was more than just an addiction, she was like a fucking drug I needed to feel in my bloodstream. The way she tasted, the raging fire her soul was made from—I needed to own every piece of her.

That thought forced the next words out of my mouth. "Tell me I'm right, and I'll let you cum."

A small groan from her was my only answer, one clearly laced with refusal. I snarled back as I forced my fingers inside of her, once again making her climb. As I lowered my lips to the sweet taste of her, I made sure to focus on that one spot that made her

body tense. I could feel it, the way she coiled. Just like before, I pulled away and waited.

Ember whimpered back, the sound almost enough to make me break. Her voice, broken and raw, finally filled my ears. "You're right."

"Louder," I growled.

"I belong to you."

Four words, and my tongue returned to her, flicking at a higher speed. I had maxed out her sensitivity, but she was held down now, allowed just enough room to buck through her release. As soon as it hit, I lapped slowly, just long enough before I stood and wrapped her legs around me before I moved us.

For a split second, I was scared to look at her without my mask but then I realized how her head hung. The sight was enough to make me smile. This was her *one* chance to take advantage of me, of the situation, and clearly, she chose not to. *She chose me.* With every sensation heightened, I pushed her back into the bookshelf and made her take every inch of me.

The feeling around me was instant as I fought against my own release.

I never wanted this to end, especially now as I fucked her up against the shelves. I didn't think anything in this world, in this *lifetime*, could stop this feeling. The sound she made, the way she clawed at my back—I forgot there was even a possibility that she could see me. I knew she wouldn't look though, she was too busy listening so goddamn well.

Pulling her close to my chest, I placed my mouth next to her ear as I pushed inside of her over and over. "You can threaten me with the cops. You can pretend other men have a chance. You can even fight back as much as you want—you should know by now that I actually prefer it that way, but just know that you're *mine,* Ember." I gave her more as I gripped harder, pouring everything into her. Wrapping my hand in her hair again, I pulled her head back, exposing her throat. Running my tongue from the base of her jaw, toward the top, I bit down on her earlobe. "Say it for me again. Say it into the fucking camera."

"Fuck!" she managed to scream out.

"Tell him that you belong to me and no one else, Ember!" I demanded, as I licked the wound from the teeth and then kissed the exposed skin on her arms and chest.

Still, she refused to say it, the disobedience ultimately pushing me over the edge and causing me to fill her. I held onto her hips as I pulsed, watching the way her body spasmed. Even on the inside, I could feel it, the way her body tightened around me.

Even like this, *especially like this,* she was so goddamn beautiful. Her head was tilted back against the books behind her as she calmed her breathing, her brown hair falling over her shoulders. Pulling the mask off her face, I settled it back around mine and watched as she opened her eyes for me. Blinking a few times, she adjusted her vision to the low light around us. I watched for a moment, before setting her down and pulling her close.

Pushing her legs open, I ran my finger over her lips before pushing my cum deeper inside of her. "Next time you think there's any chance that I don't own you, I want you to remember how it feels to be filled by me."

A choked moan escaped her, but I knew she understood what I'd said. Straightening her dress out, I bent and picked up all the books we had knocked over. Sliding the last one back into it's home, I rested my hand there for a second before standing. The air was still charged between us, filled with everything she refused to admit.

Good.

Buttoning my pants, I watched her brush out her hair with her fingers. Then, I turned to the door, unlocking it with a quiet click. I didn't open it just yet. Instead, I looked back at her. "You know the funny thing about control?" I said.

She didn't answer, and I knew it was because she was still trying to fight her feelings for me.

Taking a step toward her, I moved slow enough that she had time to react if she was going to, but she didn't.

"Everyone thinks it's about holding onto it," I continued, my voice even. "Keeping it. Protecting it." I took another step. "But it's not." I saw it in her now, the fire that refused to dim even when the oxygen in the room was thin. "It's about what happens," I added quietly, "when it's ripped away completely." I stopped in front of her again, close enough that I could see her unsteady breaths. "You don't get a choice in what happens now." My fingers brushed her arm, light at first, then steady as my hand settled briefly on her lower back. "You have claimed a piece of me because you're meant to have it, just like you're meant to be mine. You'll see."

"You're wrong," she said, her volatile side still clearly out to play.

Bracing one hand against the wall beside her shoulder, I stayed near enough that the absence of contact felt deliberate.

"Then why give in to me again?" I asked quietly. "Why let me touch you?"

Her eyes flicked up to mine, irritation flashing hot, but there was no answer. Her mouth remained closed. *At least she's not trying to lie again.*

"I'm wrong?" I repeat, almost thoughtful. "That's interesting, considering I can still taste your pretty little cunt."

"I—" She cut herself off, realizing the trap too late. "That's not the point."

"No," I agreed, leaning in slightly. "It's not."

I held her eye contact through my mask because I knew she was unable to look away, to look anywhere else. If she turned her head, she relinquished her control. That was the beauty of this whole thing, the reason why this was going to work. I *needed* the control. She needed to feel like she had it.

"How bout I make you a deal," I murmured. "You decide that you really don't want this, and you can tell me to fuck off."

"Fuck—" she said immediately.

Too fast.

"Say it now, and I won't touch you again. *Ever.*"

She opened her mouth to speak but closed it again without finishing her sentence. *Fuck, my dick was getting hard again.*

I needed her to understand how serious I was, to know that I had no hesitation. I let the moment sit—just long enough for her to process it, then I stepped back. The space between us returned, but it didn't undo anything I'd said. Nothing between us could be undone. I turned, reaching for the door to pull it open. Cool air slipped into the room, breaking the tension just enough to make it breathable again. "You should know I mean what I say. I disabled the cameras before I came in." I didn't look back as I left.

18

Ember

I pushed the door to the bookstore open and stepped out onto the small stairs, my legs barely standing from the weight of my things. I had been ravaged, again. What happened in there with Silas hadn't exactly been a *mistake,* but I had given him another chance to turn me into a complete mess.

Setting my things down, I positioned the key in our hidden spot, the one that Atlas would find it in tomorrow morning. That part was easy to take care of, I just needed to send a simple text and hope that Silas meant what he had said about the cameras.

Silas.

He was an asshole, a monster, and everything I wanted.

That fucking guy made me so angry, so confused...*and so horny.* The storm he caused inside of me was the perfect combination of rage, lust, and a continuous stream of questioning myself. Even thinking about him now caused me to descend deeper into the hurricane within my mind.

Starting the walk home, I held on to my small box and fixed my eyes on the cracks in the sidewalk like they might anchor me back to earth. They didn't, because nothing could. All I could feel was him, all I could see was his mask. *I should have looked when I had the chance. I should have let myself see his face.* But I couldn't bring myself to do it, not when he was giving me the smallest slice of trust. I wasn't like him. I needed to be better than that.

I thought the experience with him last time had been amazing, but this was completely different and just as mind-blowing. It was like he knew exactly what to say and how to touch me. There were moments with him earlier, I couldn't even think. My brain refused to form words, and afterwards? It was like he already knew how I felt. The way he got under my skin didn't make sense—it shouldn't make sense, because I barely knew him.

I exhaled sharply, shaking my head.

I came up with a plan for it to be snapped in half the moment I saw him. I could either choose to keep fighting or stop and see what happened. Either way, there was no denying to myself what he did to me. The thought made my chest tighten, something between fear and something far more dangerous. I swallowed hard, picking up my pace like I could outrun it, like I could leave him behind with every step.

By the time I reached the house, my pulse hadn't slowed. If anything, it was worse. My hand hesitated on the door for a second before I pushed it open and stepped inside. The familiar scent of home wrapped around me, but it didn't quite calm me where I needed it to. "Kinsley?" I called out, slipping off my shoes as I placed down my things.

"Not here," Bodhi answered from the kitchen.

As I walked into the room, I glanced up and found him leaning against the counter. A half-finished pizza sat next to him, one he had clearly abandoned.

"They went out to find something to give their mom," he added.

"Oh." I said, suddenly defeated. "Gotcha."

I didn't even make it two more steps before I felt the weight of his gaze. I knew he could tell something was wrong. I watched him push off the counter without saying anything and move toward the fridge. Feeling the look of confusion that filled my face, he pulled a glass bottle out and grabbed a cup.

"I made this earlier," he said, casually pouring the liquid. "Figured you'd want it when you got home."

The smell hit me before he handed it over. *Chai.*

"Thanks," I murmured, taking it from him.

He just nodded as he slid onto the stool across from me and rested his elbows on the counter. I could tell he was studying me, waiting for me to talk. I just looked down into the cup, taking a sip to avoid his stare. I definitely didn't want to talk about it.

"Who's Silas?" he asked.

Fuck.

I froze, the chai lingering on my tongue. Lowering the cup slowly, I sighed into it, like it might offer me some type of escape from this conversation. "No one."

Bodhi didn't push for me to answer, he just waited. The

longer he sat there, letting me think about my answer, the longer I wanted to tell him the truth.

A few seconds later, I gave in, and my shoulders sank in personal defeat. "He's just this guy I know," I confessed.

Bodhi raised an eyebrow toward me, silently asking for more. I wanted to comply, mainly because he never judged and I had no way to explain this situation.

I groaned softly, taking another drink and dragging a hand over my face. "I just met him, okay? It's not—it's nothing."

"Mm," he hummed, unconvinced.

I looked up at him, setting my drink down on the counter. "I mean it."

He nodded before offering me a smile, like he knew. *Of course he knew.* "Then why do you look like that?"

I blinked, trying to pretend I had no idea what he was talking about. "Like what?"

Now both of his eyebrows rose, and I knew there was no point in trying to hide it.

I opened my mouth, but the words didn't come. I just looked over at my chai, swirling it slightly. "He just—" I hesitated, trying to find the right way to explain our situation. "He drives me crazy."

Bodhi smiled faintly again, like he knew the feeling.

"In a bad way?" he asked.

I let out a soft, breathless laugh. "That's the problem. I don't know yet. I want to say yes, but I feel like I might be wrong." I finally met his eyes again and something in me caved. "It's like every time I'm around him, I forget how to think and I hate that. I *hate* it." My grip tightened on the cup. "I don't even know him, Bodhi. Not really, but I can't stop thinking about him." The admission hung between us, but I felt lighter. "I've never felt something like this before," I added quietly.

For a second, there was only silence. Then, Bodhi's expression softened completely, and he reached over to nudge my arm. "I get it," he said with a soft smile, "and I don't think that's a bad thing."

Everything inside me loosened slightly at his words "Yeah?"

His smile grew as he dipped his head in confirmation. "Yeah. I've got a girl who does the same thing to me. Sometimes I get so mad at her and what she does that I feel like my head is going to explode, but there's nothing that will change how I feel about her. You know? Sometimes fate is funny like that." He sighed and shrugged his shoulder, like he really did get it.

A slow grin spread across my face. "Kinsley is lucky to have you."

Bodhi scoffed lightly, "I think I'm the lucky one."

I smiled into my cup, picking it up again as I felt something inside me ease for the first time since meeting Silas. "So, I shouldn't tell him to fuck off?"

He full on laughed this time. "Not unless you really mean it, Em."

I nodded and moved next to him, pulling him into a hug and kissing his forehead. "Thanks for listening and not making it weird," I said.

He leaned back slightly. "That's kind of my job."

"Being annoyingly perceptive?"

"Being a good big brother," he corrected.

I rolled my eyes, but I couldn't stop the small smile that followed. The chaos in my head hadn't disappeared. Silas was still there, lingering in every thought. It didn't feel quite as overwhelming now. In some weird way, it felt exactly right.

I placed the cup into the sink and said goodnight to Bodhi before heading for my room.

19

Silas

I shouldn't have left her.

I hadn't even wanted to in the first place, but it wasn't exactly a choice. I had to basically force my feet to move in the opposite direction. My body fighting against each step, reminding me that I belonged with her.

The thought stayed with me the entire drive. For almost an hour, my knuckles stayed tight on the steering wheel, my foot heavier than it needed to be. As each mile passed, I replayed the night and every look on Ember's face. Once I watched the slimy manager touch her, I had decided to fortify my claim on her, rather than hunt him down. But still, I definitely shouldn't have left her. Pulling up the cameras, I checked on her to make sure she was home safe. From the TV in her room, I could see her curled up in bed, reading a book. The sight of her calmed some of my agitation.

As soon as I was done with this, I could go back to her. But for now, Knox was the only one I trusted to make sense of things before I did something reckless. I turned onto his street too fast, braking hard in front of the house with the white picket fence. It looked exactly like it always did—too clean, too normal. Toys

were scattered across the yard with a plastic truck tipped over in the grass. His house was the kind of place that screamed average, when the man who lived there was anything but.

I killed the engine but didn't get out right away. Clients dropping in wasn't exactly something he loved. In fact, he'd made it clear on multiple occasions that it was not allowed if you worked with him, but we're family, so I figured I could bend the rules a little. Grabbing my phone, I called him. He picked up by the third ring.

"Yeah," Knox said quietly.

"I'm outside."

There was a pause before I heard something faint in the background and then the line went dead. Staring at the screen, I hoped he was in a good mood. A couple minutes later, the front door opened and Knox stepped out. One hand dragged through his dark brown hair as he spotted me by the curb. His expression only tightened further as he walked down the path.

"You just show up here? Unannounced?" he asked the second he was close enough.

I didn't bother pretending. "I need help, and you're the only one I can ask."

His jaw ticked as his green eyes narrowed in on me. "You *always* need help."

"I need us to figure out the tracker, Knox." I cut in, my voice low and sharp. "I can't just sit here and pretend that's nothing. Something is going on with her."

That stopped him from glaring at me, but the anger didn't

disappear completely. He leaned into my car door before looking around his neighborhood, clearly weighing his options. After a moment, he motioned toward his house. "Garage. Keep your voice down."

Moving fast, we cut past the toys and around to the detached garage. Unlocking it, he flipped on the light and ushered me inside. The space was exactly what you'd expect from Knox, organized chaos. His workbench was lined with tools, and multiple monitors were mounted against one wall. Different wires and components had been laid out in neat, almost obsessive patterns. He was already moving toward his monitor before I said anything else. Waking up his system, he pulled up several windows.

"I'll give you what I've found so far," he said, as we started going through everything he knew about Ember.

Her routines, her job, anyone who'd gotten too close. There were names and faces associated with her, along with places she frequently visited. Knox had been busy, pulling records and cross-referencing information.

"No one has stuck out," he said after a while, leaning back in his chair. "No recent incidents, no reports, nothing online. Whoever this is isn't making anything obvious."

"I don't like it," I muttered as I shook my head. "People don't just plant trackers."

Knox didn't argue that. Instead, he clicked into another system. "Let me show you something. The feed you set up in her room—I can help you swap it out for something that will pick up audio."

My attention sharpened instantly. "Do it."

Clicking through multiple boxes that popped up in the interface, he navigated to the camera feed. "So, this is—" He stopped mid-sentence.

I felt it before I fully processed it, the way his posture locked. "What?" I demanded, stepping closer.

He didn't answer me, but his arm moved, tilting the screen slightly so I could see what he was looking at. My heart dropped straight into my stomach as my eyes locked on the image.

Someone was in her room. The same room she was just reading her book in.

I knew the camera angle all too well, the one I'd placed. What I didn't recognize was the person standing next to her bed, half hidden in shadow. Their face was hidden, whether it was a hood or maybe just the angle—I couldn't tell. But I could see enough. He stood over her as she slept.

Something inside me snapped as we let the live video play. The figure moved slowly, deliberately taking up the space around her. My chest ignited completely when a hand slowly reached out, pulling part of the blanket. With her legs now exposed, they slid their fingers over her skin, tracing the muscles there.

My vision tunneled. "Who the hell is that?"

Knox started typing, running something in the background. "I'm trying to identify him, just give me a second."

Clearly, it was a *man* touching her—his build and arms were proof of that.

I clenched my teeth together as he leaned closer, pulling the blanket completely off. His fingers continued to trace along her skin, lifting up her clothes as they moved. The act was both possessive and predatory, like whoever this was thought they owned her.

"Knox!" I yelled, unable to contain my frustration at having to watch this. Clenching my fists, I fought the urge to throw punches against the wall. I stepped back, then forward again, deciding whether to break something or run out the door. "I'm going to kill him," I said flatly.

"Silas." Knox's voice was firm, controlled. "I'm doing what I can, just give me a minute."

"A minute!?" I snapped, turning on him. "He could use that minute to—"

"If we don't do this right, we won't ID him, " Knox cut in, sharper now. "You think he doesn't have an exit plan? You think this is his first time?"

That hit harder than I'd expected, and now I imagined this happening to her all the time. A low growl escaped me, and my pent-up anger threatened to spill over as my gaze snapped back to the screen.

The man straightened and then lingered for a second longer. After another moment, he moved toward her vanity and out of frame. Just like that, he was *gone.*

The room was still again, and Ember had yet to stir.

Knox exhaled and immediately started pulling up more

footage. "We need to know how long this has been happening." The screen flickered as he scrubbed through recorded data, and that's when we saw it again. A different night but the same room and same figure. My stomach churned with each clip. Different positions, different times—but always the same pattern and always when she was asleep.

Knox sighed as he turned toward me. "At least a few weeks on random days."

Dragging a hand down my face, I tried not to punch through the monitor. "How did we not know this?!"

"I only gave you access. I didn't scan past footage. There was no reason to. What we're seeing now is raw data I pulled directly."

I paced the length of the garage. With every step tight, I coiled tighter. "We go there, now."

Knox stood, blocking my path before I even reached the door. "And then what, Silas?"

"I get her the fuck out of there."

"And if he's already gone? We have to know who this is to do anything about it." Knox's eyes locked on to mine. "You tip him off, and he will disappear. We can't keep her safe that way."

I hated that he was right.

I looked back at the screen one more time; toward the empty room where she slept, completely unaware.

"She's alone if I don't go," I said, quieter now.

Knox's expression softened just a fraction. "We'll keep the feed up the whole time, if he comes close again, I call the police and you head there. I need your help here, you know more about her than I do."

I felt fractured, and in more ways than one. I knew what he said had truth to it, but everything in me needed to be with her. "We keep the feed on, and you send everything you find to the app on my phone. I want every video, every picture, every detail."

"Deal. I'll dig deeper too. We'll figure out who he is before morning, and we'll have a plan."

I hesitated again because every instinct I had was screaming to leave. I forced myself to think—to see the bigger picture, the way Knox did. I had to trust him in order to keep her safe.

"Fine," I said finally. "But I'm not leaving her again once I get back to her."

"You won't have to," he replied, already turning back to his screens.

Sinking into the chair behind me, my eyes stayed glued to the monitor, watching the empty room like he might come back the second I looked away. He wasn't going to get away with this again because I wasn't going to just *go after him.* When I found out who this was, *I was going to kill him.*

20

EMBER

I woke slowly, realizing how early it was. There was barely any light coming in from my window which meant I still had time to rest. My body felt heavy, but in a good way. I laid there in the quiet for a little while, wrapped deep in my blanket. Not only did my head feel clear, but my chest wasn't tight for once. If I didn't know better, I'd say I actually slept well.

When I finally blinked fully awake, my hand drifted across the nightstand to my phone. The screen lit up as I brought it closer, seeing no new notifications. I didn't know why that made something in my chest dip slightly, but it did. In some small way, I'd hoped he would message me, but maybe this was another test, another way to show he owned me.

I clicked on the last message he had sent me as my thumb hovered over the keyboard. I stared at the screen for a second before frowning and closing out of it. I exhaled quietly, letting my head sink deeper into the pillow.

Why was this so hard? It was just a simple text to the man who'd been stalking me. I pressed my lips together, then typed again as I sat up.

Hey.

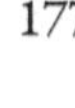

The message was a simple one, with nothing behind it. I clicked send and took a deep breath. As I did so, I registered something across my room. I pushed myself up against my headboard. My gaze drifted, unfocused at first. Then it narrowed in on my vanity, and everything in me stilled.

I moved off the bed and reached for the light switch. As brightness flooded the room, my eyes settled back on the mirror. There, on the glass, written in thick jagged lipstick strokes were the words:

I will never stop.

My body went rigid at the sight, and I knew something was wrong. A small white envelope was next to the mirrored glass.

What the actual fuck.

The paper was bright white, with my name scrawled in black across the top. For a split second, I convinced myself I imagined it. Then, I envisioned just tearing it up. The idea of torching the paper even filtered in, but I *needed* to know what was inside.

Letting courage replace my fear, I grabbed the envelope and opened it slowly. Not knowing what to expect, I braced out of instinct—like whatever was inside might explode. To my surprise, the contents seemed to be quite small and spilled out onto the floor around me. Pictures, each one falling like broken glass.

Dozens of them.

Each one was a different polaroid. Yet, in all of them I was sleeping. I bent to grab them and realized what I was looking at. In some, I had clothes on, but in others, I was completely naked. The room around me swayed as I picked up more, shots where my legs were spread open. Tears fell down my cheeks as I went through each one.

Someone had been in my room, watching me.

Someone had been taking pictures of me, taking advantage of me.

Someone who didn't plan on stopping.

The panic hit fast as I scooped the photos up with trembling hands. Clutching them to my chest, a few more tears fell out of pure, unsolicited anger. When I finally slowed down my thoughts long enough to process them, I forced myself to look at each one again. Moving over to my bed, I spread them across the blanket.

There was only one person who could be responsible for this—one person who I had almost chosen to let in. Inhaling deeply, I walked into my bathroom to find the lighter I kept next to my candles. After grabbing it, I returned to pick up the first photo. Flicking my thumb, I watched it curl and blacken in my hand. One by one, I burned them all, letting the ashes fall across my bed like dark snow. When the last picture was gone, I stared at the crumbles of what was left. "You can fuck all the way off."

A million different emotions filled me, all morphing into a combined weight that settled deep in my chest. Through shaking hands, I shuffled to the mirror and pressed against the words on the glass, rubbing once. As the lipstick smeared, I watched the lines blur into distorted red smudges. This was *my* room, my safe space. *How dare he trespass here, and how dare he take those pictures of me.*

Pulling my hand back to me, I looked down at my palm that was now crimson-stained. This was the same color I'd worn the first night with him—a thought that only enraged me further. Pressing my hand back to the mirror, I laid it flat against the sentence, dragging it down and scraping it sideways. I then moved in circles, breaking every letter into nonsense. I didn't stop until the message he left was an unrecognizable mess. The more I smeared, the better I felt.

Acting on impulse, I grabbed a glass of water from next to my bed and threw it towards the mirror as a final act of defiance. The splash coated everything, causing color-stained water droplets to run down in slow movements. Through the streaks, I caught my reflection. Angry, flushed, scared...*and done.*

I had loved the two nights with him, and every exhilarating feeling he'd given me, but this was all too much. He *was* a monster, and he was after me.

A ping notified me that a text had come through.

Ember, it's not what you think. I'm on my way to your house.

I immediately threw my phone. *I think the fuck not.*

My phone buzzed on the floor, an insistent vibration that meant someone was now calling. I didn't reach for it, but I watched the screen and the way the word **blocked** kept coming up over and over again. He wouldn't stop, just like the note had said. I stared for a while, at the way it lit up repeatedly, but then it hit me—he could see me.

I looked around my room and guessed at what gave him that kind of power. He had even told me last night that he had that kind of access, which meant he could see everything. He knew where I was, and he had just watched me open that envelope.

I grabbed my phone and ordered a car. I needed to leave. *Now.* The phone vibrated again in my hand as I set it on my bed. Flipping it over, I pressed it face-down against the comforter.

I could almost hear Silas in my head, *Answer me, Ember.*

No, I was done listening. Most of all, I was done with him.

The phone buzzed again, and something in me snapped. I grabbed it, not to answer—but to end it.

Holding down the power button, I smiled as the screen went dark. Now, there was no presence of him. I moved fast, grabbing nothing but my shoes. I knew he could be tracing anything, so I didn't overthink it. If I stopped, if I hesitated, I'd start to feel him again—like a hand on the back of my neck, guiding me back into place. I couldn't let that happen.

By the time I walked outside, the fresh air was a welcomed friend. I needed it to help me breathe, to function. Inhaling deeply, I thought about my next step. I didn't know where I was going to go, but I knew I couldn't be here when he showed up.

21

Silas

The phone rang again and again. Each unanswered call pushed deeper under my skin. "Come on, Ember!" My voice was tight, like holding something volatile between my teeth. "Pick up."

The calls continued to go straight to voicemail.

I didn't even wait for the tone before hanging up and calling again, my thumb slamming against the screen harder than necessary. My other hand gripped the steering wheel so tight, my knuckles turned white. This whole thing was a fucking mess. Knox had been unable to find a goddamn thing last night, and then this morning, I watched her walk up to that mirror and open those pictures. The engine growled as I moved faster, matching the restless thing beating in my chest.

I had left as soon I realized what was happening, but I was still over forty-five minutes away. I knew that was too long, especially now with her phone off. The moment she had jumped into a cab, I was screwed.

I didn't know where the hell she was.

The thought was like a knife to my chest. I needed to protect her, and I couldn't do that if I didn't fucking know where she was. Suddenly, I felt everything I was trying to stop. I slammed the car into park without thinking, the sudden jolt not helpful to the adrenaline that coursed through me. My breathing stuttered, like I was unable to pull in enough air. I tried to focus, but all I could focus on was the invisible weight that pressed down on my chest.

"No." The word came out strained, uneven. "Not now." But my mind didn't care as my vision narrowed, and something sharp and suffocating grew in my lungs. I knew this feeling well, and that made everything worse. Because the last day I had experienced this was the day I stood beside a casket. The day everything inside me hollowed out and collapsed in on itself as I attended my mother's funeral.

The memory hit like a blow to the chest, and suddenly, I was there again—black clothes that were too tight and the sound of people talking in hushed voices like it meant anything, like it *changed* anything. My hands curled into fists in my lap.

I squeezed my eyes shut, dragging in a shaky breath. I needed something real, something tangible to ground myself back to reality. Instantly, her brown eyes filled my vision. The warmth in them was everything I needed. The fire that lay behind them, that unyielding spark that refused to dim. I latched on to it, to *her*.

My chest loosened, but just slightly. Breathing in and out, the pressure eased just enough for me to think. Soon after, the panic loosened its grip. I opened my eyes to a world that was still a little unsteady but no longer collapsing. Reaching for my phone again, I searched for the one specific number I needed.

I scrolled past Kyrin's contact. He was useful for many things, but his heart was soft. Ember was going to fight being found. I needed someone who could handle that, someone who enjoyed the darker side of things.

Greyson answered on the first ring.

"What do you need?" he asked.

I chuckled softly, swallowing the fight I just had with myself. "Nothing. Yet."

There was a pause before his voice laced with amusement, "What do you want, Silas?"

I smiled, realizing the chaos I was about to start. "Want to play a game?"

There was a low, delighted laugh. "You're serious?"

He sounded interested, and that was all I needed to find her. "Dead."

"I'm in," he said immediately.

I started my car back up, facing all the air vents toward me. "A woman named Ember is hiding. She belongs to me, and we need to find her."

"So, she's running?" he asked, his curiosity clearly piqued.

"*Hiding*," I corrected. "She knows better than to run from me."

He hummed as if in thought. "What's the prize?"

I minimized the call, letting my eyes drift over the feeds in my phone, searching for her.

"If *you* find her first," I said calmly, "you get to run the club for the week and offer those special nights you wanted."

"Hmm," Greyson responded, before inhaling slowly. "And you're just going to let that happen?"

"If you win, yes."

A small laugh cracked through the phone. "Do we have rules?"

I appreciate the fact that he even asked. Greyson without rules could be...*inconvenient.*

"There's only three," I said, confirming she was still nowhere I could reach her.

"Go on."

"One. No one can see you. If someone spots you, you forfeit."

He scoffed in my ear. "You act like I'm sloppy."

"Two," I continued, ignoring him. "You can't hurt her."

"I wouldn't do that," he replied, as if offended.

"You would, which is why it needs to be said."

Another quiet chuckle, but he didn't deny it. "And I mean it, not even anything remotely close, or the deal is off."

Another pause, this one edged with something darker. "And three?"

"If we run into her roommates, we avoid them at all costs."

Greyson outright laughed this time. "You want to find her bad, huh?"

It's not a want, brother, it's a need.

He exhaled slowly, as if in preparation. "When do we start?"

"Now. You have a ten-second head start," I said lazily before lowering my voice. "Go."

He hung up without another word as I sat there for a moment with my phone still in my hand.

Either way, she loses.

If I found her, she'd learn hiding from me was pointless.

If Greyson got to her first, she'd learn that I was always the safer option.

I decided to head to the club first. When I did find her, I would need supplies, and I could get everything from there. Making a mental list, I thought of everything I would potentially need, including a few different masks.

Ultimately, I understood why she would do this. I wasn't angry with her for choosing this road. I actually felt the opposite. *This* was the exact thing about her that made me feel alive, that gave me the rush I craved. I looked out the car window as I pulled back onto the street. "Hide all you want, Ember," I murmured under my breath. "You're still mine."

I kept that same mentality as I ran into the club, packed a bag, and then jumped back on the road. For the next thirty minutes, I repeated that same thing in my head, over and over. Then for the next hour, I said it louder as I searched every park, coffee shop, and bookstore. Anywhere she might go, any place she might stop.

At the two-hour mark, Greyson hadn't had any luck either. We decided to join forces and follow behind each other, taking turns securing the perimeter of different blocks. The three-hour mark passed, and I finally got a ping on my phone to her location. The alert was from Ember's front security camera at her house, and the footage showed her sneaking back in. From the video, it was clear she was spooked and uncomfortable.

I turned the wheel, peeling down a side street. I smiled at the rearview mirror when Greyson followed, apparently aware that I had a lead.

22

Ember

My knee wouldn't stop bouncing now that I was back at home. Three hours was all it took me to decide that I'd rather be home with the others than freak out by myself. I'd wandered around for a while, thinking I was hearing things, thinking he would show up around any corner—I just couldn't function like that.

Being here didn't take the fear away completely, especially because I knew he could see me, but at least it was a little bit better. My plan was to stay away from my room, and my phone, which meant right now, I was sitting at my kitchen counter staring at nothing. The silence was uncomfortable, but I knew it would take one simple thing for him to find me. The only thing stopping me from freaking out completely was knowing that right now, Kinsley and Bodhi were here with me. When I came back, I found them secluded in their bedroom, where they were watching a movie with the volume maxed out like their own personal movie theatre. It was a typical occurrence, a method I assumed was used to cover up *other* sounds they were making.

I'd decided to soothe myself by pulling out some ice cream from the freezer, when the movie paused and their door opened from down the hall. I set the tub of cookies and cream on the counter and shuffled across the kitchen, making as much noise as I could to alert them that they were not alone. *The last thing I needed right now was to see either of them naked.* The sound of footsteps continued, and then someone entered the kitchen. Peering around the door, I smiled at the sight of Bodhi, who was holding up his hand to block the light.

"Em?" he asked, his hair going in every direction. "You good?"

"Yup," I replied, closing the door with a spoon already in my mouth. "Just couldn't sleep." Turning my body, I pulled a small bowl down from the cupboard.

Yawning, he scratched his head and stretched out his back. When his shoulders settled, he let out a short sigh. "Yeah, okay. Want some chai to help?"

I smiled at him with a mouthful of ice cream as Kinsley stepped in, a light blanket the only thing wrapped around her body. "Hey Bo—" She laughed when she saw me, tightening the sheet. "Sorry girl, I just needed some water."

I waved the spoon at her and took another bite. "S'all good," I managed to get out with a mouthful of ice cream.

She moved next to me and wrapped one arm around me, giving me a side hug. "Love you, Em." Then she walked over to Bodhi who was standing at the fridge and kissed his bicep before smacking his butt. "You have five minutes to recharge." Bodhi laughed as he glanced down, watching her as she stocked her arms with water bottles. After another moment, he shook his head and pulled the jug from a shelf.

Once Kinsley was back in the room, there was no more talking. There was only the sound of shuffled feet, and then liquid being poured. The cabinet doors opened as he grabbed some extra ingredients and pretty soon the smell surrounded us.

Within minutes, he set the mug near my hands and gave a small nudge to my shoulder. "You know," he said, leaning back against the counter, "you've got all of us. Always."

I finished my last bite of the frozen treat and looked at him. "I know," I said quietly.

He tapped my back in comfort and turned toward his bedroom. "If you need us, we'll be here." After a slight pause he added, "But I would highly suggest knocking first."

My fingers curled around the mug, and a smile tugged at my lips as the heat seeped into my skin. "Got it. Thank you."

I wasn't one to ask for help but *I did know* they were here for me. During my walk, I had already decided I was going to handle this on my own. I didn't need them to step in, I didn't even think I needed to call the police at this point.

Knowing I no longer had the ability to sleep in my own bed, I took my chai to the living room and dropped down on the couch. Turning the TV on for noise more than anything, I found some late-night rerun I didn't even register. The light flickered across the walls behind me in soft colors as I pulled a blanket over myself sipping slowly.

The drink's warmth settled me and my knee finally stopped

bouncing. I felt the shift as my body sank fully into the cushions and my eyes grew heavy. Pretty soon after that, I fell asleep to the sound of laughter and end credits.

It wasn't long before I was woken up by a strange feeling. Blinking into the darkness, it took a second to remember exactly where I was. A metal rod underneath me confirmed that I was still on the living room couch, and I turned to reposition myself. Out of the corner of my eye, I saw the TV was still on, but now it was some jewelry auction with low music in the background. The screen flickered once as a commercial came on, casting a pale glow around me. In the light, I noticed the front door was open.

Wide open.

My stomach dropped so fast I thought I was hallucinating. I knew I'd locked both doors, but even the screen door was swung open.

I sat up, suddenly very awake. As I focused in, I realized a figure was standing just past the porch. A slight movement in the yard activated the motion sensor, and I was hit with a sudden burst of light. When it disappeared, no one was standing there. My body locked instantly, and I couldn't move. I couldn't speak. My limbs felt like they'd been poured full of concrete.

Call the police, I screamed at myself before realizing I didn't even have my phone. I looked around to find something, *anything,* but there was nothing to throw besides my blanket and an empty cup. When I glanced back up, the figure was now on my doorstep in a Watchers mask.

Oh my god, it's him.

I tried to scream, to force him to leave, but no sound came from my throat. The figure didn't seem bothered by how upset I was, especially as they took a step toward me. Watching their feet inch closer, my heart slammed against my ribs so hard it hurt. I stood to run, but just as they approached the doorframe, they stopped. Waiting there for a few seconds, they pulled back, retreating out of view.

I didn't breathe. I didn't blink. I just sat and scanned the now empty space in front of my door, just waiting for them to reappear. Seconds stretched as the TV continued playing, until the self-timer shut it off completely, the screen going black.

This time, my voice didn't fail me and a blood-curdling scream escaped when I saw my reflection on the television. There, standing behind me, was someone else in a mask and not just *any* mask. A hand suddenly covered my mouth, and my plea was cut short as a deep voice whispered in my ear, "Found you."

Whoever that was before, wasn't Silas.

Because *this* was—the man that was now standing behind me.

I tried to fight, to push him away, but the other masked intruder appeared again. They worked together to force my body off the couch and carried me outside. Every sound I made was muffled by the large hand still covering my mouth, but I continued to fight with every ounce of strength I had.

I managed to land a solid kick to Silas. Just as he pulled away from the impact, the other captor grabbed me by my hair and twisted his wrist, yanking my head back. I cried out, and as the sound hit the air, Silas knocked him to the ground. Kicking him once to the side, he yelled down at him. "You're done. Go home."

With no one holding me, I paid no mind to what was happening and turned to run away. Just like before, Silas was quicker. In one second flat, his arms were wrapped tightly around me as he lifted me off the ground. I did what I could to make it difficult for him, but I couldn't stop him as I was tossed into his car. Within seconds, my arms were scooped up as he secured them with zip ties to the handle above the car door. Completely ignoring whoever he left on the ground, he dropped into the driver's seat and started the engine.

I was physically shaking with anger. "What the actual fuck, Silas?!"

He didn't answer me, he just turned the heat up, testing the temperature with his hand before turning the vents toward me. I thrashed around in response to his silence, trying to land another kick on him or at least put some nice dents in the leather of his car. He slammed his hand down on my thighs, halting my attempts.

I was so pissed at him that I turned and spit. As soon as he felt it hit his mask, he threw the car into park. "You already know that I love this side of you. Acting like this isn't *helping* your situation. In fact, it's making it worse." A small vein bulged out of his temple. "Do you not remember what happened when you told me you hated me?" With that question, he leaned back enough so I could see the hardened evidence between his legs. "If you continue with this tantrum, I won't stop myself from fucking you in this car."

My mouth instantly formed into a tight line. Silas was many things, but a liar wasn't one of them. Looking up at him, I envisioned breaking the plastic binding on my wrists and stabbing him in the neck. "What makes you think you can do this?!" I pulled at the zip ties as hard as I could, feeling them cut into my skin. "You're sick. You need help."

He chuckled as he shifted the car back into drive, the sound making me want to scream.

God, I really did want to kill him.

The thought enraged me, and I screamed. Trying to rip out of the zip ties, I caused the skin on my wrists to break open and bleed. My burst of anger turned into an open invitation for him, and I felt us turn off the road. As he opened his door to come around, I resituated my legs to try and put as much force as I could behind my kicks. Unfortunately, he planned for this and grabbed them as soon as my car door opened. I lost all leverage as he pulled me to the side and pushed my thighs apart.

"If you keep fighting me, you know what you're asking for." His hands gripped my bottoms in warning. "This is your one chance. Stop moving, and I'll go back to driving."

Fuck you, Silas Solstice.

I paused for a mere moment and made him believe I was

submitting, but as soon his hands left me, I pulled my knees back and kicked him square in the chest. Falling to the ground, he fought to breathe for a second before he stood back up, hovering over me.

I felt like I was foaming at the mouth now. I wasn't just infuriated with his choices. I was disgusted by his behavior. Only a complete lunatic would think I was just going to sit still and be his calm little victim.

A dark chuckle started in his chest and then got louder as he ripped my bottoms off and pulled my hips to him. "God, I think I love you."

I spit at him again which only increased the force behind his first thrust inside me. I screamed out, and he matched it with a loud groan before tilting my body up. I tried to push away, but I couldn't. With my hands bound, I had no room to move. I decided to be the furthest thing he wanted and went quiet as he pushed into me over and over again. After a minute, he caught on to what I was doing and lifted my ass up, hitting a spot inside of me that I'd never experienced before.

"Oh no, you don't get to act like you don't like this. There is no pretending with me. I know you."

Before long, I was fighting against the building pressure, and he knew that too, because he began rubbing me in small circles. The stimulation only added to the intensity, and I fought as long as I could before screaming out.

He made my body break two more times, and I couldn't help but moan with each of his movements. My body, heart, and soul were betraying me by choosing him, and I could do nothing to stop it, even now as I was being held hostage. Blood leaked down my arms, but it only added to what he was doing to me. "Stop being so damn difficult."

After my third orgasm, he finally let go and filled me before pulling out and staring at the mess he'd created. Zipping his pants, he moved to the trunk and grabbed a small towel to wipe me down, along with a pair of sweatpants he pulled up my legs. Then, he repositioned me back into my seat before returning to his.

For twenty minutes, we drove in silence as I battled the trance he had put me in. Somehow, he had won, and now I was quiet and docile. It was at that point that all my anger turned into another emotion, and my eyes filled with tears. Choking back the shame for not calling the police when I had the chance, I gave in to what was happening. "Are you going to hurt me?"

He remained silent as we pulled onto a small street. I recognized the dark bricks on the wall as the ones that surrounded his club. Unbuckling his seatbelt, he turned his body toward me and raised his hand to wipe my tear-stricken face. "Never," Silas murmured, attempting to make his voice soft. "Whether you believe me or not, I just want you safe and protected."

His words triggered more tears, and suddenly I felt trapped in a nightmare. "Is that why you wrote that message on my mirror? Why you took those naked pictures of me?"

23

Silas

"What?"

The word came out sharper than I'd meant it to, and I was suddenly glad she couldn't see the expression on my face. *She thinks I'm the one responsible for that!?*

I had no idea some of those things had even happened.

I replayed the memory of her on her bed with a lighter in her hand. Then, my memory shifted to the video of her sleeping in her room while a stranger stood above her. Lastly, I thought about her whole file that was now stored on my phone.

I looked over to find her staring at me like she was waiting for some type of confession. Her face was swollen from the tears that were still falling, and her chest was rising too fast. I would bet money she was close to having a panic attack, especially with her wrists bound in the zip ties that *I* put there. *Fuck.* I hadn't even noticed the amount of blood that was along her arms.

She must be terrified.

I opened my mouth to respond, to tell her I was innocent, and that I hadn't done any of those things. But I realized that without proof or any type of answers, it would just be empty words coming from the man who dragged her out of her home.

I needed more time, Knox was so close to figuring this all out.

The way she looked at me, I knew that I had to give her something, or I'd risk losing her forever. If I told her the truth right now, I'd only make things worse. I needed to be able to offer her something. I thought back to our last conversation, and the answer became crystal clear in my mind.

Control.

Trailing my gaze along the blood that streaked her arms, I noticed that she was visibly shaking. I could see she was trying to hide it, but it was clear that the adrenaline in her body had completely taken over. With a defeated sigh, she turned away from me in resignation. I watched as more silent tears fell down her face.

She really thinks I'm going to hurt her.

The realization settled heavy in my chest, and I was ready to do whatever I could to salvage her trust. Instead of answering her questions and creating more problems, I reached into my pocket and pulled out my knife. The movement caught her attention, and her shoulders went rigid as she sobbed again but louder—a sound I immediately hated.

I lifted my arm, and she squeezed her eyes shut and braced. Trying to avoid touching any exposed parts of her skin, I sliced through the zip ties that bound her wrists together. The plastic snapped, and her hands jerked apart. She looked up at them and then at me, like she didn't quite believe she was free.

"I'd like you to stay with me, to trust me when I say I'm trying to keep you safe," I said evenly.

She let out a hollow laugh and turned toward the door. Her hand instantly reached for the handle as her fingers wrapped around it, but just as she went to push it open, she paused. A small sound left her mouth as she turned back to me, eyes glassy. "Smart move, Silas. You almost got me—*acting* like I have a choice when I really don't." Her voice cracked. "I have no car and no phone. What am I supposed to do? *Walk back*?"

I smiled under the mask, though she couldn't see it. The tone in her voice meant she still had fire, she was still here with me. *No, baby, I'm not acting. You have full control right now.*

To show exactly how wrong she was, I lifted my hip and took out my phone. Disabling the lock screen completely, I opened the keypad and held it out to her. "Use this however you'd like."

Her eyes narrowed in suspicion, and I watched as a million different thoughts swirled in her head. I could see each one as it passed—suspicion, curiosity, apprehension. Eventually, she moved her hand forward and snatched the phone from me. I mentally kicked myself as she typed in three specific numbers. As I imagined her pressing the call button, I started naming the felonies they were going to take me down for. *Home invasion. Assault—*

But then she pulled her finger away, deleting those numbers before entering new ones. As it started to ring, she turned on the speaker.

Well, at least it wasn't the cops... yet.

A small click ended the ringing, and a voice spilled into the space between us, a voice I never expected her to willingly choose—my *brother.*

"What's up, dickhead?" I rolled my eyes at his greeting, expecting nothing less from Kyrin.

She, however, did not find his personality funny in this moment. "It's Ember. I need to ask you a question." Her voice was solid, there was no hint of emotion. I found that interesting, considering tears were still fresh on her face.

Kyrin's reply was short, like it should be with that type of question. "How do you have Silas's phone?"

In an effort to help the situation and make things go smoother for her, I stepped in. "Just answer whatever questions she has for you. Everything is fine."

He must've had some sort of guess at what was going on because his response came with light laughter. "Okay, fine. Shoot."

Ember was looking straight at me, like she could see me through the mask. "Do I need to worry about your brother hurting me?"

Kyrin's laughter was stronger this time, like he *definitely* knew what was going on. "Ember, over the last few days, I have watched that man spiral. Not only have you completely overtaken his mind, but he also threatened to kill *a lot* of people if you didn't stay safe in my bar. You have become his whole world in a very short period of time. I think I should actually be worried about *you* hurting *him*."

She didn't say anything else to him, just accepted the answer and dismissed the call. Next, she opened my messages and sent two separate ones before handing it back to me. Her body relaxed slightly as she folded her arms and looked out the window, the motion smearing blood all over the front of her shirt.

"If you *do* end up killing me, just know they were notified of where to find the body."

They. I assumed that meant she sent texts to her roommates.

I nodded once in understanding before getting out and moving around the car to her side. She watched me carefully, as if still expecting me to attack her. Instead, I pulled the door open and offered her my hand.

She stepped out and ignored it, glaring at me from the side of her eye. I should have realized that every moment I'd been with her, I'd basically been fueling that fire. I couldn't help the way my dick twitched in excitement as I motioned for her to lead the way inside. As she passed me, her shoulder deliberately hit mine, and another smile grew on my face.

That's my girl.

We entered through the back door where I grabbed a clean white mask from the extra stock and held it out. "Put this on."

She snatched it from my hand but obeyed, we pushed through the crowds and went straight to my office. Once inside, I pulled out the first-aid kit and stepped toward her. "Let me see your wrists."

She didn't move. Instead, she walked past me, ripping the kit from my hands and sat down in my chair. "I can do it myself," she said flatly.

I watched without protest as she unwrapped the gauze,

cleaned the cuts, and placed the bandages down. For now, I needed to be okay with the fact she didn't want me to help. In order to heal this wound between us, I needed to just exist near her for a little while. I leaned against my desk instead, watching her. Slowly, a reminder of everything I knew clawed at my insides.

Someone else was in her room.

Someone else had touched her.

And now I knew for a fact, I wasn't the only monster hidden in the dark.

"I'm gonna send a text, but if you need my phone again, I'll keep it open for you."

Ember waved her hand at me like she really couldn't care less. "At this point, I've already accepted that you could call for backup at any time. Just don't let it be the same guy as before—he didn't exactly play fair."

Yeah, Greyson didn't do fair. As an act of good faith, I decided to feed into the conversation by offering her a small piece of me. "That was my brother, and I'm *very* aware of his tactics."

Slowly, her head raised, and she looked over at me. "There's three Sons of Solstice?"

Bait taken, which means there's still a small part of her that cares.

I nodded as I pulled my phone out. "His name is Greyson, and he went through some rough things as a kid. Let's just say it altered his brain a little bit. Sorry about that. He promised to behave, and I chose to give him the benefit of the doubt."

Tilting her head to the side, she made a sound that was almost half of a scoff. "*Sorry*?! That's it? I don't think one apology makes up for everything you've done."

I bit my tongue as I looked down.

Everything I've done? No, everything *he's* done.

I typed a message to Knox that was straight to the point. I needed him to understand how dire this was, and I needed a timeline. I couldn't keep her here very long, but I'd be damned if she left alone.

Once the message sent, I gave my full attention back to Ember. When I looked up from my phone, she was done tending to her wounds and was waiting for my reply. She wasn't only leading this conversation, but she was actually talking to me—something I would be taking full advantage of.

24

EMBER

The gauze was too tight but I liked it. Every pulse of pain I felt reminded me that this was all very *real*, and very much happening to me. In the last hour, that's all I had focused on—what was unfolding right in front of me. Each moment felt like a new form of chaos, and it was like I couldn't keep up with everything I felt. At first it was anger, then fear. When Silas fucked me in the car, it was pure desire.

That was why I had listened to him, and stayed.

Hell, maybe I was the delusional one.

If one thing was for sure, it was that I hadn't made my mind up on Silas yet. Every time I thought that I had enough to walk away from him, I couldn't. Something made me stay, and now, he had opened up to me.

My palms itched from all the contradictions forming in my head. I decided to calm the sensation by slamming them against the desk behind me. I swore I saw him flinch from the impact as the sound echoed through his office. My words were raw as I continued, "Just tell me what you want from me."

For a second, he didn't move. Then he lifted his hand and I expected some form of punishment or retaliation for my

outburst. Flinching, I brought my hands up to my face as my shoulders hunched. I ready myself for the pain, for the proof that I was right about him all along. Just as I thought it was coming, he didn't strike me—his hand only moved up and to his head. Slowly, his fingers pulled at the buckle that kept the mask he wore secured to his face. As he pulled on one side, the plastic slid off and hit the floor between us.

He'd just broken his very first rule, for *me.*

I stared into the icy blue eyes that met mine. They weren't empty or cruel, like I had imagined. If anything, there was a quiet sadness in them that pulled me in—an emptiness I couldn't explain. Like his eyes, all of Silas's features were strong. I stopped myself from reaching out, from trailing his jawline. It was almost like he registered this, as his face slightly softened.

I had never thought about the way he might look at me, but it was magnetic. His stare was so intense, like he saw through me, *all* of me. My eyes wandered over his slightly tanned skin before moving to his dark hair. Slightly longer than what I had pictured, the strands fell forward in a slightly messy way. None of it was styled, more chaotic and unruly. Stepping closer to him, I realized that I've never truly tried to picture him. *I'd only ever thought of his mask.*

I had to look away, to remind myself that the man in front of me was not what he seemed. But as soon as I broke eye contact, it was like he was in my head again.

"Ember."

My name on his lips was soft, almost gentle. As I dragged my eyes back up to his, it was like my mind ruptured and everything bubbled to the surface. I had no idea what to do, or how to feel but I couldn't look at him anymore, I just *couldn't.*

A fresh wave of rage exploded through me, almost like a default setting within my body. Before I knew it, I was moving. My hands shoved into his chest, *hard.* "You can't just do this!" I pushed him again, harder this time. "I get to make the choices." He rocked back half a step but didn't raise his hands, which only made me angrier. When I spoke again, I was screaming. "I want *out* of whatever the hell this is."

There was no reaction from him whatsoever. He didn't block me. He didn't even speak. He just watched me as a look of understanding filled his eyes. That sympathetic expression shattered what was left inside of me.

I hit harder, balling my fists and putting my full strength into the swings. When that earned no reaction, I tore his shirt down the middle and slapped my palms against his bare chest before scratching down the exposed skin. I didn't hold anything back. I wanted him to react to this. I *needed* him to grab me, to push me—anything to prove to myself that I was right about him, that I couldn't trust him.

And yet his arms just hung there, right at his sides—which only made me more frantic. I shifted my stance and my foot caught on an extension cord coiled beside his desk. As a last ditch resort, I picked it up before he could stop me. Moving without thinking, I wrapped it around his neck and pulled with everything I had.

I could see an immediate change in his face as the cord dug into his skin. I twisted and squeezed, refusing to stop until he showed his true self. Veins bulged in his eyes and neck as his body reacted, but even then, he didn't fight back.

Silas refused to push me away, even as his face drained of color.

"Do something!" I screamed at him. "Fight back! Hurt me!"

The blue color within his eyes started to stand out against the bloodshot white around them. "N-no."

My grip on him weakened as the cord slipped through my fingers. I let go and the tool thudded against the ground as it fell between us. Silas sucked in a sharp breath, his chest expanding hard as air rushed back into his lungs. Tears flooded my vision again as I looked up at his chest. Thin rivulets of blood now trailed down his skin from the scratches I had left, weaving over the tattoo I hadn't even noticed. An intricate design, similiar to dark lace covered half his chest and both of his arms. The art was simple, but stunning, and now it was ruined, by me.

I wasn't any better than him and I didn't understand him at all.

I felt the exact moment my knees gave out and I dropped to the floor in front of him. I pressed my palms to my head like I could hold the pieces of my mind together. Not even that worked, and I was left in a broken pile of myself.

After a moment, I heard him move and realized he was lowering himself down next to me.

We sat like that for a few minutes, but my breathing kept

escalating.

Silas lifted his hand but then stopped. “Can I touch you?” His voice is rough, almost strained.

I didn’t say yes, but I didn't deny him the opportunity either. Soon, I felt his fingers graze the back of my arm. The pressure was light, but I knew he was testing me. When I didn’t immediately jerk away, he shifted closer and pulled me into his lap.

One second I was on the floor. The next, I was in his arms and against his warm chest. My body relaxed enough for me to breathe deeply, and I inhaled his cologne, the same scent that clung to the jacket that I found in my room. I closed my eyes and mimicked his breathing as he held me. His grip on me eventually loosened, as if he knew I would hate being caged in. The feeling provided just enough stability for my pieces to come back together.

When I opened my eyes, I traced my fingers against the tattooed lace of his chest. I didn't expect any reaction, but his body answered to my touch and goosebumps broke out across his skin as he shivered. I watched them move as my eyes became heavy. The last thing I felt before sleep claimed me, was the steady rise and fall of his chest beneath my cheek, and the unsettling realization that I might be in love with him.

25

Silas

Ember's breathing eventually evened out, and I could tell that she'd calmed down. After a few minutes, her shaky inhales tapered off and then disappeared altogether. With each second that passed, her breathing against my collarbone became slower and steadier.

Having her in my arms like this was an entirely different experience than the one I'd found myself in ten minutes ago. I'd take every beating she gave me, every foul word and gesture—because *that's* what she needed. From now on, I would be that, no matter what it took. Even now, I sat as still as I could. My leg was asleep, and I couldn't feel my arm, but there was no way I planned on moving away from her. I would remain her pillow as long as she was asleep, because her walls were now completely down. She had voluntarily shown me the fire within her, and I'd shown *her* that it couldn't burn me—that I wasn't scared of it.

I hoped with everything in me that she'd seen that.

The warmth of her body stung the scratches on my chest, the skin there still raw. In her rage, she'd torn several areas open, but I couldn't blame her. None of that mattered anyway, I would've

let her inflict far worse to be able to have this moment with her. The pain had been worth it because she trusted me. I could see it even now, while she slept in my arms. Her fingers had slowly uncurled from their forced grip, and her forehead smoothed over in a blank expression. Even her jaw had softened, allowing her lips to part just slightly with each breath.

This had been the goal, the entire reason I'd taken off my mask in the first place. I knew for us to make headway, I had to offer her a fragile piece of me first. In hindsight, it was the least I could do for her. There were a dozen reasons she had spiraled tonight, and most of them had something to do with me. Forcing myself to accept some of the responsibility for her, I tilted my head back and leaned against the wall behind me, careful not to jostle her. The beat from below vibrated us gently, but for the most part, the sound was hidden like always. Like us.

After warning everyone I'd be stepping away, I knew no one would come looking for me here, which meant we'd have this space for as long as we needed it. The best part was the fact she was already comfortable here. For now, everything was handled—except Knox, who was taking far too long.

Although it seemed like such a small thing, I knew the steps involved. I also knew he was taking this seriously because when I left, he promised me he would find answers. I was now waiting on that to crack this mystery wide open.

I lifted my hand and traced the curve of her cheek. Her body twitched in response to my touch, as if she still guarded in some way. Each of the layers that I planned to rip away were mine to keep safe now. I wanted to know everything. I wanted to hear her thoughts, her fears, and I wanted to take them all away.

Here in my office, nothing was going to touch us anyway. *I could bet my life on it.*

Settling into her with that thought, I closed my eyes. Would it be smart to rest now, with her in my arms? Just for a few minutes? If I didn't sleep while she did, I would have to create time for rest later—that was a luxury I didn't exactly have at the moment. Figuring it was for the best, I shifted her higher on my chest and let her weight settle against me. I had just closed my eyes when vibrations erupted in my pocket.

I sucked in a sharp breath, tightening my hold on her. Looking down, I noticed Ember stir from the sound, but thankfully, she didn't wake.

Groaning as quietly as I could, I slid a hand down the back of my jeans, fishing the phone free without moving her. The screen's immediate glow lit the dim room around us in a pale blue.

Message from Knox

I clicked as soon as I saw it, trying to control my anxiety.

All three phones of the roommates have been cleared. There's no sign it's any of them. I'm running through the others who have been at her house recently. Apparently, teammates are in and out a lot. I'm handling things as fast as I can. Just keep her there with you and don't let her out of your sight.

I read the message over and over, especially the last sentence.

That was the plan, for however long she would let me.

The text came with a rush of disappointment. He hadn't found much to go off of, but at least it wasn't *nothing.* If it wasn't her roommates, that could help us narrow the potential list of people down by quite a bit. The fact it could be any potential number of teammates made it harder. If they were in and out, that meant a lot of access and even more opportunities for them to be in her room. My jaw flexed as I realized way too many people had access to her.

I slid the phone onto the floor beside me instead of putting it back in my pocket. One less interruption was one less risk of waking her. She shifted slightly as I did so, her nose brushing against my collarbone. A quiet, unconscious hum left her, and the sound vibrated straight into my chest. The quick jolt I felt as a result had nothing to do with the wounds on my chest and everything to do with her. Gently locking my arms around her, I cradled her head beneath my chin and tilted us up against the wall behind me.

The thought of letting myself rest pulled at the edge of my vision. The door was locked, and no one could come inside. Knox was busy, figuring out all the things I couldn't do. In every way I thought about it, taking this time to close my eyes would only benefit me in the end.

I let myself drift, just slightly, keeping my arms firm around her as sleep edged closer.

26

Ember

I woke feeling the farthest thing from panic. My eyes weren't even open yet, and I was already calm from being wrapped in the smell of him. For a moment, I stayed still, listening to the beat of his heart. Both of his arms were looped around me, like he'd fallen asleep making sure I was comfortable and that I wouldn't disappear. His head was tipped back slightly, his dark hair pushed to one side. With the black mess falling into his eyes, he looked almost childish. Next to me, at this moment, he didn't look like the dangerous man I'd made him out to be. *He just looked exhausted.*

Lifting my neck slightly to look up at him, I let my gaze drift across his skin. The tattoos that covered him in different places were truly beautiful. The inked lace curled in the same directions as his muscles. I hadn't noticed exactly how much ink there had been before, but then again, I hadn't exactly *let* myself look either.

As carefully as I could, I moved my hand from his chest, down to his arm. My fingers grazed over the skin just below his wrist, and I traced one of the veins that ran up his arm. I moved slowly, following the path up his forearm, and the faint pulse proved he was actually real. His arm twitched the higher I went, and the sudden movement reminded me of my own bandaged wrists and how I'd felt toward him in the car ride over here.

Was this the same man?

I swallowed and gently lifted his arm from around me. Shifting my weight, I crawled out of his lap like I was extracting myself from something fragile. The air instantly felt colder without him, and I wasn't sure how I felt about that.

I crossed the room to the first aid kit, looking down at my bandages. I could see I'd already bled through one of the gauze pads, and the other seemed to be ripped open, *probably from me attacking him earlier.* Although I could potentially wait to change it, I do it anyway. I decided to let the task distract me from the confusion in my head. Kneeling over his desk, I had just popped open the case, when Silas suddenly shot upright. The sound making me jolt and causing me to drop the supplies. The plastic edges snapped loudly as they hit the ground, but that wasn't what startled me—it was *him.*

His breath came out hard as he pulled himself away from the wall. Both eyes wide, scanning the room like he was searching for something. His fear was immediately palpable *and genuine.* I couldn't help the way my eyes widened from his reaction. If I was really someone he was going to hurt, he wouldn't wake up *like that* looking for me.

His gaze found me across the room, and everything within him changed. His shoulders instantly dropped as the panic drained from his face. Dragging a hand through his hair, he exhaled slowly, looking down at the items I had dropped. "Sorry," he muttered toward me, voice rough with sleep.

I responded simply by shrugging my shoulders at him. Then, I bent down to pick everything up and set it back into the container before peeling off the dirty gauze that was attached to me. He watched me intently the whole time, like he didn't want to let me out of his sight. It was only when I'd finished and closed the kit that he looked away.

I walked back over and stopped in front of him, waiting for his blue eyes to come back to me. For a second, we sat in silence as his gaze settled on me, neither of us knowing what should come next. I hesitated before speaking, debating on how I wanted this to go. To my surprise, he knew my thoughts before I did.

Without me saying anything, he shifted his back up against the wall again, lifting his arm slightly as a silent invitation to sit in his lap. There were no words spoken between us, but it was clear he wanted me to go back to where I was while we slept. *He wanted me back where I belonged.*

I decided to take a chance, because honestly, I wanted that too. When I settled, I realized this time felt different—it was *intentional.* He silently confirmed my thoughts as his arm settled around me again, but slower now, like he was making sure I was comfortable. I let out a small sigh as I felt his fingers slide into my hair, brushing through it gently and massaging my scalp. The motion almost absentminded for him and calming for me.

This was a part of him I never thought existed, a soft side I never realized I craved until now. His hand stilled for just a second before he looked down at me. "Thank you," he whispered softly, "for allowing this."

We sat in silence until an idea popped into my mind. *One that could get me some more answers.* Pulling away from him, I created just enough space so I could turn and fully face him. I quietly sighed again as I crossed my legs, placing my hands in my lap. "I think it's probably time to get to know each other a little more," I said. "Don't you think?"

He nodded once, like he'd already decided that.

I raised one eyebrow and looked him square in the face. "Truth or dare."

A small smile curved his mouth, and I was ashamed to admit that it did something strange to my chest. "You sure this is the game you want to play?"

I nodded enthusiastically because it was the *exact* game I wanted.

"Truth," he said, voice still rimmed with sleep.

I tilted my head. "Have you been watching me?"

His smile disappeared, but not in a dramatic or angry way—it just faded as he rubbed his eyes. "Yes," he said, his voice low and flat. "Your turn."

Okay, at least now I know I was right about that.

I bit the inside of my bottom lip. "Truth."

He studied me for a moment, but whatever question he wanted to ask died before it formed. "Pass," he muttered.

I narrowed my eyes as I threw a playful punch into his

shoulder. "That's not how this is supposed to work."

As my fist made contact with him, a faint smirk hid whatever emotion he was battling. "I don't want you to tell me things because you *have* to."

"Fine." I leaned closer. "Dare, then."

His brows lifted slightly as if he was trying to gauge how I felt about playing. "I dare you," he said carefully, "to give me a compliment."

My smile was involuntary, but my tone was almost sarcastic. "Seems easy enough—"

He scoffed loudly, as if there was no truth to my statement.

I narrowed my eyes at him, a piece of me slightly offended. "What's that sound for?"

His eyebrows rose as he feigned innocence. "Nothing. Go for it."

I looked at him suspiciously before giving a dramatic thumbs up, "You're kidnapping skills? Real ten out of ten."

His eyebrows lowered as his smirk turned into a full smile. "Okay. Now I want a dare too."

Running my hand through my hair, I decided to test how much information he would give me. "I dare you to show me a piece of you that no one has ever seen."

The question took him by surprise, and his smile faltered. "A *piece*, huh?"

"Mhmm," I hummed, enjoying the fact he actually had to think about this answer.

For a second, I thought he was going to shrug as he lifted his arm, but I watched him use his hand to point down at his collar. Among the small amount of bare skin there was a puzzle piece. A tattoo that didn't match the other ones he had. The style was simple, one that looked almost like it was drawn by a child.

"Greyson used to draw a lot—it was how he coped with certain things. Sometimes, it was small doodles that didn't make sense, but other times it would be patterned things like puzzle pieces, where he could zone out and fill them in for hours at a time. This specific one was from a napkin we had during our first family dinner. It stuck with me, and I ended up getting it tattooed. Sometimes, it was nice knowing we're just a small piece in the grand scheme of things… and other times, it was better knowing that no matter what, we had somewhere we belonged."

I stared at the shape, at the meaning behind it, and at another layer of Silas Solstice.

"I didn't think much about the fact I had gotten it done, until both my brothers came home with the same one. Dumbass one and two had a high school friend do it over a kitchen table as a surprise for me."

Another wave of emotion rolled through him, and this time, I was able to catch it before he buried it. His blue eyes filled with nostalgia, and his face softened, as if that memory was one of his favorites.

This Silas was everything the other version was not, a view that I didn't think a lot of people were privy too. Lifting my finger, I traced where the piece laid. "So what you're telling me is that you guys *all* have a lifelong reminder of the questionable decisions you make."

"It wasn't all bad. The tattoos ended up infected, and Kyrin found out he had a knack for medical things." A soft chuckle from him made my body shake and without thinking too much about it, I suddenly wanted him to know things about me too.

"Can I do truth again?"

He nodded as his fingers traced the back of my arms, his question coming out soft, almost like he was scared of the answer. "Why are you here with me, when you could have run?"

My whole body clenched, but it wasn't because of the question. *It's because of the truth behind it.* "Sometimes there's a voice that turns on in my head,"—I bit my lip as I watched his fingers graze my skin,—"and against every fiber of my being, it told me to stay."

A small nod was his only response, and for a brief moment, I wished I could see into his thoughts. I formed my next thought as he processed my previous answer.

"I dare you to touch me."

His body stilled as he answered with one word. "No." His tone neither angry, or defensive—just flat, and exactly what I'd expected.

I nodded once in his direction. "Okay." I didn't push him, but that didn't mean I was giving up. "I dare you to close your eyes, then."

He looked at me like he knew I was up to something, his blue eyes full of suspicion. After exhaling loudly, he closed them.

"Keep them shut," I added, sitting up and pulling away from him.

It was apparent he didn't like me leaving his arms. As I moved, he outstretched them toward me until he couldn't feel me anymore, and then he said my name, a word full of warning. "Ember—"

I grinned, even though I knew he couldn't see me. Moving quietly across the room, I dragged a chair just to throw him off.

One eyebrow twitched and I giggled. The sound felt foreign but light. I circled the room once and then darted to the other side to grab his mask. With every sound I made, his head turned in that direction.

"Ember," he warned again, but this time, his voice was starting to sound playful. I liked the sound of it.

"Sir. Eyes closed."

Shaking his head slightly, he sighed in defeat.

I fastened the mask on my face and bolted out of the room. Slipping out of the office, I sprinted down the hallway with my bare feet slapping against the floor. I didn't stop laughing until I reached the main level. I knew how ridiculous this was, how ridiculous I probably looked in this crowd. For the first time since I met him, I wasn't running because I was scared—I was running because I *wanted* him to chase me.

27

Silas

The door to my office clicked shut with a sound that was barely audible, but as soon as I heard it, I knew she was gone. For half a second when I opened my eyes, I stared at the empty room around me.

I assumed she hadn't left because she was running. So, what were the chances she would reappear with that crooked smile? The more I thought about it, the more I quickly realized that was not the case.

I hadn't imagined it, the bond that had solidified between us. There was no way she didn't feel it now, that she didn't feel the fact we were made for each other. Moments before she'd asked me to touch her, but I had said no—would that be why?

My eyes locked on the door to my office as I stood. Up until this moment, I had given her every bit of control I could. If she was comfortable now, that meant I could take some back. Knowing her, that's what she wanted—*to play.*

She didn't just get to surrender everything to me and then leave me. She belonged by my side, right next to me. I grabbed at the spot where my mask had been, only to realize it was gone. I studied the empty space and rolled my eyes at her. If

her goal had anything to do with something outside of playing, she wouldn't have grabbed that. If it was any negative emotion, she would have done anything she could to break my rules out of pure spite. A cold, razor-sharp clarity sliced through me, and I knew she wanted to be hunted.

I should have known right away, because this was her—this was *my* Ember. She was trying to play a game with me, one I had originally refused by saying no.

I laughed to myself as I grabbed a different mask. I had two options. One was a fun form of primal play where I could hunt her down through the crowd. This method would probably be her favorite, but selfishly, I knew it would be faster to use my security cameras. For a second, I considered how to fuse both. I moved to the balcony and looked out at the crowd. The music swelled as I stepped out, and the lights streamed across bodies as they moved. Everything below me churned with sin and sweat, with my girl now hiding somewhere within it.

Smiling, I realized it should be really easy to spot her. Her shirt was stained with blood, and her bandages were not easy to conceal. Both of those things would call out to me like a warning label. My eyes searched, cutting through the crowd. I scanned past all the masks and bare skin. Interestingly enough, it was her hair that caught my attention first. For a brief second, it was almost as though she felt the connection and turned back to look at me. I swore I could see the smirk on her face underneath the black mask.

My pulse picked up speed as I watched her. I was trying

to be what she needed, and at this moment, I wasn't sure if she knew what *exactly* she was asking for. The last thing I wanted to do was regress back to where I'd been with her. The moment she ran from my office, she had started a dangerous game, one she was apparently confident in. She walked in the opposite direction of my office, with no signs of fear for what was coming. I lost sight of her as she ducked into one of the side rooms, but not before she looked back at me one more time and nodded.

Blowing out a breath, I pulled away from the balcony and headed back inside. One side of me was obsessed with this, the other was angered by the amount of people she was around.

Still, I didn't just answer her request—I threw myself into the role. It took all of two seconds before I had crossed my office and tore open the door. The closer I got to her and to the room she was in, the harder it was to control my thoughts about how to punish her.

As I hit the dark hallway, I found the exact door she slipped through and opened it slowly. To my surprise, I found her right on the inside of the door, completely transfixed on what she was watching. Three people occupied the room. There was a man in a Dom mask lying on his back on the padded floor. A Volunteer woman rode him while taking another volunteer in her mouth. At first glance, it looked like she was being used, but the more you watched, the more you realized she was being worshipped. Two men and one woman, completely in sync with each other.

Ember stood just off to the side, watching like she was studying something sacred. I moved up behind her and placed the mouth of my mask near her ear, just close enough that she could hear me over the music. "Why run?"

She stiffened slightly, turning her face toward me, like she didn't want to look away completely. "Why say no?"

Because I wanted to say yes.

When I didn't answer, she turned her head back toward them, and we watched as the woman came undone, filled by both men. They then moved around until she was in the middle of an Eiffel Tower situation, still filled completely.

I placed my hand across her lower back. "I said no because you just had a panic attack. You aren't stable enough to make *this* kind of decision yet, and I don't want you to regret it."

That broke her concentration, and she fully faced me. The heat that came off of her shot straight to my dick.

"If I'm staying with you," she said evenly, her voice laced with irritation, "you need to learn you do not make decisions for me. *Ever.*"

Before I could respond, *or hide my hard-on,* she stepped away from me and toward the center of the room. In a way that only she could, she walked straight up to one of the men. In one smooth motion, she faced me and lifted her hand. I held my breath as she moved it toward him, placing it on his shoulders. Slowly, she rubbed his back, like he was something she owned.

Breathe, I reminded myself, fully knowing she was trying to push my buttons.

When I didn't react, she leaned into him, her hand trailing

across his skin. I balled my fists as I watched her whisper something in his ear. *Breathe*, I tried to say again even though I knew it was useless. The volunteer moved his hands to play with the woman he was inside of. The room immediately filled with wet, choking sounds as Ember looked down and watched.

Without a single doubt, I was absolutely and entirely fucked. This woman not only had the ability to command rooms, but she had the same power over my soul.

Shifting her attention to the woman, she bent down and gripped her jaw. Looking at me, she rubbed her thumb across her cheekbone as if in approval. Then, her hands moved again, and I could feel myself take a step toward her. Ember decided to push even harder when she took the woman's hand and placed them inside of her pants. The demand was intentional and meant to rile me. She had definitely succeeded, and my eyes were now glued to that area.

She was mine and mine only. She knew that.

Ember's head lifted, as if she was actually pleasured by this. Then, it tilted toward me, as a reminder that I was the one being challenged. Every fiber of my being was on fire as I watched her do this, but still, I refused to move. She didn't have the power over me she thought she did, *right?*

I was proven so very wrong as the girl I was obsessed with, stepped toward the *man* next to her. My fingers twitched as she extended her hand toward him, like she was about to let him touch her too. Every muscle in my body went rigid at the sight. This was the fucking part she knew I'd fail at. The second I saw his hand raise, something in me snapped.

NO.

"Out," I said, my voice cutting clean through their sounds and the music.

The man standing next to Ember froze, as the woman pulled her mouth off the other and looked toward us. The Dom's initial reaction was to protest, but then he noticed Ember's mask and figured out that this wasn't a simple request from another member.

"Now," I repeated, the edge in my tone sharp enough that even Ember looked at me. One man backed up, helping the woman to stand, and the other one collected their things. They all moved together to the next room, avoiding eye contact with Ember as they passed her.

At least she wore the correct mask this time.

As the door shut behind them, silence settled heavier than it ever had between us. I smirked from the stillness in the air, it was clearly an extension of her angst. I walked toward the door and locked it, letting my hand rest there for a moment.

When I turned around, she was still casually standing in the center of the room like she didn't just intentionally douse me in gasoline. "What," I asked, keeping my voice low and controlled, "do you think you're doing?"

She shrugged, *actually shrugged.* Like this was no big deal, like it was all just funny to her.

In response, I let the darkest part of myself come free. Three strides erased the space between us. Unsurprisingly, she refused to back up, leaving us completely flush against each other. A smile tugged at my mouth as I planted one hand beside her head. *She had planned this from the start. She wanted me to touch her.*

Her breath came out in short pants as the air shifted from thick to suffocating. I lifted my arm, letting my hand graze her neck and her jaw. As my fingers slid into her hair, I pulled just enough for it to hurt. The tension forced her head to turn up. "You will always be allowed to make your own decisions, Ember."

As soon as the words left my mouth, I wrapped my fingers around the base of her skull and let my fist close slowly. The motion wasn't a threat, but a promise. "And sometimes, I will end up making decisions for you, like now." A small moan escaped her as I pulled again, holding her in place. "Do you understand what I'm saying?"

I felt the pull from her hair as she tried to nod, but her head stayed from my grip. When she couldn't answer that way, she began to step backward toward the wall behind her. A dark chuckle of approval came out of me as I moved with her. The moment she made contact, I released my hand and placed it around her throat. I held it there for a moment and counted to ten, waiting for her to show any sign of remorse, but she didn't.

I flexed my fingers and tightened my grip as I leaned down to whisper to her. "I am trying really hard to be the person you need me to be right now." My thumb shifted against her soft skin, slightly rubbing the space below her ear as a reminder.

"I am *trying* to make sure you stay in control so you feel comfortable around me." Inhaling her smell, I exhaled the next words slowly. "Do me a favor and don't light the fire between us until you're ready for it."

She didn't move at first. In fact, it was the most still I'd ever seen her. Even her breathing had stalled. I knew exactly what was happening inside her head, even without seeing the thoughts behind her eyes. Every option, every outcome, she weighed them.

Slowly, her hands landed on my chest. Then, she shoved me as *hard* as she could..The force from her push was so strong that I had to take a step back.

Before I could even register what happened, she stepped up to me and put her chest against mine. Next, she ripped off her mask and looked at me. I could feel the heat rising in my body, pooling low and dangerous. Every choice she made was another button of mine, pushed.

A small smile tugged at the corner of her mouth before she spit on me.

It landed on the cheek of my mask and slowly slid down. The impact made the last bit of restraint melt away. I couldn't see. I couldn't think, and the feral need to have her climbed faster than I'd ever felt before. I watched her expression change from playful to victorious, and instantly, there was nothing I'd like more than to peel that smile right off her face.

This time when I forced her against the wall, the force made her head smack against it. At this point, I was shaking, trying to restrain myself from what she had loosened. "I'm not going to say it again. Stop."

Ember looked straight up at me and wickedly licked her lips. My whole body spasmed, and a rough groan fell out of my mouth as her hand suddenly gripped me through my jeans. I completely forgot how to function as she stroked me. All of my thoughts ceased to exist besides her and the drug she was to my system—the one I would never recover form.

Closing my eyes, I tried one more time to talk sense into her. "Ember."

A soft hand tore my mask off and then yanked my chin down. When I opened my eyes, I didn't see her. I saw the goddamn pyre I would spend the rest of my life burning at.

Staring into the depths of her flames, I leaned in to trace her bottom lip with my tongue. Her approval was instant as she groaned into my mouth. As I pushed my lower half into her, her whole body melted into mine with a slow, aching desperation.

Bringing my hand up to the back of her neck, I anchored her as I kissed her. This time, I didn't hold back, I gave her everything she could handle. *My possession over her. My need for her.* The feral energy between us grew from one form of chaos to another as she started to claw at tmy back. Leaning her back, I grabbed the hem of her shirt and threw it to the floor. The sound sent another jolt through my dick as my eyes raked over her.

The light hanging above us highlighted every curve of her body, and I fought the instant urge to lick every inch of her skin. I wanted to start at the divots from her collarbone and then move to every spot of sweat that was starting to form. Eventually, all of those spots would be claimed. Every single part of her would be, because she was *all mine.*

I groaned as I moved my mouth to her neck, tasting the skin there. Demanding more from me already, she bucked her hips and moved my hand to her waist. Letting it stay there for only a moment, she eventually placed it on her lower belly and then pushed it down.

The snap within me ricocheted through my entire body. Pulling my arm free, I gathered her into my arms and carried her to the back wall of the room. Pushing against one of the mirrored panels, the wall gave way and revealed a hallway. Holding her, I walked the ten feet I knew led somewhere else entirely. In this new, hidden room sat a four-poster bed with buckles attached to each of the columns. I carefully set Ember down, before I walked to the corner of the room and unplugged the cable from the back of the camera.

Now that she had given herself to me, I was going to take my time. She would be worshipped, like she deserved. With that being said, there was no way anyone else was going to be able to watch what I was about to do to her.

28

Ember

The restraints he'd put me in felt equally exhilarating as they did unfair. Attached to each corner of the bed, they separated my limbs completely, which only allowed me a small area to move. The leather bit just hard enough to remind me that I wasn't going anywhere, but that also meant I couldn't touch him, and it was already driving me crazy. Every time I pulled, my wrists burned against the bindings. I knew it was because they were buckled over the gauze that covered my injuries.

None of it mattered though, not when I was focused on the fact my body buzzed from him. Both of his hands slowly made their way to different parts of me, moving across my skin and massaging each place they touched. The act was both incredibly sensual and unexpectedly arousing.

This was the exact type of thing I wanted when I had chosen to run. Despite him trying to remain in whatever form he *thought* I needed, the truth was that I just needed him.

In the last twelve hours, he'd shown me exactly who he was, and I had finally settled on how I felt about him. In his time with me, he had had every opportunity to take advantage of me. There were multiple times he could have used my vulnerability

against me, and he hadn't. In those moments, his one goal was to create a safe space for me. Every time I thought he would take the chance to be the villain, he would do the complete opposite of what I had expected.

In fact, all that I'd ever felt from him was comfort. Our experiences together never blinded me to the dark parts of him. I was fully aware of the way he handled things. Silas could be a bit... *excessive,* but he made it so I always felt comfortable and safe. That was what my mind had been trying to tell me all along. He was unconventional for sure, but he was everything I wanted. He gave me air in a world where I'd always held my breath.

Not once had he let his frustration or anger bleed into his interactions with me. I kept waiting for it, counting on it—where his control would become cruelty. I thought his restraint would snap and he would remind me of what truly came with darkness...but that wasn't who he was.

With every choice he made, he had shown me that. From when he gauged my reactions to being concerned of how I would feel—it was clear I came first. In just the short time it had been, he had already assessed, learned, and mastered what I needed from him. His instinctive ability to know me better than I knew myself was layered over his desire for me, and I could see that now.

He was so very twisted and full of broken parts, but so was I, and somehow, it worked.

His methods in the beginning had been a little unorthodox,

but he never pretended to be anything he wasn't. Silas had simply waited for me to accept the darkness—to choose it for myself.

As his hands continued to run over my body, I realized the truth that had now settled deep in my bones. I didn't want him waiting to see where I stood anymore. I wanted him to know he didn't have to be gentle with me, because I'd accepted him. *Us.*

"Do you know how infuriating you are?"

His question ripped me from my thoughts as he murmured it. With each word, his hands ran over my thighs and dipped between them. He repeated this motion over and over again, never quite crossing the line my body begged him to.

The repetition was pure torture, and I found myself pulling on the restraints more than I meant to. Every time he touched me, it was just enough to promise everything but give nothing. I was whimpering before I could stop myself. He continued until my breath was uneven and my pride was long gone.

"Silas," I pleaded, the word breaking apart as it left my mouth.

A dark sound slipped from his lips as he brought his mouth down to mine. The kiss was light, barely enough to feel before he moved down between my legs. Slowly, he licked up my center, and my body jerked from the pressure. I was completely at his mercy, and I didn't mind one bit. Taking his time, he coaxed my body. With each pass, I tensed.

The first night he touched me, I was repeatedly shattered and then pieced back together nine times. I had barely survived, and I knew that tonight, we were on a completely different level. Everything he was about to do to me was going to be worse, and I was ready for it.

Within minutes, I could feel myself building, and he had only just begun.

29

Silas

In the few hours I had her restrained, I learned many new things about Ember.

She had a total of five scars hidden throughout her body, most in places you couldn't see. There were also a few scattered freckles that dusted her chest and shoulders. When she moved her left arm, a large dimple formed on her back, one that most people didn't have.

She was wildly ticklish on the left side of her body, and the laugh she gave while being tickled was not the same one she gave when she was uncomfortable.

Every time she claimed a release, I explored more, touching and tasting her as I pleased. As much as I wanted to make everything about her, I quickly became selfish. By the time I finally let her rest, there was no area on her body I hadn't thoroughly examined. By the time I took off the restraints, I'd memorized every sound she made. Even though I didn't think it was possible, I felt even more devoted to her now.

I hadn't taken my eyes off her, even now as she slept. With one arm tucked under her pillow, her hair fell in an uneven mess around her. Sweeping some behind her ear, I picked up her wrist

and held it carefully, examining the bandages. I'd forgotten about her wounds, but there was no fresh blood, which meant the gauze had acted like a protective layer against the straps.

I moved my thumb in slow circles over the bruised skin there, pressing gently along the dark marks originally left from my zip ties. My hand drifted up her arm, tracing her shoulder, where my fingers paused against one of her scars, a two-inch line on her shoulder. It was thin and pale, barely noticeable unless you were looking for it. I followed the line with my fingertip, tracing it over and over again, memorizing it.

Her body twitched slightly before her eyes fluttered open for a brief second. After registering that I was still next to her, they closed again. Her voice was scratchy, almost like she was dehydrated. "I need food."

I laughed quietly at the statement because I honestly couldn't tell if she was asleep or not. Regardless, I stood and carefully slipped away from her. Walking over to my phone, I pulled up the closest restaurants and clicked through the menus to find something to order for her. As I finalized some items and received a confirmed delivery time, several messages began to come through. At first, it was a text, then videos.

The vibrations kept going, even as I opened the thread. I noticed Knox's name and narrowed my eyes on each item that flashed on my screen.

Thirty-seven times total over the course of the year. I went as far back as I could go and sent you everything. You never see his face, and he never fully takes advantage of her, but I would suggest thinking about what you might see before watching the clips. Everything has been downloaded to the file on your phone as well. Give me two hours, I have a lead and the police on standby.

And just like that, the temporary world we had created came crashing down as a feeling of grief slammed into me. Thirty-seven times. That *number*, that thought, made me want to vomit.

The other thing about this situation was that I was trying to build our relationship on sturdy ground, and yet, I hadn't told her anything. Ember was strong, stronger than most people, but this news wasn't something anyone could take lightly. Learning this could make her spiral in a direction that was *away* from me. How was I supposed to tell her without cracking the foundation we had just built? I tried to push aside the overwhelming feelings that I'd already let her down.

The messages Knox sent contained seven different files, including videos. I frowned when I noticed the preview images were all identical. Each tiny box showed her sleeping in different positions. Nothing could have prepared me to learn that there were this many instances. I tried to focus on the fact he had a lead. Two hours would go by pretty fast, and it seemed like a reasonable amount of time to keep her occupied. If I could do that, I could provide her with everything she would need to know, and we would go from there.

A cold sensation slid down my spine as I convinced myself to tap the first video. I paced in the corner of the room as I watched the footage play.

The angle was unmistakable. Knox had pulled footage from the camera in her bedroom TV. I was now viewing everything from a high vantage point in the corner of the room, pointed directly at the bed. In this video, Ember slept in only a tank top, tossing slightly in her sleep. A black blanket was wrapped around her waist, and it was clearly the middle of the night.

I was too busy figuring out if she had pants on when I noticed someone step into the frame. Just like before, the figure quietly moved next to her bed. Same broad shoulders, same dark clothes. As if in some weird form of deja vu, I watched the blanket slowly peel back—

I clicked the screen and paused the video. All the contents of my stomach threatened to come up because I knew, *I knew,* what I was about to watch and looking at Ember now, I didn't think I could follow through.

With one large inhale, I forced myself to push play and observe as a hand slid over Ember's leg then moved higher. They weren't just touching her bare legs, but her chest too. Grabbing the light fabric of her shirt, they lifted it over her head, exposing her body underneath.

The video was shut off before I even realized I had been the one to do it. I debated throwing my phone across the entire room. It was like I was right back in Knox's garage. I couldn't think. I couldn't breathe, but I needed to know *everything* in order to help her.

With shaking hands, I opened the next video to the same cover and the same room. Again and again, I watched as boundaries were pushed and Ember was touched. On the final video, I only made it thirty seconds before I had to stop completely. There, on the phone screen, was a frozen image of his fingers deep inside of her.

My stomach rolled violently as I placed a hand against the wall. I needed to throw something, to strangle something, to *hurt* in some way so that she wouldn't have to.

The thought of going upstairs and ripping apart my office surfaced in my mind, and my hands ached in response, begging for that type of release. Making it two steps toward the door, I stopped and looked back at the beautiful woman who was sprawled across the bed.

I couldn't leave her.

Not now. Not *ever.*

Balling up every emotion, I promised myself that she wouldn't have to worry. No matter what happened after I told her, no matter what it took, I would find this person and kill them for violating her.

Knox had said that he had never "fully" violated her, but these things were equally unforgivable. I just hoped she would understand why I kept it from her for so long. I paced the room, trying to convince myself that everything would be fine, but the videos played repeatedly in my head. As much as I fought them, the images began to sear themselves into my brain. A type of pain washed over me that I had never felt before—one I couldn't identify. I knew that even this was nowhere close to what she would feel when she found out.

Through the entirety of my mental breakdown, Ember didn't stir. She just laid there, completely unaware of the crumbling walls around us. Blind to the fact that someone was touching her while she slept, *because she still had no idea.*

I couldn't help the avalanche that was occurring in my head. Truthfully, I knew that when it came to this situation, my feelings and thoughts were irrelevant. Nothing about me mattered because *this*, this was going to destroy her, and I could do nothing but let it.

The mattress dipped under my weight as I settled back next to her, scared to touch her. "How come you never woke up, baby," I whispered under my breath as my hand slid into her hair, pushing it gently off her forehead.

I just sat and stared at her, fighting against everything that twisted in my chest. Using my thumb, I brushed over her temple until I had slightly calmed. By then, I'd convinced myself that I needed to tell her as soon as I got the name from Knox.

30

Ember

The smell pulled me from a dream I didn't want to leave.

Warm waves of salty cheese permeated my senses. The image surrounding me rippled away, rushing me back into reality. My eyes fluttered open as my lashes stuck together, but soon, the room came into focus. The ceiling, the bed, and Silas, with a plastic container between us.

Propped up on one elbow, he was lying on his side next to me. His expression was cautious but focused. It seemed as if he was watching me like he'd been there for a while. A small smile curved his mouth when he realized I was awake, but something was off about him. He pushed the large bowl toward me and handed me a fork. "I'm not sure if you just talk in your sleep or if you were actually asking me for food, but I got some anyway."

My stomach answered him before I did, growling loudly between us. I'd definitely asked for food on purpose, considering how this man was making a habit out of depleting my energy. Taking the fork from him, I stretched my arms, reaching over my head until my back popped. "Well, I have been quite busy."

Silas huffed quietly, almost amused. Then he shifted, reaching over to a side table that wasn't there before. Grabbing two

cold water bottles, he turned back to me. "Plan on being *busy* for most of your life now." His smile grew wider as he handed me one. "Drink."

My throat felt like I swallowed sand, which made sense—considering how many times I'd screamed out his name. Naturally, I wanted to fight him and his damn instruction, but I twisted the cap off and chugged half of it immediately. As I pulled the bottle away from my mouth, I noticed the food between us.

My eyes widened as my mouth began to water. "Oh my god." I ripped the bowl into my lap like he might take it away from me, as drool continued to form. *Fries.* Not just regular fries, but multiple stacks drowned in thick country gravy. I couldn't help the smile that took over my face, and suddenly, I felt like a child who'd just received an ice cream cone. "*Silas.*" His name came out as a sigh before I shoved the first bite into my mouth and groaned with instant approval. Every bite was a continuous flood of hot, crispy perfection. "Is it weird if I say I forgive you? For *everything*?"

Instead of answering, he looked down, leaning back against the headboard beside me. "Don't say that just yet," he muttered to himself. I barely caught it but paid it no mind because for the next few minutes, I was solely lost in fries. He just sat there and watched me devour them with his arms resting loosely over his knees. It wasn't long before I'd finished the entire container. I had just wiped my mouth when he spoke.

"Can I ask you something?"

Completely content, I snuggled into the blanket and shrugged. "Go for it."

"Your friends," he said, bringing his eyes up to me. "The ones you live with. Tell me about them?"

I gave a shallow nod and closed my eyes as I started talking. "Kinsley is easy, I guess. I mean, we get along well. She's always been everything I'm not, because life has always come easy for her." I snorted, opening one eye at him. "Which has always been slightly annoying."

Silas's eyes slightly narrowed at that comment, like he was cataloging everything I said.

"She's funny and doesn't take no for an answer, been that way for as long as I've known her, but sometimes, it's like we live in two different worlds," I added.

He nodded slowly before moving to the foot of the bed and taking my leg into his hands. Focusing along the muscle there, he massaged my calf.

"And Bodhi is her other half, basically my brother. He's a quarterback and stays with us when he can. Sometimes it's weekends, sometimes just the summer. He's basically like, the house dad when he's there, making sure everyone is taken care of."

Silas's jaw tightened slightly at that, but his hands kept moving.

"Kolby is Kinsley's brother," I opened my eyes, feeling myself smile, "They're fraternal twins but honestly, they couldn't be more opposite from each other. I'm surprised he's survived this long with how he acts sometimes. Between his impulses and that mouth of his, he tends to get in trouble a lot." Dropping the blanket, I dramatically brought my hands up to my throat. "Kinsley choked him multiple times. Like, *physically*, with her bare hands."

The memory of that night played out in my head as I mentally watched Kolby get tackled by Kinsley in front of me, for just merely existing. I laughed involuntarily at the image.

Silas's hands stopped moving. "His mouth, huh?"

Of course *that's* what he would take from that conversation.

"Mouth as in the *words* that seem to fall out of it—not because of what he can do with it. Despite his multiple attempts at that, I never looked at him in that way." I leaned toward Silas playfully. placing my hand lightly on his before I tapped twice. "But honestly?" I said in a light tone, winking. "He probably couldn't manage half of what you do."

There was no instant flare of anger in his face. If anything, his expression turned to one of sadness, but his hands twitched, tightening around my leg, and I took that as a win. After a moment, he blinked a few times and casually picked a piece of lint off my leg. "And they all live with you?"

An odd feeling crossed over me then, and I straightened my body. Something told me this wasn't just an average conversation. He wasn't just trying to learn, like he did with my body earlier. The questions he asked felt weighted, as if this talk was more like an interrogation. In just the last few seconds, Silas's body had tensed and his eyes seemed colder. I tilted my head, very aware that something had changed. "Yes?"

A slight pain shot up my leg as his thumbs suddenly dug into the muscle there. A short sound of pain escaped me just as he looked down and realized what he'd done. His hands stilled as he looked up at me, gently rubbing over the area before kissing it. "Sorry."

I pulled my leg away, keeping my eyes on him the whole time. Now I *knew* something was off. "Well," I said lightly, brushing my hands over the blanket on my lap, "while we're asking questions...Am I allowed to ask when I can go home?"

This time, my words pulled a reaction from him. Silas held my gaze for a moment before his eyebrow twitched and he stood. "Why? It's not like you have a job anymore. Am I allowed to ask how you feel about us?"

My jaw dropped at his first response but I wasn't sure why. Silas had been watching me, so of course he knew about that. To be fair though, I had never actually resigned from my job, I had just left the keys out for Atlas. A clear indication I wasn't coming back.

Deciding to let it go, I considered his next question as I watched him gather the trash around us. When he turned back toward me for my answer, my body automatically shrugged even though my thoughts on that subject were anything but casual. "I'm still thinking about everything," I admitted. "You aren't exactly an average boyfriend." The words sounded silly when I said them out loud, but they were the most honest ones I had.

Silas clicked his tongue once as he tied the bag and unbuckled the restraints from the bed before throwing them into a pile. "I don't think the term *boyfriend* fits me very well."

"Yeah," I said in full agreement, "I know." My confession made him stop completely. I stopped fiddling with my fingers to look up at him.

"I think *husband* would be better."

I replayed his words just to make sure I heard the right ones, but even then, I was in shock. "I'm sorry, *what*?!"

He held eye contact for another second before continuing to strip one side of the bed. "I guess that's something we can discuss later." His tone left no room for argument, which made me blush and become incredibly uncomfortable.

I stood, trying to change the subject. "If I can't go home, am I allowed to *debate* the terms of my stay? Like maybe access to a hot shower?"

A slow exhale came from him, as if it was something he hadn't even thought about. Handing me my clothes, he pulled me into his chest. "If I say yes, will you stay with me longer?"

My cheeks flushed as I pushed up against him and then stepped around his body to get dressed. While I slipped each leg into my bottoms, he stripped the bed of the dark sheets and threw everything together in the corner of the room. Then, he walked to the opposite corner and reconnected the wires hanging out of the bottom of the camera. Twisting together two cords, he stepped back just as a blue light flickered on. A few seconds passed before he was facing me again and closing the space between us.

"What do you think?" he asked as he grabbed my hand.

I furrowed my eyebrows at him, avoiding the question. "I need a shower, Silas."

He nodded, pulling us toward the door we entered through. Once we left the hidden hallway, I assumed he would take me to a reserved space in the club, a place meant to wash off the sins that were regularly committed there, but ten minutes later I found myself in his car.

I didn't say anything as he opened the door for me, and I remained quiet as we pulled off onto the road. The more Silas drove, the more the engine created a steady vibration—one that traveled up through the seat and into my spine, weirdly soothing me. Outside the window, the world had dissolved into long stretches of dark road and scattered lights. I decided to focus on that. Resting my head against the cool glass, I watched the night slide by.

The air was too quiet between us and I wasn't sure what to say. Silas was Silas, but *not.*

As if he heard my thoughts the exact moment I had them, Silas's hand moved to my thigh and gently squeezed. My eyes moved to his face, where I found him staring straight toward the road. I shifted my gaze down his neck and shoulder, following his arm until the tattoos stopped at his wrist.

I quietly scoffed at myself and the fact I was sitting here, worrying about Silas. Realistically, he was the person I was supposed to be nervous *about,* not worried *for.* For all I knew, we were driving straight to the middle of nowhere, but here I was, trying to figure out what was going on inside his head. A quiet breath of amusement slipped out of me before I could stop it.

As I watched him from the corner of my eye, Silas repeatedly glanced over at me. Each time was quick, barely a second, and then his attention snapped back to the road.

I turned my head slightly, studying him in the dim glow of the dashboard lights. The faint blue light caught along the edge of his jaw and the bridge of his nose. "This feels weird," I said, rotating my hand in a circle between us.

"What does?"

Shifting in the seat, I pulled one leg up underneath me as I leaned back into the leather behind me. "The part where I should probably be panicking again."

One dark eyebrow lifted, just barely. "You want to *panic* again?"

"Maybe," I muttered back.

Silas went quiet again, focusing on a stretch of empty desert around us.

And just like that, it was back again—the strange, subtle tension that had been clinging to him since I'd woken up. I watched from the corner of my eye for a few seconds longer before letting my head fall back against the seat. "It really just depends on you."

That grabbed his attention.

Dark unreadable eyes slid toward me before returning to the

road. “Do you feel panic right now?” he asked.

I gave a slight shrug, watching the side of his face. “Oh, I don’t know,” I said mockingly. “I was actually enjoying your presence and personality before it was replaced by a slightly more brooding version. I don't like this one, he seems *disconnected.*”

A quiet breath escaped him through his nose. “I’m right here.”

“Yeah, *okay,*” I said, turning my attention back out the window.

Normally he’d have some type of reply—a sharp comment or a dry insult. His arsenal was always ready to remind me that provoking him was a terrible idea, but that was the end of the conversation. There was nothing else besides the silence that stretched between us.

I eventually decided to fill it. “Do you kidnap everyone, or am I just special?”

A short breathy sigh of an answer told me he didn’t approve of me trying to lighten the mood. “This is not kidnapping. You asked for a shower.”

“So maybe I’m the only victim that’s been smart enough to ask for basic human needs, but still gotta know—am I the only one to get zip tied?'

Silas’s hands tightened on the steering wheel, his knuckles turning white. “You are not my *victim.*”

“I bet you have a punch card,” I grinned at the windshield, having way too much fun now, “Kidnap ten girls, get the eleventh free. Maybe you should have just put me to sleep, it probably would have been easier."

"STOP."

Silas's voice wasn't just stern. He was angry. This was the first time I'd ever heard him raise it and I hated the feeling it gave me.

I chose to stay quiet and let him deal with whatever the hell was going on. When we eventually pulled up into a driveaway, I didn't even have time to look at the house before the car shut off and Silas got out, slamming the door behind him.

31

SILAS

I left the door open for her as I walked inside.

I knew I should apologize. She had no idea of why that verbiage would upset me, but I still couldn't knock the feeling that she'd somehow compared me to *him* in the car. I tried to get over it as I moved straight to the kitchen and set my things down. *I should have taken the time to explain why I brought her here of all places.* I could have shown her around and talked about why I'd chosen *my* house to stay at, but now I felt like it wouldn't be the same.

I didn't like keeping things from her, especially *this.* Knowing I couldn't tell her was making me uneasy, so much so I was turning volatile and it was affecting my communication with her. I owed her so much more than just an apology once this was done.

I looked around at what she was about to walk into. My house was simple, but I thought she'd like it that way. Because she was still outside, she'd be able to see the paint—a deep charcoal grey I'd picked out, with the bottom lined in a dark lattice that matched the trim. I bet she'd notice that my windows were tinted like the ones on my car. Knowing her, she'd probably

have something to say about that.

Her favorite thing, though, would probably be the yard out front. I ran sprinklers year-round to promote the vibrant green landscaping, including my yellow rose bushes that lined the side wall of the house. A smile lined my face as I realized the correlation between those flowers, my mom, and Ember. I had never put it together, not until now. *I bet they would have liked each other.*

Turning to look at my cupboards, I quickly searched for a vase. Finding one on the top shelf, I jogged out of the kitchen and retraced my steps to her. From the hallway, I saw her outside through the open door. It was almost like she'd sat in the car for a while before getting out. She had barely made it into the yard.

She stared down at the walkway as she moved, smiling every time her foot crossed over one of the pavers. I could tell she was studying the diamond patterns carved into them. Her gaze only lifted when she noticed me standing there. I held the vase out, along with the scissors I'd grabbed.

"Wanna help me with something?"

"What, did you run inside so that you could take your crazy pills? Are we calm now?"

I didn't answer, just walked over to the side of the house with the vase. When her eyes landed on the rose bushes, they widened before glancing back at me. I nodded as she ran over to it, carefully touching the large yellow roses that were sprinkled throughout the leaves. I shook my head at the way she instantly fell in love with them. *I should have known, considering yellow was both of their favorite colors.*

I walked over next to her and cut off six roses, sliding them into the vase, along with some foliage. "You like them?"

"Yeah, I do." She carried them to the door with the biggest smile then looked up at me as we stepped inside. "I'd like them even more if we could talk about why you got upset?"

Walking through the door, I stepped to the side and let her take in the space. "Nope."

She just sighed, smelling the flowers as she passed me and looked around.

"This is my home."

Almost dropping the flowers, she stuttered on her next words before looking around. "What? You brought me to your house?"

I just nodded and moved past her into the living room, where I sat as she looked over everything. She noticed the ceiling first and how it was broken into small sections from dark exposed beams. Following each one with her eyes, she moved on to the soft lighting that was tucked into the edges of each one. Her focus moved again, down to the dark wood floors that matched the beam's color above. I wondered what her thoughts were, considering my home was completely different from my office. "What do you think?"

She eyed me, like she couldn't figure out what my next move was, and I realized it had been a while since the last time I'd received that look. "I didn't take you for a modern house kind of guy. The fact it doesn't look like a jail is commendable, but I *did* expect neutrals. That's not surprising at all."

"Yeah well, it *was* painted yellow." I answered before disappearing down the hall to find a towel. I grabbed a few from the extra closet and then some of my clothes for her, realizing she was probably going to need new ones after she showered.

When I came out, she was standing in front of a shelf in my living room. Somehow, I knew the exact picture she was looking at, I'd known that was the one she'd be drawn to. As I moved closer, I saw the picture from over her shoulder. The photo she held was of three boys, huddled together on a broken tree. The tallest one was me, and I could see she'd figured that out because her thumb was rubbing my face. Beside me in the image was Kyrin and Greyson.

"Your brothers?"

"Yeah," My shoulders dropped slightly when her gaze met mine. I wanted her to know everything about me, and yet, I was hiding something from her about her own life. I offered her the folded towel and clothes. "My mom took that."

She smiled softly and leaned against the wall next to me. Turning the towel in her hands, she brought it up to her chest and wrapped her arm around it. "What's she like?"

There was a quick tick in my jaw as I pushed past the discomfort I was starting to feel. The discussion with her about *him* and what he was doing to her would be ten times worse, so I needed to start with this, *even if it made me want to be sick.* I took the photo from her and ignored all of the bad feelings coming back. "She was everything good in this world—the type of person that lit up a room. Everyone loved her."

Ember's whole demeanor changed, but not in a bad way. She seemed to pick up on the fact that it was a really sore subject for me. "I'm sorry, Silas. She sounds amazing."

I pulled my eyes up so she could see how I was laying down my shield for her, how I too could be exposed and vulnerable. "She *was*, even though she was the sole reason why everything in this house was painted yellow." I laughed, feeling the sting inside my body from actively talking about her.

A look of realization crossed Ember's face, just like I was hoping it would. "*Yellow*?" She blinked at me a few times. "Like my dress?"

I smiled one more time at the picture before placing it back on the shelf. "There were a lot of reasons I couldn't get you out of my head, even from that first night. I think I knew though, even then. Finding someone like you is extremely rare. I know that, because when she died, the world lost part of its light and so did I. When I saw you in the club that night, in that yellow dress—I couldn't help but get angry. I hadn't felt that warmth since I was sixteen."

Ember's arms wrapped around me, and the towel she held pushed into my side. The hug was foreign and I wanted to reject it, but I'd take anything from her as long as she stayed with me.

"What was her name?" Ember asked from my chest.

Another imaginary wound was inflicted from that question. Instead of retreating, I wrapped my arms around her back.

"Lacey."

I felt the exact moment she put everything together about my tattoos. "Silas, I'm sorry that I—"

"It's fine," I replied, not wanting any type of apology from her.

"Was it just you guys and your dad, then?"

That question hit the hardest, and the pain wasn't just a sting, it was a gut punch. "My dad was the one who killed her." The words echoed like a scream in the quiet kitchen around us. "I think it's safe to say the world is full of really shitty people." I mumbled into her hair, "I raised my brothers after that."

With that information she pulled away and looked back at the picture. "You did that alone?"

I shrugged slightly. "Someone had to. I wasn't going to let them get taken from me."

When she looked at me, it was like she truly saw me for the first time. There was no wall between us, none whatsoever, and now it was my job to *keep* it that way.

When she turned, I thought she was stepping away to shower, but to my surprise, she walked a few feet away and pulled out a barstool from my counter. Once it was out far enough, she sat down and placed her elbows on the towel, holding her chin in her hands.

I pointed in the direction of the bathroom before moving to the fridge and pulling out a bottle of water. "I thought you needed a shower?"

Tapping a finger on her chin, she smiled up at me "That can

wait a few more minutes. I want to know about you. Is that okay?"

It was definitely okay, but as she said that, I cursed internally at Knox. After a few seconds of making her wait, I let her win. Grabbing an extra bottle out of the door, I handed it to her and took a seat in the barstool next to her. "I'll tell you whatever you want to know as long as you drink this."

She raised an eyebrow and twisted off the cap with two fingers before chugging the whole thing. Not once did she take her eyes off me, even as she set the empty bottle on the counter. "When did the club come around?"

Throwing the empty one away, I walked back to the fridge and set a new one down in front of her, just because I could. "I was a kid raising kids. I found an outlet that eventually turned into a hobby. When my dad died, I inherited our family money and invested into a few companies. One came to be mine, and the other two went to my brothers when they were old enough."

I could tell that she was processing everything. She wanted to understand, and the best thing was, there was no sympathy in her expression, which I appreciated. She briefly looked down and then back up at me. "How do the masks fit in?"

I straightened, stretching through the restraint my body was trying to give. "A lot of my childhood was being who others needed me to be. I spent a large portion being my mother's protector and then my brother's guardian. My face became one people looked at with remorse." I took a moment to swallow and collected the rest of my thoughts. "I just wanted to create a space where I could be who I was, make my own choices, without anyone judging me." The words seemed simple as they left me, but that was all it really boiled down to. "Trauma affects everyone differently, and mine just manifested as masks."

"It all makes sense now. Why you want control"—a light shade of pink flooded her cheeks, and she tried to hide her smile—"and why you play a certain way. Is that why you shared me with Kyrin that first night?"

"Let's be crystal clear about something.." I couldn't help the look that settled on my face, the expression was one of pure objection. "I did not *share* you with my brother. *You* needed to learn a lesson, and *I* needed to touch you. *Kyrin* was just there." I knew that night would eventually come back to bite me. "I am not the type that *shares*."

She shook me off with a simple hand gesture. "I don't want that. I already have a hard time keeping up with all your dueling personalities—I'd be stupid to add anyone else to the mix."

Grabbing an empty envelope, I threw it at her, and she flashed me one of her amazing smiles. We sat in silence for a few minutes until she began to pick the skin on the sides of her fingers.

"I didn't go through the same thing you did, but my parents weren't the best either. They were never home, and when they were, they were on drugs. My grandmother raised me, which is where I learned to never back down. I had to move out when she passed away because I couldn't afford things on my own—that's when I found Kinsley."

With a small laugh, she lifted the towel and pointed down the hallway for direction.

I answered by motioning to her where to go. "Second door on the right." As she stepped away, I couldn't help myself. I lightly grabbed her jaw and pulled her into me. She instantly relaxed into my hold and looked up at me with those eyes, the eyes that I pictured every time I closed my own. I almost said everything then, almost told her the complete truth of what we found and why she was with me. In order to stop myself, I let my eyes drift to her lips. Lowering my head, I rested my forehead on hers. It was only a moment later that her mouth crashed to mine.

Every time I felt her lips, I knew our kiss wasn't simple or average, because *we* weren't. I let her lead, and at first it stayed soft. Then she ran her tongue along my bottom lip and let out a sound, one that I had to push myself away from before I literally threw her on the counter.

I didn't say anything as I kept my face down to control my breathing. She giggled and rubbed my dick once before heading down the hall toward the bathroom.

32

EMBER

Steam filled the bathroom as I slowly stepped out of my clothes.

The bathroom itself was massive and so was the shower directly in front of me. Tall glass walls surrounded the area with dark tile, and a rainfall showerhead poured warm water down in a steady curtain.

I stepped under it and let the hot water hit my shoulders. God, I didn't realize how tense my body was until now. Well, I *did*, seeing how that kiss almost pushed me off the deep end.

To be fair, I'd already jumped into those shark-infested waters all by myself, and now I was just trying to stay above water and not drown.

As I showered, the muscles in my shoulders loosened one by one as the heat spread down my back. I tilted my head forward, letting the water soak through my hair, pushing everything down the drain—sweat, bodily fluids, and the weird emotional whiplash I had experienced lately. If someone were to ask me to sum up the last twenty-four hours of my life, I'd have a lot to explain. I was introduced to a world where someone could be kidnapped, have the best sex of their life, eat delicious fries, and then forgive the kidnapper, *all because he had emotional*

trauma.

I reached for the bottle of shampoo on the shelf, squeezing some into my palm before working it into my hair. The scent was clean, something close to laundry detergent, and it immediately reminded me of Silas. I didn't mind the fact that the scent was now filling the entire bathroom.

I closed my eyes as I massaged it through my scalp, thinking about everything that was going on. I knew Silas was quiet and controlling, intense in such a way the air changed when he walked into a room. Now *every* piece of him made sense. His mom. His dad. His brothers.

He was sixteen years old, raising kids.

My hands slowed in my hair as my heart broke for him. No one should have to carry that kind of weight that young, which was why he was made into this type of person. Craving that type of control over everyone...*It's because he never had any.* The way he studied everything around him like he was calculating every outcome...*He had to do that for his brothers.* A life like that would shape anyone into the same kind of mold. I rinsed the shampoo out, watching white foam spiral down the drain as I replayed our conversation.

He said he never felt seen, but the weird thing was I felt like I *only* saw him. Despite the fact he stalked me and then forced me here, I wanted to know more. I wanted to know everything about his family, his brothers, about what kind of kid he was before the world broke him open.

After a few more minutes of washing my body, I shut the

water off and stepped out of the shower. Swirls of steam radiated around me as I dried off. Once I was no longer dripping, I picked up the clothes on the counter and spread them out. A black tank top and dark sweatpants, obviously Silas's.

Pulling the top over my head, it hung loose on me. I didn't mind the comfort, and I appreciated the fact it was not ridiculously oversized. The sweatpants, however, were a different story. The waistband slid halfway down my hips the second I let go of it. I laughed quietly to myself and rolled the waistband twice until they stayed up.

Barefoot, with my hair still damp, I opened the bathroom door and stepped into the hallway. When I entered the kitchen, Silas was exactly where I left him. Sitting at the counter, he was now looking down with his head buried in his hands. I walked up behind him and ran my hands over his back and across his shoulders. Something about the way he looked now was heavy, like something was weighing on him that I just couldn't see.

"Silas." The moment I spoke he jumped.

Standing abruptly, he gave me a small kiss on my cheek. "I'm going to shower. When I get out, I want to talk more. I have something to say."

Before I could respond, he was already walking past me down the hallway. The bathroom door closed behind him a second later.

Staring in that direction for another minute, I guessed at what personality that was. "...okay, then." Weird, *but whatever.*

I leaned against the counter and grabbed another bottle of

water from the fridge. Twisting the cap open, I took a long drink. My eyes drifted down to the counter and settled on his phone. It was there, right where he'd left it *unlocked.* Picking it up, the screen instantly lit up. Part of me considered hiding it, just to cause trouble. Another part was trying to convince me to just put the phone back down. The gremlin part of my brain pushed me to go through it and find out more things about Silas on my own. *That* was the side that won, like always.

My thumb swiped across the screen, and the messages opened. Kinsley's number popped up immediately at the top of the app, because that was the last message sent. Opening a new text to her, I started typing and watched my thumbs move across the keyboard before I could overthink it.

I'm alive. Long story. Don't freak out.

I stared at the words for a second, debating whether or not to send the message in general. Half of me knew she was already freaking out, and the other half believed she hadn't even noticed I was gone. I was about to hit send when something else on the screen caught my eye.

A folder, right beneath the messages.

A folder with *my* name.

EMBER V.

My brows knitted together as my heartbeat picked up. Knowing Silas, this could be so many different things. I took one steadying breath as I tapped the icon and watched the screen instantly fill. At first, I only saw photos, but then videos started to load in—*all* of me.

My stomach dropped, like I'd just stepped off a ledge I didn't realize was there. "What the hell?"

Looking through the beginning, the first few images appeared to be screenshots. I stared at them, trying to make sense of what I was looking at. It was my room, with me sleeping in my bed. The angle was familiar enough that it took me a second to place it. My eyes narrowed in, tilting the phone closer. The TV mounted in the corner of my room, that was what this was from.

A slow breath left my lungs.

Okay. *Weird,* but not exactly shocking from him.

I already knew Silas had been watching me, he admitted to it—that part wasn't exactly new information, but I still didn't like the feeling it caused. As I tried to shrug everything off, I found another photo, but this time, it was something small with numbers.

Shaking my head, I swiped through the rest of the album before coming to the videos. My pulse started to race, beating faster as I stared at the screen. For a moment, I considered not opening them, but the gremlin won again, and I pressed play.

The video loaded, and I was viewing my room from the same angle, but this time, the lighting was different. A dim glow cascaded down from my lamp and spread across me and the blanket I was under. I watched myself sleep, shifting slightly every few minutes.

At first, that was all the video was. A few minutes passed, and it was still just me and the darkness, but then there was movement. Someone entered the frame, and my entire body stilled when a man stepped quietly beside my bed. His moves were slow and careful, like he knew exactly where every creaky board was.

My pulse started to hammer in my chest as the figure reached down and gently pulled the blanket away from me. At this point, I could hear my heartbeat in my ears, but I kept watching anyway. My eyes stay glued to the screen as a hand reached out, grazing my leg.

No.

No, no, no—

The hand moved slowly upward along my thigh and then dipped between them. The sight of it made my chest tighten so painfully it almost knocked the air out of me. I paused the screen, clicking on it over and over again, as if it would erase what happened.

Eventually, I moved on to the next one. I watched as the same figure returned on a different night. This time, I was on my stomach, watching him spread my legs wider to play.

Each video blurred into the next, the pattern becoming sickeningly clear. Each one was worse than the last, every video making the knot in my stomach pull tighter.

Realization slammed into me, and all other thoughts left my head. Not only had Silas been watching me, but he—*this* was something else entirely. He hadn't just been coming into my room, standing over me. He violated me, *touched me.*

The water bottle slipped out of my grasp before I even realized my fingers had gone numb. I didn't watch it hit the floor because I'd lost all control of my body. The sound of plastic cracking against tile echoed around the kitchen as water burst across the floor, splashing outward in a sudden small wave. I didn't notice that either, not when my hands were shaking so badly that the phone threatened to slip from my grip.

My chest was too tight, like a vice has been placed around me. Each breath came faster than the last, like my lungs couldn't pull in enough air to keep up with the panic surging through my body.

A body that had been taken advantage of, over and over again.

I never saw his face in the videos, it was always hidden with a hood, but I knew it had to be Silas. There was no one else it *could* be. I held on to the counter as more dread filled my mind. At one point, my legs threatened to give out over the fact that I'd just let him—*because I had thought that—*

I swallowed a scream that was threatening to explode from the inside. Opening up the dial pad, I debated calling the police. *But how was I supposed to explain this? How could I defend sleeping with him?* Even now, I was still in the same house with him.

My hands moved as I thought of the next person to call. Kinsley's line rang once, then twice. On the last one, it went straight to her voicemail. "Damn it." I pulled up the dial pad, knowing it had to be Bodhi next. *If anyone was going to answer, it would be him.*

"Hello?"

"Hey," I said quickly, my voice shaking. "I need you to come get me."

There was silence, then his voice came out rushed and anxious. "Ember? What the hell! Where have you been?!"

It was clear he was angry with me, and I deserved that, but right now, I really needed his help. "Bodhi, please come get me. Now."

His voice softened immediately. "Where are you?"

I described everything I could remember, starting with the drive.

"I'm coming, hold on," he said, clearly already moving on the other side of the phone. "Stay there."

"No, I can't. I—I'm going to start walking down the main road."

"Ember—"

The phone was already out of my hand and back on the counter. I didn't grab anything, I just walked straight out the door and away from Silas.

I remembered some turns we took, along with the general direction from where the car had come. At this point, I'd rather end up anywhere else than here, *with him.* Fifteen minutes passed, and I'd made it pretty far. My legs started to ache just as headlights pulled up beside me.

The passenger door swung open, and Bodhi leaned across the seat. "Get in, Em."

I listened, climbing in immediately and sagging into the seat.

My body was fully numb now, matching the feeling inside my brain.

The moment the door shut, he looked straight at me, and I could feel the anger radiating off of him. "Were you trying to get yourself hurt?!" he snapped.

I stared down at my hands, but they only reminded me of the others that had touched me. "No."

He opened his mouth to say something else, but his eyes dragged over my clothes, clearly displeased. Then suddenly, he frowned, "Where's your necklace?"

"I... don't know."

Bodhi just exhaled sharply through his nose as he shifted the car into drive. We sat in silence the rest of the ride. Bodhi simmered in his anger, and I continued to shatter in silence. By the time our house came into view, I was now heavily bleeding from the broken pieces within me.

Bodhi parked and cut the engine. "Kinsley and Kolby are with their family," he said flatly. "I had to leave to come get you."

Guilt twisted at my stomach, which only made the bleeding worse. After he was done saying that, he opened the door and slammed it shut as he headed toward the front door.

Bodhi had never been this angry with me before, and that was how I knew I'd messed up.

He hated me as much as I hated myself.

33

Silas

I let the shower run longer than it should, focusing on the scalding heat burning my skin. The air around me was thick, but I barely noticed. I was too busy yelling at myself. My hands braced against the wall in front of me as I stood there. I'd been in this same position for a while, not wanting to move. I just couldn't make myself...because the second I stepped out of this shower, I *had* to tell her.

I had convinced myself to wait. First, it was because I didn't want to ruin the simple happiness that a measly pile of fries gave her. Then, I didn't want her to feel trapped in the car. Now, we both had opened up and—I couldn't wait any longer. It wasn't fair to her.

But how the hell was I supposed to tell her the truth?

Dragging my hands down my face, I pushed away from the wall and shut the water off. As the bathroom fell silent, so did my mind. The only sound was the faint drip of water hitting the tile. With each drop, I pieced together one more word of what the conversation would be. As I grabbed the towel from the rack and dried off slowly, my mind was still trying to figure it out.

There was no good way to tell someone their privacy had been ripped away from them.

There was no gentle version of that kind of heartbreak.

I pulled on clean clothes, dragging a shirt over my head, fingers slower than usual. When I stepped into the hallway, I tamped down everything to focus on her. "Ember?"

No response.

As I turned toward the kitchen, I realized it was empty. So were the living room and the bedrooms. Opening the back door, I called outside. "Ember?"

Still nothing, which caused a strange tension to spread inside me.

When I stepped back into the kitchen, the first thing I noticed was the floor. Water pooled across the wood, and a bottle had cracked open. My gaze snapped to the counter and onto my phone, where the screen was open and *glowing.*

I stopped breathing altogether when I saw the screen.

The background was toggled between the call log and my folder on her, with a video paused. My mind instantly locked me out with panic because she saw it—she watched *everything.*

"Fuck!" I screamed, grabbing everything within my reach and throwing it to the ground. Shards of glass exploded around me, but I kept going until I felt a fraction of the anger dissipate. It was only when I looked across the room and saw the photo of me and my brothers, that I stopped.

What the fuck am I supposed to do now, guys?

Not *only* was she gone, but she left without me explaining

everything to her, which made it all *so* much worse. I was the man who kidnapped her, who watched her, who kept a folder full of that footage. *She's going to think it's me in the videos.* My grip tightened around the phone as I stared down at the mess around me.

I had to find her, to explain. She needed to know the truth before she got hurt. Before—

The phone suddenly vibrated in my hand. The caller ID showed Knox, which caused my blood pressure to spike to dangerous heights. "*Please* tell me you got him."

"Yes. I couldn't do it using face recognition in the database, but I got a match from the ring he's wearing. You can see it in the video on his hand, a championship ring from last year. *Football.* The emblem is for the quarterback—I double checked that information with the tracker you found. The necklace was registered as a gift and labeled under a woman named Kinsley."

I bit down on my tongue so hard I tasted blood.

That Mother Fucker.

It was her "brother," the quarterback.

"Do you want me to call the police?"

"No," I ground out, my voice radiating with rage. "I got it."

For a few seconds, everything in my brain went black. I forced myself to inhale as the wrath living in my chest begged for escape.

The fucking quarterback.

As Knox ended the call, I stared down at my phone and the call log that was now displayed on my screen. Blinking through my red vision, I looked at the numbers listed at the top. There had been calls made *this* morning, while I was in the shower. Kinsley's name hung there, now a permanent contact, but that was not what my eyes snagged on. Above Kinsley's timestamp was another number, the last one on my outgoing call list.

If Kinsley hadn't answered, she would have called someone else for help. I ran for my keys when I realized it wasn't Kolby, that number I had looked up after going through her texts.

"FUCK," I yelled out again, running to my car.

Ember had called Bodhi, thinking *he* would be the one to save her from *me.*

34

Ember

Bodhi walked straight inside, without saying anything else to me.

I figured it was best for both of us to take a few minutes before I followed him in, considering we were both dealing with strong emotions. I understood his frustration and where he was coming from, I knew it was because he cared. Unfortunately, I was still trying to cope with what I'd just learned about myself. *Something that I couldn't just outright tell him, at least not yet.* I stood in the entryway for a few minutes, staring into the darkness as I willed it to swallow me, just so I would stop feeling for a little while.

When I finally stepped inside, I could tell Bodhi had moved into the kitchen. Soft golden light spilled out, stretching across the floor in a warm rectangle. I kept my eyes on it as I slipped my shoes off and walked toward him, my body moving automatically even though my mind was still somewhere else.

As I walked under the light, I heard the faintest clink of a metal pan, and that was when the smell hit me—*Chai.* Even though he was upset, he was still making me my favorite drink. I watched him work from the doorframe as he stood at the

kitchen counter with his back to me. He poured the contents of the pan into two mugs that sat on the counter in front of him.

Taking a few steps, the floor creaked under my weight. Bodhi glanced up and over his shoulder at me. The second he saw me, the tension in his posture disappeared and he turned toward me with both cups in hand. I could still see the anger and agitation within him, but it was softer now. His eyes searched my face as he held one of the cups toward me. "Want some?"

A smile draped over my face as I walked toward him, taking the cup. My hands wrapped around the mug, welcoming the familiarity. "Thanks," I murmured.

The steam from my cup curled upward between us as Bodhi watched me take a sip. As soon as I swallowed, he cleared his throat once and started to speak. "I'm sorry." I looked up at him over the ceramic rim as he continued. "I shouldn't have snapped earlier." He rubbed the back of his neck as his eyes roamed over me and then dropped briefly to the counter. "I was just scared."

The moment those words left his mouth, my heart hurt and I set my cup down to reach out for him. "I was fine, I promise. I'm sorry."

For a second, it looked like he might say something else, but he pulled me into a hug instead. "You left in the middle of the night and all we got was a text. I would have appreciated a call to hear your voice, to make sure you were alive." His arms wrapped around me tightly, a solid and familiar feeling—safe in a way that made my throat ache because *apparently*, I didn't know what that word meant.

I let my forehead rest against his shoulder.

"I love you, Em. You know that, right?" he murmured into my hair as his hand started to soothe me, moving up and down across my back.

I closed my eyes, taking a deep breath. "I know," I whispered again, debating if I should tell him everything or maybe ask him to help me go to the police station. *But what would happen? Him killing Silas? Us going to court?*

We stood together like that for a few quiet seconds while the warmth of the chai spread through my chest. Eventually, Bodhi pulled back, his hands settling on my shoulders. "You look exhausted," he stated, studying my face. "Why don't you try to get some sleep?"

Sleep.

The word alone made me want to run in the opposite direction, but I nodded anyway. "Yeah, okay."

Taking the last swig from my mug, I stood, turning toward the hallway. Each step toward my room felt like I was walking a plank to my death. I didn't want to go in there. I didn't want to be in that room *at all.* Standing at the half-open door, I saw my bed exactly how I'd left it. My blankets still slightly rumpled, and one corner hung loose over the side. Suddenly, I couldn't stop seeing it, me asleep under the sheets while someone stood above me, beside me, or behind me—using me.

Pushing open the door, I continued to stare at my bed like it had personally betrayed me somehow. I wanted to walk back to the kitchen, grab a butcher knife and shred it into tiny pieces.

I stepped into the room instead, quickly moving to the edge of the mattress. Yanking the blanket off, I ripped it in one angry motion. The sheets followed, along with the pillows. Everything came off as I pulled all pieces of my bedding free, ripping them before throwing them to the floor in a messy heap. The mattress was now naked, staring back at me, bare and accusing.

My room felt too small now, the space taken by something I never offered to give.

I sank down onto the edge of the bed and let everything hit me. The anger was first, then anxiety and regret, *everything.* Quiet sobs escaped me as my mind started to process everything. Bending forward, I gripped my hair with my hands as I balanced my elbows on my knees. Another round of involuntary sounds left me, followed by a massive body quake, making my arms unstable. Tears began to blur everything as I cried so hard the edges of the room softened in my vision.

After a few more large body tremors passed, I tried to steady my breathing, but it still came out broken. Forcing myself to stand, I felt my head grow fuzzy from the hyperventilating. I inhaled deeply, but just as I did, my knees threatened to buckle underneath me. The feeling spread from my legs and moved through my torso. Urging my limbs to move, I fought against the fact they felt like steel weights. Trying to gain my balance, another wave of fuzziness clouded my mind.

Something wasn't right.

The room began to spin slowly as I fell back onto the stripped mattress behind me. Every single part of my body now too heavy to move, like each area was filled with sand. The emotional pain that had infiltrated my chest just moments ago, the one that had set my veins on fire, was gone—now, in its place, was an overall numbing sensation. I started to battle against my eyelids, forcing them to stay open. My body no longer wanted to stay upright, and even though I was screaming for control, my shoulders started to sway back and forth. Consciously, I was very much awake, doing everything I could to wake my body up. But physically? Everything refused to listen, like it had no choice but to shut down.

I continued fighting with everything I had, but eventually, I couldn't keep myself up any longer, and my back hit the bed. I'd lost control over my neck as well, my head falling to the side. Now facing the door to my bedroom, I see him standing in the frame. Bodhi—or at least I thought it was, because this man seemed like a totally different person from the one I knew. The smile covering his face was the definition of pure corruption, and his eyes were now blank, as if there was no emotion behind them.

This person, whoever it was, stood watching me with a large smile as every last drop of feeling drained from my body. With his hands in the pockets of the hoodie he was wearing, his stature was so casual, like this was something he watched all the time. The position he was in made it seem like everything was normal, and we were having an average conversation.

After waiting a few more seconds, he moved forward and

pushed the door completely open with his foot. Stopping when he landed directly in front of me, he crouched down. His eyes rested on my lips as his hand lifted to trace the side of my face. Pushing a lock of hair behind my ear, he clicked his tongue a few times as if in appreciation. "I know it typically takes a full fifteen minutes, but I couldn't wait any longer."

I forced my mind to process his words, to take in exactly what he'd said. Through my sluggish thoughts, I understood. He wasn't just a roommate or my "friend." He was the predator. He was the guy from the video, the person who'd been violating me repeatedly—*not* Silas.

Bodhi had been the person I needed to stay away from, *and I called him.*

I couldn't scream. I couldn't fight back. I couldn't do a damn thing except let a single tear fall down my cheek—the last attempt of refusal from my body as I was shut inside of it. His voice carried on around me as he ignored the fact I was now paralyzed. "All this time, I've been the perfect brother figure, the protector—the one who stayed right next to you. You have no idea what it was like for me, Ember."

I felt a light pressure on my chest, then the feeling moved as something trailed against my collarbone. For a moment, I couldn't feel it anymore until his voice cracked with something raw and he kept talking.

"I was always right here."

My head was hammering with how much I was screaming inside, but to him on the outside, I looked like a lifeless doll—the same unconscious toy he had played with before.

I wished I could go to sleep. I wished I could do anything not to have to experience this. Most of all, I wished I'd never left Silas.

There was a tug on my shirt as it was lifted above my head. "You think it felt nice for me to have to fuck Kinsley all these years, pretending it was you?" His cold hands cupped my chest and then tugged, too hard. "You should be proud of me. I've been so fucking patient, Ember. You have no idea."

I tried to force my thoughts away, to make them retreat as his hand moved to my sweatpants and pulled them down. I tried to visualize Silas, to convince myself it was him touching me. I did everything in my power to prepare myself as his hands moved up and down my legs.

Just as I thought he was done talking, he spoke again. This time, his voice was full of anger and resentment. "I haven't even truly felt *you* yet. Did you know that?"

The sound of shoes being kicked off and a belt buckle rang in my ears. "I was too busy learning about what you like," he said quietly as my legs were aggressively pulled apart, "and how to make your chai lattes." I felt weight on me then, just as hot breath fanned over my neck. "How to drug them just right so I could play," he whispered, kissing behind my ear.

I was so completely and entirely numb inside and out.

There was no other way to explain how I felt.

"I tasted you. I took pictures. I recorded the way you look when you're nice and plump."

Instead of listening to him, I forced myself into the best place I could find in my mind, somewhere I could stay until this was over.

"Now I get to finally fucking feel it," he muttered into my ear as one hand started stroking my hair. The moment he kissed my cheek and pushed my legs up, I disassociated completely.

35

SILAS

Swerving into the driveway, I barely put the car in park before I was out of it. There was no time for anything besides getting to Ember. They had come home, *together*, and too much time had already passed.

Every second was another deep stab into my chest, and I knew the pain wouldn't subside until I saw her and made sure she was okay. With one kick, I slammed my foot into the front door, forcing it to crack off its hinges. The sound instantly rippled through the house like thunder, and I hoped that he heard it. That sound wasn't just a warning—*it was his death call.*

I ran straight down the hallway and into her room, where the door was already open. As I entered, a savage growl ripped from my chest at the scene in front of me. He was on top of her naked body, lining himself up to her opening. She was clearly limp underneath, completely unresponsive.

This would be the last fucking time he touched her.

Everything in my line of sight went haywire as I launched forward, tackling Bodhi off her. We crashed to the floor, and I pinned him down, each of my movements turning absolutely lethal. There was no choice in the matter. He didn't get to walk

away from this. He was going to die by *my* hands. That single thought was on repeat as my fist made contact with his face, the crack not nearly as satisfying as I thought it would be. In a defensive move, he brought his elbow up, trying and create room to protect himself. I fought through it, getting two more solid hits in before he landed one on me. I was knocked off, giving him time to grab his pants.

It didn't matter what he was wearing. By the time I was done with him, he wouldn't be able to use anything, *ever again.*

We continued to wrestle, crashing into the furniture and ultimately knocking over her vanity. "You think you will have the ability to change anything. She's already ruined." Bodhi sneered up at me, spitting blood in my face.

Absolutely the fuck not, was he allowed to talk about her like that.

The air in my lungs froze as the thought of murder invaded my whole body. It was no longer just a thought in my mind. It was now a challenge I needed to complete as fast as possible.

"I'm going to fucking kill you."

Bodhi focused in as my words cut through the room like a blade. A new type of rage flared in his eyes as they narrowed. Lunging at me, his hands went straight for my throat. I dodged, but he guessed at the direction, digging his fingers into my flesh. For a moment, his grip tightened and stars threatened my vision. Moving quickly, I slipped my knee up and knocked him off balance.

With as much brutal force as I could muster, I slammed

myself down on him. My fists moved like clockwork, pounding again and again against his face.

One.

Two.

Three.

I lost count once blood started to splatter on me. The warmth hit my face as Bodhi tried to do what he could to stop me. There was no chance of that happening, not now that he was in my grasp. The sound of his pained grunts mixed with the thud of flesh on flesh, and soon, there was only silence.

At some point, I realized Bodhi was no longer fighting back, but I kept going. I hit him for every photo there was, and then for every video Ember would have to watch. Drowning myself in her rage, I couldn't stop.

By the time I pulled away, his face had been completely pulverized and there was not one recognizable thing about him. The blood covering me was proof that I'd accomplished my goal, that Ember was now completely safe from him.

An unfamiliar scream pulled me away from my thoughts. I turned, moving off of Bodhi's corpse.

Kinsley stood in the doorway, her face etched in a mask of horror. As her eyes tracked over what was left of Bodhi, mine moved to Ember, who was still on the bed. Kinsley didn't even acknowledge her naked body. Her whole focus was on the man on the floor behind me. When I moved out of the way, she jolted forward and dropped to her knees beside him. Her voice was a mixture of utter shock and suppressed wails.

"Oh my god! What did you do to him?!" she screamed, over and over. "You killed him! You fucking killed him!"

I moved closer to Ember as I started to feel the places on my own body that took a beating. My eye was definitely blackened, and blood dripped from my nose. Ignoring both that and Kinsley, I moved to the bed and focused on my girl. Grabbing her clothes off the ground, I put them back on her, wincing as my shoulder protested. I didn't stop until her body was completely covered.

Kinsley's volume had now maxed out, and the fact she hadn't even noticed Ember pushed me over the edge. I screamed at her, thickening my voice with venom. "As much as I don't want to, I understand that you are probably a victim in this as well. But the truth is, *you* are as much at fault for what's happened to her."

Kinsley's face crumpled as realization crashed in. A fresh sob making its way out as she forced words into a question. "Wh-Why were her clothes off?"

I shook my head at her. "You don't get to ask fucking questions," I snapped. "Not until you understand the damage of what you and that pathetic piece of shit have done. This is something that she will now have to carry for the rest of her life because you *thought* you knew him. If you choose to call the police over this, just remember that you'll have to explain to them what kind of a man he was. You'll have to admit you loved a rapist. If you're smart, you'll do both of us a favor and use whatever money you can access to clean this up. After that, plan to stay out of her life *forever.*"

Kinsley looked from Ember to Bodhi and then threw her body over his, clearly making her choice. Picking Ember up and ignoring everything else around me, I carried her through the carnage and straight to my car. I had to fight myself to physically let her go, even though I knew it was just to lay her in the seat next to me. That feeling stayed with me as we drove away. I kept looking over at her every few seconds, as if she'd disappear.

Activating the speakers through my phone, I called my brother.

"Hey."

"Greyson," I said, trying to keep my voice low. "I need you to go to Ember's place for me and grab everything from one room. It's the one with a stripped bed. Don't ask questions to anyone there. Just go in, find the tan room, and grab everything you see of hers. Clothes, bags, photos, all of it. Bring it to my house when I ask for it. There's a body there and a woman with it. Ask if she needs help disposing of it. If she's not there, feel free to light the place on fire."

There was no hesitation from him. "Give me 45 minutes."

Ending the call with a click, I sat in the stillness. Looking down, I eyed my hands that not only had blood but pieces of tissue on them.

Will she let me hold her with them? Or will she run for good?

Glancing over at Ember, my eyes lingered on her frame and then her face. I hated how fragile she looked. She was nothing close to that word. She was the *farthest* thing from it. With every rise and fall of her chest, my haze lifted. A few more in, and I finally let myself breathe. As oxygen flooded me, so did a unique sense of clarity.

There was not a goddamn thing in this world that would ever touch her again. I would make sure of it.

When I pulled up to the house, I let the car run for a few minutes as I sat there looking down at the blood that covered me. Almost transfixed, my eyes followed the drips that fell down onto my seat and floor. Watching as it puddled, I'm reassured that there wasn't anything I wouldn't do for that woman next to me. My eyes stayed glued to the crimson color as I dialed another number, the only person I knew that had any kind of medical experience. The ringing pulled my thoughts back to reality and I looked over at her, just as Kyrin answered.

"What's up? I'm in the middle of my break and I—"

"She was drugged Kyrin. I need to know what to do to help her. She's asleep." The panic was definitely there—even I can hear the way it's laced into my voice, despite my best efforts to keep it hidden.

"Fuck man, hold on." There's some shuffling as he moves to a quieter area. "Okay, depending on what she was given and the dosage, it can be anywhere from two to three hours before she wakes up. Watch her closely. If it goes much past that, you'll have to administer an IV of reversal agents."

When I answered him, I'm pissed off at my own words. "I don't have the things needed to do that."

"It's a simple IV starter kit. I can bring one now if you want it, but her body will need time to process through whatever drug is in her system. What the fuck happened man?"

I don't have any desire to answer that question, especially when it's not my story to tell. "I'll call if she doesn't improve. Keep your phone on, yeah?"

"Yeah," is all he says before the line disconnects.

Taking a deep breath, I pushed open the door and made my way around the car to get Ember. Once it's opened, she's cradled against my chest. The blood instantly smeared over her skin, but I didn't even think about that. His blood didn't matter, just like his death didn't matter—*only she did.*

Once inside, I moved straight to my room and placed her on my bed. I trusted Kyrin and his knowledge, which meant I didn't need to worry about triggering her right now. By the time she woke up, we wouldn't be anywhere near a bedroom, not until she could handle that. Carefully, I stripped her down and replaced her clothes with clean ones of my own—the ones she would always belong in. Tucking her into my comforter, I moved to the bathroom and positioned myself so I had full sight of her. Quickly stripping out of my shirt and pants, I stepped into the shower and scrubbed my skin as I counted her breaths. Her chest rose a total of sixteen times by the time the water was running clear. By then, most of the blood had washed down the drain and I worked on washing everything else away. As soon as I was done, I was out and dressed beside her.

I sat next to her on the mattress and straightened my back against the headboard. Moving my hand over hers, I gently grazed my thumb along the skin on her knuckles. I knew that the only answer was to wait, to sit in this silence until she was back with me. As a last ditch effort to calm myself, I started talking.

"About a year after my mom died, Greyson got really sick. We thought he had caught some weird stomach flu but Kyrin researched the symptoms when they got worse. He was convinced Greyson was severely dehydrated. After working a double, I came home and figured out rather quickly that Kyrin had taught himself how to administer an IV. I don't even know where he had gotten the supplies, but it was one of the first times I had seen him actually be serious about something. After another hour, Greyson had stopped vomiting and was able to hold down water. Kyrin slept in his room that night." I took another breath and held her limp hand, letting my mind move to another memory. "That year on Easter, Greyson found a chocolate bunny in the freezer. He tried to cut it, and the knife ripped into his thumb. That was the month that Kyrin learned how to stitch. It wasn't long after that, I figured out he was volunteering a few hours at a hospital to swipe their supplies—all because we had no health insurance. I made him promise to stop and found another job that offered benefits." On the end of that sentence, a small uncomfortable laugh escaped me. I paused my story when I realized she still had the inept ability to make me open up, even unconscious.

For the next little while, I just continued talking. I started with my childhood and went from there. I reached for every piece I could of myself and offered it to her. Even if she didn't hear, even if she didn't remember, I wasn't going to let her be the only one that felt uncomfortable. I talked until I'd carved myself out for her. Every fear, every dream, every thought I've had——including the ones I originally had about her. Once I finished, I just sat with her, tracing her fingers.

Soon, an hour and a half passed and my phone vibrated with a text from Kyrin.

Any updates?

I went to type my response when I felt it, her hand giving a slight flinch. In my head I thanked her, relieved I wouldn't have to kick my brothers ass for poking her with needles.

Quickly typing the reply, I thanked him for checking in and then wrapped my arms around her body. I carried her the fifty feet to my couch and laid her down as I walked back to the kitchen. Grabbing some washcloths and a bowl of cold water, I returned to her side and dropped to my knees. Dipping one of the cloths into the bowl, I rung it out and began to move the material over her skin. I started slowly at first, doing what I could to bring her back to me. Repeating the process in different areas, I encouraged her to wake up the only way I could. When I finished with the skin on her arms, I then transferred to her neck and chest. After about twenty minutes of this, she started to stir more. Eventually, she opened her eyes. Blinking a few times, she clearly tried to pull herself from the depths. Before I could stop her, she attempted to move off the couch, but her body denied her. I was right there, though, grabbing her elbow for added stability as she tried to hold her own weight. Fear clouded her eyes as she focused her attention on me.

"Bodhi-" she said as she lifted her hand to her head and winced.

I cut her off before she could finish. "He's dead."

Blinking at me, she nodded as she looked around. Her eyes went in and out of focus as she mouthed a word in response to me. I couldn't hear exactly what she said, but I guessed the word from how her mouth was angled.

Good.

"He can't touch you ever again," I said, moving my hand from her elbow to her waist. I readied myself for her to pull away from me and my touch, but she instantly moved toward me instead. Her hands shook as they clutched around my biceps. I gave her a second to adjust before offering to pull her in. When she didn't deny me, I let my arms lock around her with one of my hands cupped protectively over the back of her head.

The moment my arms closed around her, she completely shattered. Each fragment of her, carved into different parts of my body. I refused to budge. I just absorbed them all as I tightened my grip on her. I didn't mind sharing the pain, not when every single shard of her beautifully broken soul was mine. I would happily hold on to them until she was ready to reclaim them.

Neither of us said anything as I held her. In fact, there was no emotion whatsoever. As her silent tears fell, Ember just stared into the space in front of her, completely in shock. At first, I thought that maybe this might be a good thing, like the stillness between us could undo the damage that had happened.

As that thought crossed my mind, her body started to spasm. One by one, the muscles along her arms tensed and then released, causing her to shake violently. I pulled back just enough to see her. There was nothing I could do to help her besides just be here. Even with the adrenaline fading, she wasn't fully here with me yet.

I swallowed the apology that crawled up my throat. It would be selfish to say right now—to make this moment about my guilt when she couldn't even unravel herself properly. This was just the first step. Her brain hadn't processed anything because it was still trying to protect her.

The quakes intensified as her body released more adrenaline, and soon, the shaking in her arms turned into whole body convulsions. I watched it all as she suffered in silence. There was no sound coming from her other than her teeth chattering together.

I didn't say anything, I just sat patiently and waited with her through it. The only time I touched her was when I intertwined my hand with hers. We sat there well after midnight, when she finally gave into sleep. Only after that, did I finally take out my phone and send a text to Greyson, telling him to bring her things over. With one quick reply, he informed me he was on his way with a total of seven garbage bags full of her belongings.

Seven bags, that was it. That was everything she now owned.

I waited next to Ember for him as she slept, convincing

myself it was better if I didn't touch her—regardless of how bad I wanted too. I just observed her small movements until a sound from my pocket alerted me that he'd arrived. Shifting her slightly, I moved to the door and found Greyson standing there.

Red drawstrings were wrapped around both of his hands, the ties cutting into his skin from the weight of the bags. Attached to the ties were two gigantic white sacks that were filled to the brim with clothing. Three more lay at his feet, each one tied closed. Just looking at the outside, I could tell one was bedding but the others seemed to be a combination of items. He threw a nod back as he lifted the bags off the ground. "There's two more in the truck."

Bending to grab the ones at his feet, he met my eyes for a brief second before they zeroed in behind me. "Kyrin called me on the way over here, told me to check in on her. Is she okay now?"

I followed his gaze and looked over my shoulder for a brief second before I moved to grab the bags. "She will be."

I froze as my hand touched the plastic. I didn't want her to have any of this. *I didn't want her around it.* I wanted to give her a complete fresh start, where she wouldn't have to think about anything attached to her past.

Greyson must've had a similar thought process, because as he finished unloading the bags, he went back to his truck for one more thing. When he handed it to me, I couldn't help but gawk down at the *empty* red gas can.

"There was no woman when I got there, but there was a

body. The house had been rummaged through, like maybe she had packed her shit and ran." He shrugged then, as if it was just a random Tuesday. "It doesn't matter now, I made it look like it was the dead guy."

It took me a second to process that information. Because of him and whatever screws were loose in his head, some of the leftover strings that Ember would have had to deal with had quite literally been burned away. "Thank you."

He nodded once before looking past me at Ember, who was still sleeping. "Just take care of her, yeah?"

That was no longer a question to me. "Yeah."

He shoved into me then, pushing inside to drop the bags. "Hopefully, she makes you nicer. You can be kind of an ass-hole."

36

Ember

Trauma.

A word I used to make fun of. One I thought people used as an excuse.

Turns out, it affects *every* part of you. Not just your mind, but your reality as well, blurring everything together right in front of your eyes. Not in the dramatic way either, the way that sometimes came across in movies. There was no slow motion and no sudden clarity—everything had been layered between dense fog and sudden spikes in anxiety.

At least, that's how it was for me.

I would think I was okay, and I didn't have to remind myself to breathe. I could sit with Silas on his couch and let him hold my hand without wanting to rip it away. The next second, I would freeze up because I couldn't stand the thought of being touched. *I felt crazy.* Especially because in those moments where I sensed myself shift, it was due to my own inner voice—a new one, one that told me I was unworthy of him.

Sometimes there was just silence, and that voice didn't exist. When that happened, I found myself hollow, which pissed me off even more. I wanted to *feel.* I wanted to *move on.* I

wanted to be *myself* again, but it was like something was there, stopping me—like I was locked out of my mind and I didn't have control. That was the only way to describe it...a thick wall of numbness that had settled into my body and refused to leave. Everything on the inside of the wall felt heavy, weighed down with questions I'd never get answers to.

How did I not know that was happening?

How long did it go on for?

Am I the one to blame?

Some questions were answered instantly, starting with the day Silas saved me. I only remembered so much, but I had been aware enough to listen for a while as Silas took care of me. I heard him say Bodhi was dead, and I knew that Greyson had helped. It was after *that,* where my body had finally went to sleep.

Eventually, I figured out some more things. The necklace I had worn, the one I thought was from Kolby, had been from Bodhi—another way he had manipulated us all. We also knew that Kinsley chose to cover up the murder and not call the police, seeing how we had no one show up. I'm plagued by what I still don't know. I've tried to force myself to openly talk about things, but I don't think I'm ready, at least not yet.

A week slowly passed, and the haze in my mind started to clear. I still felt like I was fighting against the same thick wall but now, I could at least be present and hear those around me. I hadn't noticed right away, but every day one of Silas's brothers would bring us food and give him updates on the club.

I began to look forward to them coming. When I found myself surrounded by them, I felt like the wall was starting to crack and I actually had a chance of removing it.

Today when the knock came, I was the one who opened the door. I expected it to be Greyson with some type of pasta, but instead, I found a detective standing on the porch. The moment I registered the badge, my face paled and my hand dropped to my side.

"Good afternoon, Miss Vale, I need to ask you some questions about Bodhi Williams."

I made eye contact for about ten seconds. After that, the very little amount of my soul that I had regained, locked away again.

Bodhi.

The name triggered a response in my body I couldn't fight off. I watched as the detective's mouth moved more, but the words slid past me like rain on glass. No matter how much I fought for control over my mind, my brain just went on autopilot. I felt something this time though, as I was thrown into mental darkness again—a faint glimpse of emotion, of my old fire.

Hearing that name out loud made me remember what it was like to be angry.

Luckily, Silas approached and could immediately tell something was off. Without me saying anything about who was at the door, I felt his eyes lock on to the stranger. His energy becoming palpable, coming off in waves as he stepped forward to protect me without even knowing who I was facing. I turned my neck slightly, just to witness him and the force he was. With his arms crossed over his chest, he looked down at the officer in front of us. There was no surprise on his face. With both shoulders straight, and his voice controlled in a way that almost sounded like he'd expected this. "What about him?"

The officer looked between us before addressing Silas's question. "He seems to have gone missing, and you are an emergency contact. Have you seen him lately?"

I shook my head slowly and pretended to think about it.

The detective across from me eyed Silas before raising his eyebrows in question. "Were you aware of the fire that took place at his residence?"

His residence?

I felt Silas's hand move to my lower back, a silent reassurance that it was all going to be okay. I focused on the warmth of his skin as I ended the conversation. Siphoning strength from him, I looked directly at the officer, "I have no idea why I would be his contact. I don't know where he is, and frankly I don't care." Surprisingly, my voice sounded a lot like *me*—the girl who went missing when Bodhi did. Silas apparently agreed, by the way his hand patted my back in approval.

The detective briefly glanced up toward me and I forced a smile, solidifying my statement.

"I understand. If anything else is needed, I will call."

I watched as the officer retreated to his patrol car that was parked across the street. I could feel Silas's eyes on me as he waited to see how I'd react. "Did he say *his* residence?"

Silas answered as we watched the car drive away, "I have a cousin that's good with stuff like that. He wiped your name from the lease and fixed some other paperwork with your name on it."

I shifted toward Silas, realizing that was probably how he had the videos of me. "Good with *what* stuff?"

Silas leaned in to wrap his arm around me, pausing to make sure it was okay. When I nodded, he pulled me close, talking into the top of my head before kissing it. "Stuff that help keep you safe."

When I looked up at him, I saw just how exhausted he was. His fatigue was not only external. I saw it in his shoulders and in the lines of his face. The more I looked at him, the more I realized that he had drained himself. "Have you been sleeping?" The only response I got was when the corner of his mouth tugged up as he grinned at me. A slight pain ran through my heart when I realized how forced the gesture was. I missed seeing his genuine smile. *I missed him.*

Another flare of something erupted inside of me, and I was angry again. How dare one person think they had the power to take away other people's happiness. I didn't deserve that, and neither did Silas. He had done nothing but be patient with me. He had also given me all the time I needed, extending his time off work to just sit next to me in shared silence. Not once had he tried to make me speak or do anything that would upset me. In fact, every physical interaction we'd had, he waited to be given some kind of permission. Even though he was not the one to do this damage, he was the one repairing it—staying hyperaware of how things could affect me. The words were out of my mouth before my brain had time to stop them. "Thank you."

His eyes widened so fast I thought I'd imagined it, but then they softened, along with his face. I barely heard the words he mumbled as he exhaled. "Don't do that."

I swallowed, pulling at the strings inside of me, the ones I'd recently contemplated hanging myself with. "Thank you for everything you've done for me." My lips trembled as I pushed out the next words. "And really, I'm just sorry about everything. I don't want you to feel responsible for healing me."

Even I could hear it, how fragile those words came out. As he listened, he pulled away, looking down at me—his eyes completely widened with disbelief. After a few seconds, he frowned before slowly exhaling and closing the door behind him. When he looked back toward me, I was scared of the look on his face. There were so many things he could say. My fingers moved anxiously, fiddling with what nails I had left. This was our first real conversation about what happened and I knew I needed to apologize more. I needed him to hear everything I had to say. "I'm sorry for leaving," I whispered. "For not asking you about the videos and for not staying long enough to talk." A new emotion forced through the wall that kept me excluded from him—*guilt.* I was overcome by the sheer strength of it, but I continued, "I was scared. I didn't know that he—"

"Stop." The word cracked in the air along with his voice as his hands wrapped around me, pulling me into his chest. "Please just stop, baby."

I closed my eyes and focused on the feeling he gave me. The ease he brought wasn't something I'd ever learned about, nor could I define it. The comfort he offered by just being him made me feel like anything could happen and I would be okay. As long as his arms were around me, just like this—*we* would be okay.

After a few seconds, he pulled back and our eyes met. The bright blue staring back at me was flooded with tears. My chest tightened at the sight, at what was happening to him. He shook his head slowly at me, making sure I was fully aware that he didn't want any more words. The movement of his head caused a few to fall onto his cheeks and I just watched them as they trailed down his skin.

He went to open his mouth but stopped. The words didn't come until he tried again a few seconds later. "I don't ever want to hear you say that again." He moved his hands to my cheeks and brought his mouth to my forehead, kissing the skin there. I could feel more tears fall as he spoke. "*I'm* sorry, Ember. I'm sorry I didn't get to you fast enough. I'm sorry I didn't know you sooner. I'm sorry that you waited so long for me to find you."

When he pulled away to look down at me, the intensity was so raw. The prison my mind had been forced into, started to crumble. The wall came down first—the one I had been stuck behind. I could see everything clearly now. *I could feel everything.* As the pieces crashed down around me, his voice became louder, drowning out all the others I had recently battled.

"Don't you dare apologize to me. *Ever.*" Silas leaned in yet again asking for my permission before his lips softly touch mine. "This will be the only lifetime I let this happen to you. In all our others, I promise I will find you faster."

I nodded into him, feeling my own face wet from the emotions I'd buried.

As his lips moved against mine, his words came out as a whisper. "I'll just follow that god-awful yellow color every time, until I get to you."

A sound much like a laugh escaped me, but I was surprised at how alive it sounded, and it was all because of him. That sound meant Bodhi didn't win and I hadn't been carved out hollow like I'd thought. There was still hope, so I swallowed hard, grabbing onto it with both hands. "You still want me? Even after—"

Before I could finish, he hoisted me into his arms, pulling my legs around him. The movement jarred me enough that I stopped talking. Turning us, he placed my back against the door, so I was supported, but there was still the slightest amount of space between us.

"Ember," he said firmly, his grip tightening around the backs of my thighs, "I will *always* want you." He smiled, and this time, it felt real. "I think I get it now, why everything happened in both our lives. I was put here for you," he said quietly. "That fire you have? The one that makes you loud and stubborn and impossible to control?"

A faint spark flickered inside me, the same one I'd felt over the last few days. I grabbed it, refusing to let go as he beathed life back into it.

"I'm not letting anyone take that from you. *Ever.* It's my job to keep it lit."

37

SILAS

Just over two weeks had passed, and Ember was starting to come back. Little by little, I watched as she rebuilt herself and started to thrive in our life together. Each step she took forward was not just her simply stitching the broken parts of herself but welding the pieces I offered her into place. Each day that passed hardened her fragility, until the woman standing before me wasn't just healed—she was forged into something far more resilient than she ever was before.

If you asked me at the beginning if I even thought this was possible, I would have laughed. Not because I doubted her, but because it took some people an entire lifetime to recover from things like this. Turns out, my girl's fire had room to grow.

When I first brought her home, I thought there wasn't going to be a chance in hell of getting her back fully—at least, not for a long time. But just a few days in, she'd opened up to me, allowing me to be part of this process with her. What started as an apology turned into me proving I wasn't going anywhere, and we've taken it day by day since.

Considering the events that unfolded were enough to rewire *anyone's* brain, I waited for the days where she might regress,

but this woman, this goddamn goddess, had yet to yield.

At first, we spent a lot of time just existing in each other's silence. I felt it often, how the quiet would turn against her. Every particle of the air surrounding us would go stale, and she would stiffen. When those moments crept in and I saw her slipping into her own head, I did everything I could to pull her back out of it. I talked about anything that came to mind—stories about my brothers and the stupid things we did growing up, like the time I duct-taped them to the wall. I rambled about my plans for the club, about the future I wanted to build for us. When she needed it most, when the quiet became the loudest, I told her how I felt about her.

Each time that conversation came up, I wished there was a better way to explain things. There was no word that described my connection to her. Every emotion felt too small, too soft for something that had rooted itself so deeply inside me. Having her in my life wasn't just something I wanted—it felt vital, like the breath in my lungs.

It was during these specific talks she made me realize that I'd never truly lived before her. I simply wandered around a black-and-white world, refusing to see the color. I think something inside me died when my mother did, and it was only after Ember found me that I started to notice it. Somewhere along the way, without me even realizing it, she became the reason I looked forward to the idle moments. The times when I could just sit, feel her skin and be in her presence. Those moments became pivotal to her recovery, and as time went on, I realized just how important they were to me too. They gave me purpose. *She* gave me purpose. Every chance I was given to help her helped heal a small part of me.

This became our routine, at least for a little while. Soon, I felt comfortable taking phone calls about the club without worrying about her. On days I needed to attend meetings or go over numbers, I grabbed the blankets from our bed and made a little nest on the floor next to my chair. She seemed content with that, and it became our daily thing. I'd load her up with a variety of snacks, along with different books, and she'd snuggle into the blankets around her. At times, I wished it could be *me* giving her that comfort in our bed, but little things like this made her happy.

After my meetings ended for the day, I looked down at her. "How does a shower sound?"

Tilting her head back and forth, she considered the thought before pulling the blanket from around her to stand. Walking toward my bathroom, she looked back over her shoulder once at me before turning the corner. Shaking my head, I heard her yell, "You coming or what?"

I stiffened at the offer before answering. "Are you sure you need help?"

A mess of brown hair popped out from around the corner along with a very naked collarbone. "Well, I need you. So..."

I stood from my chair faster than I probably should have, and she squealed before moving back toward the bathroom. Against my better judgement, I followed her.

By the time I opened the door, she had the water running and was standing next to the shower, waiting for me. There was a towel wrapped around her, and from what I could tell, her body seemed tense.

Closing the door, I looked over at her. "Are you sure?"

Nodding once, her eyes hardened, and she dropped her towel.

I moved closer, letting my eyes roam over her skin. I had missed this body and the feeling of it in my hands. I brushed my fingers over her hips and around her back. Reacting to my touch, she stifled a breath, and I paused. Sensing my doubt, she moved her hands to mine and continued the movement. Her brown eyes slowly raised to mine and I swore I could tell exactly what she was thinking.

With a small smile, I guided her under the falling water. As the drops rained over her, she held my gaze before grabbing my hand and pulling me under too, fully clothed. At first, I thought it was because she was uncomfortable, but then her hands moved to the button on my jeans, and she pulled them down. Stepping out, I kicked them into the corner before pulling her close. Flattening my body against her back, I wrapped my arms around her. Careful to avoid any sensitive areas, I lowered my head to her neck and just held her. She accepted me and tightened her arms over mine.

When I noticed the water start to drop in temperature, I pulled away and grabbed the shampoo bottle. Pouring some in my hand, I watched as the foam slid between my fingers. Once it was soapy enough, I gently worked it through the strands of her hair, massaging her scalp. Rinsing it out, I repeated the process with conditioner.

Next, I carefully washed her body. Her eyes closing as she made sounds of approval. When I reached her thighs, I handed her the loofah, but she pushed it back toward me, lifting one leg up against the wall. I breathed deeply at the sight of her exposed in front of me and channeled everything I had into controlling myself. I washed her thigh down to her calf, easing the sponge across her. I then moved to the other leg and she let out a low moan. The sound instantly made me hard and I looked directly at her, to make sure I didn't imagine it.

I caught her eyes for the slightest second before she pulled my shirt off, pushing me up against the shower wall. I kissed her deeply, letting my hands finally feel her. The rush was exhilarating and I hadn't realized how tense I had been. I kissed her more, before moving my lips to her neck and chest. The sound she made amplified, and soon, it echoed around us.

Turning her, I pushed her chest up against the glass wall and moved her hands up above her head. "Tell me what you want." I pushed into her backside, as she tried to slide her hands down, but I gripped her wrists.

Throwing her head back, she pushed into me with her ass. "You, Silas. I want *you*."

I placed her hands against the glass, telling her to stay while I bent to take off my boxers. After only a second, I was back behind her with my hands against hers. This time though, I placed my hands over hers and intertwined our fingers. "Ready?"

She nodded as I pushed inside and it felt like I'd died. The moment she took my full length, I literally had to fight myself from cumming. I thrusted inside her, watching the leftover suds on her skin, the way her chest moved against the glass. *This* was where I belonged. *This* was where I would always belong. I brought my mouth down to her ear and whispered to her as I pushed in harder. "I love you so fucking much."

The moan that resulted was more of a cry, and she began to fight me to turn around. Allowing her the movement, I brought her legs up around me, and kissed her hard as her hands roamed over me. It was only when she tried to pull away again that I let her tear her mouth from mine.

"I love you too, Silas."

Those words engrained themselves in my soul, in my very *being* as I kissed her again. I took my time with her, pausing to check in. We finished together as I held her under the water that was now cold. She stood with her eyes closed, but not in an uncomfortable way. Her body had relaxed in a way I hadn't seen before. *She had needed this.* The sound of the nozzle turning off caught her attention. She made a small defeated sound in my direction.

I chuckled quietly as I stepped out, grabbing a towel. Wrapping it around her, I motioned for her to go into the bedroom. "Better?"

She didn't respond but looked up with a content smile as she leaned into me. "Your clothes are still bagged in the room, do you want to go through them?"

She looked over the piles that had remained untouched and then to the dirty basket full of the clothes she'd been wearing. Nodding, she went to the drawer and pulled out some of my boxers and a shirt. I did the same, and we dressed before settling onto the bed, *another first.*

Soon, we were surrounded by different piles of shirts, blankets, and jackets. There was a clear indication that she wanted to get rid of most of it, but the more time that passed, the more she became uncomfortable.

"What's wrong?" I asked, as she held up a dress, staring at it.

"I guess I just realized I don't even have anywhere to put this stuff now, you know?"

Wanting to stop whatever thoughts were in her head, I walked over to the closet and grabbed a handful of coat hangers from the rack. Tossing them onto the bed, I took the dress from her and threaded the hanger through it. "What do you mean? There's lots of room in the closet and my dresser," I explained, laying the dress down and grabbing a shirt. "Well, *our* dresser."

I lifted my eyes to her to find her smiling. *Smiling.*

The jolt that hit my heart was instant. "Because you'll be moving in with me."

The grin on her face only grew as she followed my lead with the clothes, reaching between us for more. Together, we hung the rest of the random piles and then sorted through the ones she wanted to donate. As I threw the bags away, she picked up one of the last pieces on the bed.

My jacket.

The one I'd originally left in her room.

I watched her from the corner of my eye as I gathered more hangers. She looked down at the black fabric for a few seconds before pulling it on and rolling up the oversized sleeves. Shifting the items in my arms as they started to fall, I walked the contents over to the closet. *The one that now belonged to both of us.*

Sliding my dark items to the back, I made room for all her things. Each top I lifted was different from the last but all made from bright ass colors. There was everything from glitter fabric to chevron patterns. By the time I was done, I found myself quietly laughing at the colorful chaos in front of me. My closet wasn't just full of clothes now; it was full of *her.* I scoffed at myself as I placed the last hanger. A few weeks ago, my plan had been to bleed this color out of her completely because I didn't want to see it. Little did I know I would let it saturate my life.

It felt good. *Right.*

Now I would just have to work on restoring her flame.

When I returned, she was collecting the clothes left into one single bag. Some she hadn't recognized, and some she simply didn't want anymore. There were so many times through this process that I wanted to just stop and offer to buy her a whole new wardrobe, but I restrained myself—that would come in time.

As she tied the bag and set it against the wall, I swore her eyes seemed different, lighter in some way. Looking down at the bed, she fluffed one of the pillows before grabbing my attention. "I think our backs would appreciate sleeping in here from now on. I call the left side."

38

Ember

Three months.

That's how long it'd been since everything fell apart... *or so I thought.*

In a lot of ways, I loved my previous life, but everything with Bodhi had cracked me open in a way I didn't know was possible. Even though he was dead, I still lived with a constant level of anxiety. Before him, I was never scared of anything, and now something inside of me was cautious of almost everything. I refused to let that part grow, especially when I had someone who made it his mission to make me happy.

I actually figured it was better to not think of my life before Silas. I thought I had a family, I *thought* I knew what happiness was. Turns out, I knew nothing.

I was so angry for the longest time about that. I just couldn't understand how Kinsley could choose a man like that over the friendship we had created and how Kolby could just *disappear.* I swore I would never forgive them, and then one morning, Silas handed me his phone with a weird look on his face. Looking down at the screen, I understood immediately. There was a voicemail waiting to be played, one that was from a number I

had memorized so long ago. I stared at the name for a minute before looking up at Silas. Annoyance was written all over his face, so I knew he had already listened to this. As my finger moved to push play, I paused and decided to have the message transcribed instead. As much as I wanted to know what Kolby had to say, I didn't think I could handle hearing his voice.

"***Hey Em. I um, well I hope you're doing okay. I just wanted to call because,.. well, because I-I'm sorry. I couldn't just sit here and let you think that I walked away from you. I need you to know that I had no idea he was doing any of that. Neither did Kinsley, not until she.. she figured it all out. It broke her, Em. She went off the rails and blamed herself, went after her own wrists because of it. I took her to treatment and she's okay now, but I guess what I'm trying to say is if we would have had any clue, we would have stopped it. We would have kept you safe. I'm sorry. I hope you're well and that you're happy. I know you have him and I know that he'll never let anything bad close to you, including us. I get it, I do. Please just know I'll always miss you and I'm here if you ever want to reach out. I love you. I always have.***"

When I finished reading the message, I looked up at Silas.

"You want to know what I think?"

I nodded slowly as I handed him the phone, still searching for my own thoughts on the matter.

"I think he's being genuine and I think him calling proves that they did care, but I will never allow them back around you."

"Silas."

"What?" he asked, as he stepped closer to me.

Instead of finishing my sentence, I watched as he protected me from some invisible threat. I sighed, and wrapped my arms around him. Honestly, I agreed with everything he was saying. I knew that voicemail had been genuine and I was really actually kind of glad to finally hear from Kolby. I was sad for Kinsley, but for a long period, I had convinced myself that they must have known, or that they truly hadn't cared. Hearing this, I knew that wasn't the case. Shaking my head, I finally felt something I had waited for—*closure.*

As more time passed, the anger over everything subsided, and I realized that I was truly happy. Silas had been right, our lives had turned out the way they had so we could find each other. That was the biggest thing I had learned. Everything had happened so that I could experience this life I have now.

I was so goddamn happy in every way, even on the random days I struggled. Through it all, Silas refused to leave my side. From the nightmares that plagued me to the therapy sessions he talked me into—he was there. Somehow, in the quiet days that surrounded us, we built our life together.

Fantasy books were now stacked on the shelves in our house, and my favorite snacks littered the pantry. Fries with gravy became a weekend staple, and to my surprise, Silas even asked if I wanted to pick out new colors for the walls. I practically jumped at that chance, eager to replace the neutral, boring tone. We settled on the first color I mentioned, *yellow.*

As far as work, I ended up pursuing my career in photography. Silas had the idea to open a room up inside the club for me to take pictures in, it ended up becoming very popular among the members. We had fun with it—making different themed nights, scavenger hunts, etc. Eventually, working this space within the club became full-time and Silas was able to create another company with me as his partner. I would work, and he would watch me.

It was within this space, I'd learned just how in tune Silas was with me. Somehow, he always knew what I needed before I did. If I woke up restless, he would ask if I wanted to go for a walk. If I went quiet for too long, he would remind me how much he loved me. A love that I knew for sure was rare. Not many people experienced it, not like *this.*

There were other things too, things I had never been able to be involved in before. His brothers immediately accepted me as family, and in just a few short months, I had moved our monthly dinners to every other week with each of us taking turns. Tonight we were hosting, and all I felt was excitement as I pulled out the roast.

I knew that he'd never admit it out loud, but Silas enjoyed these nights, even though he was currently trying to talk me out of hosting. *You would think seeing me twenty-four seven, he would be glad to see other people, but that wasn't the case.* Trying to convince me to cancel so we could go to the bedroom, he started kissing up the side of my neck. "Don't make me be the one to text them. I'm not nice when I don't want to share."

I turned my neck slightly to glance at him and rolled my eyes. "You have me every single day. Besides, Kyrin *knows* that. Now grab the stuff from the fridge," I added, glancing at the clock, "they'll be here in twenty minutes."

Silas slowly exhaled through his nose and pulled away from me, like he really thought he could win. The way he looked standing in front of me was almost *mopey.* I laughed at the thought, reaching up to run my fingers through his dark hair.

He glared down and his face changed as he felt my fingers shift. "*Don't.*"

"Too late." I replied, rapidly moving my hand back and forth, causing his hair to instantly stick up where I'd rubbed it. Reacting instantly, he moved fast and wrapped his hands around me, caging me in to tickle my sides. I squealed in response, but he didn't stop until I bent at my waist, allowing him to do the same to my hair. When I straightened back up, I was breathless, and for a moment we just stood there looking at each other, the warm kitchen light reflecting in his blue eyes.

In some twisted way and through unfortunate circumstances, fate had brought him to me. Standing here now with him, I knew that with absolute certainty. I would easily live through that life five hundred times over if it meant I ended up here again, *with him.*

Silas pulled me in with a mischievous smile and lowered his mouth to mine. I felt his breath as his lips slightly parted, and I grabbed the collar of his shirt to pull him into me. His body instantly welcomed me, and we both deepened the kiss just as rapid knocking came from the door.

Silas eyes flicked to the door before he kissed me again. "They're early. They can wait." Then, in one swift movement, he flipped me around, bending me over as if he planned to use that time wisely.

I screamed, which made the knocking come again, louder this time. "It's open!" I yelled in between laughing and pushing him away.

Reluctantly, he pulled away from me as his brothers entered, hovering in the doorway. I swatted at him one last time before walking toward our company. "Behave."

Silas immediately grinned before slapping my ass. "Or what?"

I couldn't hide the smile on my own face as I approached Kyrin. When he saw me, his head snapped in my direction before picking me up in a giant hug. "Ember!"

I was instantly lifted halfway off the floor. I laughed from the sheer impact and the look of annoyance on Silas's face. "Okay, crazy. Drop me before your brother kills you."

Kyrin set me down and let out a loud laugh after looking over at Silas. "With what? His dick?"

Silas looked straight at me and tucked the hard-on he had gotten from playing into the waistband of his pants. "Control him, before I kick them out to take care of this problem."

I laughed, pushing into Kyrin. "Go to the kitchen, trouble."

"Missed you too," he said casually as he walked away, like we'd known each other forever.

Greyson followed next and I hugged him, receiving only a

side pat but it was still progress. I knew that Silas was very thankful for the things he had helped us with but through all of that, he was still in the doghouse for hurting me that *one* time.

I squeezed him as I looked up at him. “Glad you're here.” He gave a small smile in return before nodding at Silas as he headed into the kitchen.

Silas and I readied the plates, as we all took our seats around the table. Passing the food back and forth, it all disappeared rather quickly while conversation flowed between us. Kyrin talked the most, giving insight into a new idea that he had for the bar. I couldn't help but laugh at him and the expressive faces he made.

Kyrin eventually retaliated by throwing a spoonful of mashed potatoes at me, but I ducked out of the way. Greyson was the first to defend me, grabbing a fistful of his own potatoes and smashing them in Kyrin's face. Silas ended the fun there, by making them call a truce.

The next few topics came and went but we all took turns updating the others about our lives—random stories, arguments about new movies, and inappropriate jokes by the time dessert was ready.

I was halfway through teasing Greyson about the way he ate his brownie when I noticed Silas wasn’t talking. He just sat at the head of the table, with one arm resting casually against the back of the chair. I glanced over to find his eyes locked on me.

“I think the 23rd is a good date, yeah?”

I questioned him with a mouth full of brownie and ice cream.

"For what?"

"Our wedding."

I choked on the food in my mouth as Kyrin hollered congratulations and jumped out of his seat to slap Silas on the back.

Gasping for air, I waved my hand around, shooing Kyrin away. "No, stop. There's no wedding." Reaching for my glass of water, I glared at Silas who was still staring at me.

"It's not a joke, *Mrs.* Solstice."

Swallowing water in big gulps, I rolled my eyes at him before pulling the cup away from my mouth. "That's not something you can just decide. It takes two to enter a marriage."

Kyrin looked back and forth between us before taking another bite. "I disagree. It's actually just as easy to call Knox for the marriage license."

This time, it was me throwing things. My spoon hit Kyrin in the shoulder, splattering the ice cream it held against his shirt.

"Actually bro, maybe marry someone a little crazy or just with better aim in general."

As soon as I settled back in my seat, Silas's hand found the leg of my chair and pulled me directly next to him. "No, she's my problem now."

I tried to push him away, but he kissed me repeatedly, blowing into my face as I tried to bite him.

39

SILAS

The club smelled like sweat and whatever new disinfectant spray they switched to when I was gone. I didn't mind the lemon scent, but it definitely took some time getting used to when I came back. Other than that, everything was completely the same and Ruined was thriving, even in my absence. I had returned a few months ago and now I was able to experience this every day with Ember by my side. Leaning against the edge of the bar, my eyes scanned the crowd, looking for her.

I loved being back in this atmosphere, but I'd grown accustomed to having her next to me. Sweeping my eyes over the room again, I caught many flickers of movement. As a strobe of green reached across the room, my eyes finally landed on her and my heart swelled with pride.

Ember, *my ember,* was walking through the crowd toward me. She was wearing a white dress tonight, one that I had bought her for our honeymoon. I knew the lights would catch it just right here, especially with the new mask she'd been given. Made from a black material that mimicked mine, hers was almost an exact replica but instead of a purple crack, she had an outline of yellow flames that danced across the bridge of her

nose and cheekbones. The design was so perfectly her and the one she wore here at work, marking her as the new co-owner.

The crowd swirled around us, bodies colliding and pressing together, but I never looked away from her. In fact, I didn't breathe until she was close enough for me to touch. The feeling that rushed through me as she entered my arms was identical to the one I had the first time she left my club—overwhelming obsession.

Even then, she had ruined me completely.

Acknowledgements

To my readers, thank you for falling in love with my flawed characters and their stories. I can't thank you enough for loving the ones that cut a little deeper. Your support means more than I could ever put into words.

To my team, thank you for helping bring this story to life. From my editor, to my team, I'm endlessly grateful to have such passionate people in my corner.

To my husband, thank you for being the first person to protect my spark. Thank you even more for forever feeding my flames.

And finally, to everyone out there who has went through hell and never lost their fire—this book is for you. You refused to give in when the world tried to break you, and for that, I am forever proud.

May you never apologize for the way you burn.

www.ingramcontent.com/pod-product-compliance
Lightning Source LLC
LaVergne TN
LVHW091141150826
845672LV00005B/1003
9798999607843